S0-BKR-290

OMNIVM
LVX
CIVIVM
MDCCCLII
MDCCC
LXXVIII

NIGHT SCREAMS

Also by Bill Pronzini and Barry N. Malzberg

THE RUNNING OF BEASTS
ACTS OF MERCY

NIGHT SCREAMS

BILL PRONZINI
and
BARRY N. MALZBERG

PBP
A Playboy Press Book

 Published simultaneously in the United States and Canada by Playboy Press, Chicago, Illinois. Printed in the United States of America.

FIRST EDITION

Trade distribution by Simon and Schuster
A Division of Gulf + Western Corporation
New York, New York 10020

Designed by Tere LoPrete

Library of Congress Cataloging in Publication Data

Pronzini, Bill.
Night screams.

I. Malzberg, Barry N., joint author. II. Title.
PZ4.P9653Ni [PS3566.R67] 813'.5'4 78-27166
ISBN 0-87223-525-4

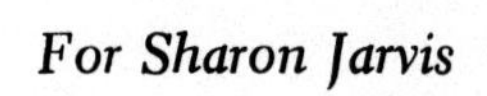

For Sharon Jarvis

Lamentings heard i' the air; strange screams of death,
And prophesying with accents terrible
Of dire combustion and confused events
New hatch'd to the woeful time. The obscure bird
Clamour'd the livelong night: some say, the earth
Was feverous and did shake.

Shakespeare, *Macbeth*

PART ONE

After the Beginning

CHAPTER 1

Wednesday, January 17

TWIN FORKS, CONNECTICUT—8:30 P.M.

In the darkness, using the beam of his flashlight to guide him, he moved at a measured pace through the marshland. The trail he followed wound at random angles, was nearly obliterated in places by rootsnarls and huckleberry shrubs and underbrush; the ground was firm though muddy, no longer frozen after four days of an early January thaw. Even at this hour of night, the air was brisk without being chill—forty-five or fifty degrees. His breath tingled in his lungs when he inhaled, made little plumes of vapor that shone mistily in the light from the flash when he exhaled.

Heavy black shadows that were cedar and pine trees loomed around him as he moved, shifting and retreating with his passage. Patches of dirty melting snow gleamed in the darkness, like paint spattered on the landscape. From time to time a bird would scream in the thick marsh growth, soar upward with a great beating of wings; but he moved so noiselessly, so well, that he knew his movement wasn't connected with their flight.

The trail skirted the edge of a shallow brook where little

collars of ice spread inward from the edges, outward from stones in its center. The moving water made soft giggling sounds in the night. He felt an answering giggle build within him, but caught it before it could come out and pushed it down. Nothing funny in this, he reminded himself. Nothing funny in death and salvation.

Beyond the brook the trail climbed to a hillock. And beyond the hillock, against the hard black of the sky, he could see the pale shimmer of light from the farmhouse. He switched off the flashlight, put it into the pocket of his overcoat. His fingers touched the smooth surface of the cord, the blue velvet cord, and lingered for a moment. But it was not time yet. Soon, but not yet. He knew exactly when he would take the cord from his pocket because he had seen it all before in the vision.

Everything was there in his mind and in the mind of the host. Each of his actions and reactions. The few lines of dialogue that would be spoken. The stark image of the woman's face after he strangled her: distended eyes, blue-purple skin color, protruding and blackened tongue, saliva coating the edges of her mouth.

Yes—and the sound of her screams.

He listened to the screams as he moved toward the top of the hillock; they were like faint echoes trapped between his brain and his eardrums. He shivered once, wrapped the collar of his coat more tightly around his own throat. No, nothing funny in what he was about to do. He hated it more and more each time. But if he didn't go through with it, then both he and the host would die instead. He didn't know why this was so; it just was. Obey the visions or die. Protect the secret or die.

And he didn't want to die again.

Four deaths and four salvations. Until the man in New Jersey last month, just the one in Concord in 1964 and the woman in Albany in 1972. But this new vision had come after only twenty-seven days. Did that mean they would happen more and more often now? That it would be a matter of *days* instead of years or even months? He was afraid it did. Terrified of more visions, more deaths, more salvations.

But there wasn't anything he could do; he was helpless.

Obey the visions or die.

Protect the secret or die.

When he neared the top of the hillock, he heard, for the first time, the faint melody of her flute. Yes. The vision. He moved into the shadow of a stunted pine, looked down at the farmhouse, and listened. He knew little about music, but the tune wasn't modern. Classical, that was what it was. It made his ears hurt; he had never liked the flute, it was a shrill instrument, and he had never liked classical music either. He imagined that the sounds of it were little beads of crystal, hovering in the cold air, cracking, pelting him with tiny shards.

Time to move again.

Slowly he started down the far slope. The farmhouse was typically New England, made of wood and painted white, with a covered front porch and a screened-in rear porch. Light glowed in two of the facing windows—the front parlor. It was a solitary place, without close neighbors, although a country road passed in front of it a hundred yards to the west. It would have been simpler if he had parked his host's car off that road and made a direct approach, instead of taking the rutted marsh lane and leaving the car a quarter-mile away. Except that that was not the way he had seen it in the vision.

The flute music grew shriller as he came down off the slope and started through the vegetable garden. The sound of it now was like a scream.

He raised both hands to his ears. This had been the most painful part of the vision, but it would not last long. In a little while now the flute would stop and her own screaming would begin.

He moved more quickly, at an angle toward the nearest of the lighted windows. The glass was misty from the warm air inside, but when he came up to it he could see her clearly. In profile, looking at her music stand, the flute at a right angle to her face, she was absorbed in her playing. And she would keep on being absorbed in it, he knew, until he entered the parlor.

For a few seconds he lingered, watching her. Sandra Harris. An attractive woman in her late thirties, dark hair, milky skin that shone in the ruddy glow from a fire on the hearth. Delicate-looking, fragile, small breasts and small hips. Quiet person, inoffensive. The kind of woman you might not notice immediately in a group, but whom you remembered when she was gone.

Why her? he thought. But he knew why. The secret, to protect the secret. The visions had told him that. The visions told him everything.

And they told him nothing at all.

He stepped away from the window, went around to the rear. At the door to the screened-in porch, he paused to pull on a pair of thin black gloves. Then it was time, and he took the velvet cord from his overcoat pocket, held it loosely in the palm of his left hand. The anxiety vanished; he felt calm and prepared. Even the wailing of the flute no longer bothered him.

He reached out and opened the screen door.

It was unlocked: the vision. Here in the northern Connecticut countryside, Sandra Harris lived without fear. An open door was a symbol of warmth—it would admit a neighbor or a friend. Except tonight. Tonight it admitted Death.

With silent steps he crossed the porch, opened the door to the kitchen. Warmth surrounded him, made his cheeks tingle. He stopped for a moment to unwind the length of cord, stretch it out between his hands; then he went through a swing door into a narrow hallway and along there to the parlor.

The flute line wavered, broke to silence, and began again seconds later. Something different now, less piercing, a sad melody in uneven rhythm. Something she had written herself, he thought, or maybe just *something*—an unplanned flow of random notes which were taking the last breaths of her life.

He stepped inside the parlor.

Her back was to him as she blew into the mouthpiece of the flute. He watched her continue to play for a dozen seconds, her fingers moving in a steady tempo. Then, when she sensed that she wasn't alone, he watched her stop abruptly and swing around to face him.

"Hello, Sandra Harris," he said.

Her eyes were wide, surprised, but there was no fear in them yet. Not yet. Recognition came first, slowly, and in a bewildered voice she said, "What are *you* doing here?"

"I'm sorry," he said.

"Sorry? I don't understand—"

"For what I have to do. But I have to protect the secret, I have to obey the visions." Sometimes he talked to them this way and sometimes he didn't; it was never his choice. "I don't want to die again."

"What are you saying? I—"

That was when she noticed the velvet cord.

The fear came all at once, froze her expression and made her face look like something fashioned of brittle glass. Her hand closed tight around the flute and then, in a spasm, released it; the bright silver tube reflected glints of firelight as it clattered to the floor. She backed away, shaking her head, saying the word *no* over and over, soundlessly.

"I'm sorry," he said again, and went after her in quick, powerful strides.

She tried to run, but he caught her and held her thrashing body against his, bending her over his knee so he could bring the cord up around her neck from behind. She fought him wildly, with amazing strength for such a small woman, but his strength and his purpose were greater. He pulled the cord over her sweater and against the softness of her throat, preparing himself for the first of her screams.

It came an instant later, half-strangled by the pressure of the cord. He jerked it tighter. Her struggles became frenzied; she tried to scream again, but she had no air and it was stillborn. She clawed at the cord, fought desperately to dig her fingers under it so she could breathe.

He didn't want to do what he did next, but what he wanted meant nothing. Obey, obey. He eased the pressure, let her draw one last lungful of air, let her use it for a final terrible shriek that seemed to hang in the bright, cheery room, echoing and reechoing in his ears.

When he couldn't bear it any longer, he retightened the cord, twisted it at the nape of her neck. Quickly now. He had to do it quickly. Her struggles became spasmodic, then weak and tremulous, then quit altogether; she sagged downward in his grasp. The bowel stench of death came to him and made him gag.

He let go of her, let go of one end of the cord. She dropped at his feet, body convulsing in death spasms as if trying to assume a fetal position. Then she was still, and her eyes stared up at him, blood in little ridges at the corners, distended—distended blue eyes, blue-purple skin color, protruding and blackened tongue, saliva coating the edges of her mouth.

The vision.

It was silent in the parlor now. He stood motionless, listening, waiting for his heartbeat to slow to normal. He felt drained. Relief would come later, and after the host took control again he would sink deep inside, where there was little pain and little fear. Where there was peace. Where there was *life*.

Until next time.

No, don't think about that.

Until next time.

He folded the cord carefully, put it away in his coat pocket. Bending, he managed to lift the body into his arms. Carried it out onto the rear porch. The coil of clothesline was where he had known it would be, inside a storage cabinet; he tied one end of it around her neck, looped the other end over one of the dark rafters above, laboriously hoisted the body upward until it was suspended a few inches off the floor, and fastened the other end of the clothesline around the kitchen doorknob.

The vision.

And it was done.

The images and the sounds began to fade from his mind. He could no longer hear the echoes of the flute; he could no longer hear the screams. The first feelings of relief began to move through him as he opened the screen door and went outside. Away from the dead thing, blue and black and red and white, hanging from a rafter in the house where Sandra Harris had lived.

WHITEHALL, VERMONT—9:00 P.M.

Leslie Abbott was in her kitchen, making coffee and baking cornbread, when the vision struck her.

It began in the solar plexus, at the center of her, as the frightening visions always did: acute and without warning. Her knees turned weak; she caught onto the edge of the stove to steady herself. Colors swirled across the screen of her third eye, the psychic eye that seemed to exist between her brows. Blue and black, red and white. They came together briefly, like a kaleidoscope forming a pattern, and she saw, as if through a bright haze, the exterior of a farmhouse. Auditory impression: the faint melody of a flute. Then the image fragmented into more patterns of color, the same four hues—

Someone began to scream.

The sound seemed to come from behind the vision, as if it were she herself who was screaming. At first it struck her as feline, but when it went on and on, climbing in decibels, she understood that no animal could shriek like that, no animal could express that much pain and terror.

Terror welled inside her, too. And there was a sudden pressure at her throat, biting pain; for a moment she couldn't breathe. She wanted to cry out, but had no voice.

The pressure was suddenly gone and her chest heaved and her lungs swelled with air again.

Odors assaulted her, sharp and foul. Waste products, feces. Her stomach churned, she felt as though she were going to vomit.

Make it stop, dear God, make it stop!

The colors streamed faster, congealed, and took on another set of visual outlines. A room with a fireplace, a bright silver tube on the floor, the dark shape of someone moving as though in shadow. She felt herself being drawn deeper into the room, compelled to move closer to the dark shape, to see its face—

Another scream. Different voice but filled with the same terror.

Revulsion swept through her, a fresh surge of fear. She felt herself retreating, away from the dark shape, away from the room, into the swirling colors. Blues and blacks, reds and whites—so bright they were painful, like the hot, shimmery glare of the sun at noon. The odors remained strong and sickening, the screaming went on and on.

Until an even higher sound, a piercing whistle, penetrated. Then, all at once, the colors dulled and the familiar trappings of the kitchen reappeared: crockery stacked on the drainboard; her own unframed paintings pushpinned to the walls; the stove and the steaming teakettle.

The teakettle.

She fumbled at the knobs on the stove, turned off the gas. The shrieking merged with the dying whistle of the kettle and died along with it. The colors faded altogether, the lid of her psychic eye closed; the odor of waste transformed into that of hot cornbread and boiling water.

Over. It was over.

Trembling, she caught up a towel and rubbed perspiration from her face and hands. God. One of the strongest and most frightening visions she'd ever had. Much worse than the one a month ago; that one had been similar to this, but without such intensity and clarity.

She sat at the table, drank coffee that made her gag, and tried not to think about the dark shape she had seen. Upstairs, in her studio, there was another dark shape, this one on canvas, part of a painting she had begun two weeks before Christmas and which she hadn't been able to bring herself to finish or destroy. It had started out as another of her Vermont landscapes: a winter scene of her own house by night, blanketed in snow, snow falling all around. But then that other vision full of streaming color and foul smells and terrifying sounds had struck her, and inexplicably she had found herself sketching in the figure of a man standing in the snow on the north side of her yard, between one of the elms and the woodshed.

A figure without a face.

Why? she thought again. Why?

It was snowing outside now, and she sat listening to the wind hurl flurries against the windows. The wind blowing beneath the eaves of the old house.

A tremor passed through her.

It sounded like someone screaming.

PART TWO

The Middle and the End

CHAPTER 2

Friday, January 19

WHITEHALL, VERMONT—4:10 P.M.

The new landscape was not going well at all.

Leslie had been working on it all afternoon, and in four hours she had done nothing more than to add a fawn with expressive and rather frightened eyes. The fawn was all wrong: The frightened eyes were a jarring note in the pastoral scene. Landscape buyers didn't want strong emotion in their paintings, any more than they wanted modern buildings or machinery. What they did want was a sense of the antiquarian—a capturing in oils of the age of the land, its dignity and softness and durability. Which was exactly what the best of her work expressed.

So why had she done the fawn this way?

You know the answer to that, she told herself. Sandra Harris, that's why. Sandra Harris and Tony Murray.

Both dead—both murdered. Tony a month ago in New Jersey, and now Sandra two days ago at her Connecticut farmhouse. Both garroted and then hung from rafters. Both members of PSYCHICs, just as she herself was a member of the small group of paranormals led by Oscar Koskovich.

Both of whose deaths she had experienced psychically.

That was what the two visions before Christmas and on Wednesday night were all about; that was what the terror and the screams and the smells were all about. She'd understood that last night, when Oscar called to tell her the news about Sandra, and there had been an edge of fear inside her ever since.

She hadn't told Oscar about the visions yet. Or anyone else. She hadn't seen anything definite, couldn't identify the dark shape; she had no control over her psychic gift—no clairvoyant did—and she couldn't will another vision that *would* identify him. If she went to the police, they would probably write her off, as too many people had in her life, as some kind of oddball crank.

But sooner or later she would have to tell the other PSYCHICs, tell *someone*. She couldn't keep it locked inside her. Oscar was convinced that someone, for whatever insane reason, was bent on destroying members of the group; he had called a meeting for tonight—right here in Whitehall, of all places—to discuss the possibility. And what if he was right? What if all their lives were in jeopardy? They each had a right to know she had been sensitive to the murders; tonight was the time to tell them. Wasn't it?

She didn't know; she didn't know what to do. She had always thought of herself as a strong, decisive woman, and in most ways maybe she was. But in this situation she felt uncertain. And uneasy. Because there was evil in it, and it was an evil that she couldn't begin to understand.

Pointless to keep on working. Unless she could alter the look in the fawn's eyes, she would have to destroy the canvas anyway; and the north light coming in through the studio windows had already begun to fade and darken with dusk shadows. She put down her brush and palette, wiped her hands on a turpentined rag, and set about mechanically straightening tubes of paint and cleaning brushes.

Once this building had been a country church, but it had been converted by an enterprising architect/painter in the

1950s, and the studio had been fashioned by enclosing the choir loft. At the inner wall were the stairs leading up from the main floor, and boxed in at the north corner was a second set of stairs that went up to a dusty belfry where she stored virgin canvases and odds and ends. Wooden beams criss-crossed the ceiling. The studio was sparsely furnished: an old couch, a long catchall table, two fluorescent lamps, and four easels for painting and drying canvases; the walls were filled with framed and unframed landscapes of different sizes, arranged in neat rows or hung selectively.

Orderly and *organized.* Those were the words, she imagined, that people would use to describe her working and living quarters, and to describe her—along with *quiet, sensitive, self-sufficient.* But they were just words; they said nothing about the real Leslie Abbott. No one really knew her, not her few acquaintances in Montpelier and in New York, not the men she had known and occasionally been intimate with. Sometimes she felt that she herself did not even know the real Leslie Abbott, she of the psychic gift.

Or curse. Psychic *curse.*

When she was finished with the brushes, she shrugged out of the smock she wore over a sweater and a pair of jeans, crossed to hang it on a wall peg. Her watch said the time was 4:30. She wondered if Oscar and the others had arrived at the Colebrook Inn; the meeting was scheduled for 6:00. She was already beginning to dread it.

Restlessly she went across to the north windows and looked out. It hadn't snowed since last night, but there were black-edged clouds moving in from the east. The wind was sharp, gusty, and it would be bitter-cold when she went out into it. Snow mantled everything in plumes and puffs, fingers and waves of white: the woodshed and garage and stark leafless elms in her yard, the house boarded up for the winter nearby, Ephraim Buell's antique shop and Quint's Country Store and the Colebrook Inn a quarter-mile distant along the village's one-block Main Street. There were no cars moving anywhere that she could see; Whitehall was thirty miles from the nearest ski resort and off the beaten track anyway, so got little winter traffic. The stillness seemed absolute, as if she were looking at a hologram. Indigo shadows on the snowdrifts; the cold, slate-colored mountains in the distance, capped in silver where rays of dying sunlight touched them through the clouds —it all had a brooding, lonely aspect.

Behind her the telephone rang.

The sudden sound startled her, turned her jerkily from the window. Nerves. She had promised herself weeks ago that she would stop reacting to the telephone this way, and here she was doing it again. The anonymous caller who had plagued her during her first six weeks in Whitehall—"*We don't want your kind here, miss bitch, you better just pack up and leave, you know what's good for you*"—hadn't called again since early December, and before that only at night. Whoever it was had apparently realized she wouldn't be intimidated and had decided to leave her alone. It had been unpleasant for a while, and if she had had anywhere else to go she might have given in and left this place where "her kind" weren't wanted. Only there wasn't anyplace on earth where her kind *were* wanted. She had suffered one kind of abuse or another in New York City and Montpelier, and now Whitehall—they were all the same.

She listened to the phone ring again, for the fourth time, and then went over to the extension mounted on the wall.

"Hello?"

"Leslie? Is that you, darling?"

She recognized the voice: Jo Turner, who operated a small New York theatrical agency and who was one of the five remaining members of PSYCHICs. Jo was a sometimes pleasant, sometimes abrasive person, with a penchant for Tallulah Bankhead dialogue. Leslie neither liked nor disliked her; Jo was merely an acquaintance.

"Yes, it's me," she said. "Who else would it be, Jo?"

"Well, your voice sounded odd. Leslie, I'm in a strange little village called Stonestown, about twenty miles from you, having a bloody flat tire fixed. So I'm afraid I'm going to be a little late for the meeting."

"I'll tell Oscar."

Jo sighed audibly. "Dear Oscar. I do wish he had persuaded you and Gloria to come to Manhattan, instead of talking me into popping up to Whitehall. Not that I don't *like* the place, sweetheart; it's a lovely little village. But long drives and flat tires and pointless silly meetings in the Vermont wilds are not exactly my idea of the perfect weekend."

"Why do you say the meeting is pointless and silly?"

"Because it is. Don't you think so?"

"I don't know. Sandra's dead too, Jo."

"Yes, poor Sandra. And poor Tony. But really, the idea that someone is deliberately murdering members of the group is preposterous."

"I hope you're right."

"Of course I'm right, darling," Jo said. "Besides, what are we going to accomplish by getting together and discussing it endlessly? We'll only frighten each other. And become suspicious of each other, too, I imagine."

"Suspicious?"

"Certainly. After all, if Oscar is right, it could be one of *us* who is responsible, couldn't it?"

My God, Leslie thought. She couldn't think of anything to say.

"Well, I'd better let you go," Jo said. "This is long-distance and the flat is already costing me a fortune. These garage people here are *highwaymen*. See you soon, darling."

Leslie put the handset back into its cradle. She wrapped her arms across her breasts and chafed them beneath the sweater sleeves. The studio, despite its heating ducts and insulation, seemed very cold now.

One of us, she thought. The possibility simply hadn't occurred to her before. Plump, white-haired Oscar? Annoying, immature Neal Iverson? Flighty Gloria Mason? Jo herself?

No, it was ridiculous. She had known them all for more than

a year, and if they were all less than delightful companions, they were certainly harmless enough.

Weren't they?

For the fourth or fifth time that afternoon she found her eyes drawn to the cloth-draped canvas standing alone against one wall. The winterscape of her house, with the faceless figure on the snow outside. Whose face was it? Someone she knew? Innocent figure, or menacing figure? Real event or symbol? Had there been a dark figure watching her house in the past, or would there be one sometime in the future?

She shook her head and thought again, as she had several times, of destroying it, burning it in the fireplace downstairs. But she knew she wouldn't. Or couldn't. Something compelled her to keep it as it was, where it was, because someday it would play a role in her life.

Predestination, she thought.

In most things you had free will, the power to control your own destiny, but some random events or series of events seemed to be preordained by whatever forces controlled the universe. Not all psychics believed in that, or in any kind of predestination, but she was one who did. There had been other times when she'd been psychically compelled to do or not to do certain things. It happened to everybody, but she sometimes knew when it was happening to her; her gift/curse let her feel the impulses with her mind. The day she had been driven to a friend's house, unannounced, minutes before a water heater accidentally exploded and gave her and the friend a bad scalding. The day she had been compelled to take a long trip to an unfamiliar hamlet in New Hampshire and arrived just in time to stop a little boy from darting out in front of a truck. She was *supposed* to be in the friend's house. She was *supposed* to be in the village.

She was not supposed to destroy the painting.

For reasons that were good or for reasons that were evil? Anything could be predestined; you had no way of knowing until it happened whether it would be good or bad. And no way of changing it in any case.

She pulled her gaze away from the covered painting and hurried out of the studio. She wasn't going to tell the other PSYCHICs about her visions of the two murders, she knew that now. She wasn't going to say anything to any of them about her sensitivity.

What she didn't know was whether or not the decision was hers.

6:00 P.M.

The Colebrook Inn's large main lobby was furnished—not very harmoniously, Oscar Koskovich felt—to create the impression of a rustic Vermont inn circa 1920. There were a dozen heavy chairs and couches, a chess table, a trestle desk, brass and milk-glass lamps, a rosewood china cabinet, an antique Simon Willard tall clock (and a television set that looked out of place). The walls were decorated with Vermont landscapes, none of which were Leslie's, Oscar knew; the floor was bare except for a scattering of colorful hooked rugs. Across the side wall was a massive eight-foot-broad stone fireplace with an old-fashioned hanging kettle crane inside it. The other rooms that opened off the main lobby—a small bar, a dining room, a reception foyer—contained similar accoutrements.

This evening a birchwood fire blazed merrily enough inside the fireplace. Oscar was sitting in front of it in an armchair, sipping at his second hot buttered rum. Gloria Mason, who drank nothing but white wine, sat restlessly in another armchair next to him. Neal Iverson, who drank nothing but Coke, was slouched on a sofa across a round glass-topped table. Oscar had been there since 5:30 and Neal and Gloria had just arrived, independently of each other because Neal lived on Long Island, in Massapequa, and Gloria just across the Vermont–New York line in Storm Junction.

Neal was a thin, intense man in his late twenties who wore thick horn-rimmed glasses over protuberant eyes and, almost always, a checked cloth cap over his straw-colored hair. He called his cap his "vision hat" and claimed it allowed him to have more vivid and powerful psychic experiences. Which may or may not have been an exaggeration; Dykshoorn used a wire loop, after all, to aid him in his work with police and other agencies.

Most psychics were uncomfortable with their talent, having learned early on that it was a source of pain, fear, and rejection; but Neal gloried in his gift and told everyone about it. He worked as an accountant with one of the large computer corporations, but believed that one day he would make a professional career for himself as an entertainer, a mentalist like his idol, the Amazing Kreskin. He was working up an act with his wife, he said—Oscar had often wondered what the wife was like; Neal never brought her to meetings—and was forever pestering Jo to find him a booking. He had even picked out a rather florid name for himself: the Prince of Psychics.

Gloria, on the other hand, seemed mostly unconcerned with her ability, perhaps because it was the weakest of any in the group. She was forty, twenty pounds overweight, and already beginning to look and act matronly: She wore shapeless dresses and colored her brown hair with a silver rinse. Once she had had theatrical ambitions; now she contented herself with managing a playhouse in Storm Junction. She still retained an actress's flightiness, though, a certain giddiness that Oscar had always presumed was typical of theater people. She had been a widow for four years, and, because he himself had been a widower for nearly two, they had occasionally turned to each other for comfort and sexual release. But it was the most casual of affairs. Neither of them needed or wanted it to go beyond that level.

Oscar had grown to accept his own gift. Unlike that of so many clairvoyants, it seldom involved frightening or unsettling experiences. Mostly his visions were concerned with animals of one kind or another; he had always loved animals, was content in his job as editor of a trade journal for pet dealers. Until his wife died of cancer, he had been, he thought, a supremely happy man. After that, to counteract the loneliness, he had formed PSYCHICs by seeking out information on clairvoyants in the New York and New England areas, sending out feelers, conducting persuasive interviews. None of the members were professionals; professionals were too busy to join a social group. They were all just gifted people who preferred to keep a low profile, who had never been tested by eminent parapsychologists, and who had no interest in becoming trance mediums or giving readings or making public predictions. Except, of course, for Neal—but Neal was a special case.

PSYCHICs. The Parapsychological Society: Yankee Clairvoyants in Humanistic Ideological Concord. The acronym was his, too. Some of the others, Jo Turner in particular, made fun of the name, called it labored, but he liked it. He liked everything about the group, and through it he had recaptured some of his old happiness.

Or he had until the murders of Anthony Murray and Sandra Harris.

Oscar's contentment had been shaken; he felt threatened and apprehensive. Why would anyone want to brutally murder two members of PSYCHICs? Jo believed it was a terrible coincidence, but he found that difficult to accept. Tony and Sandra had obviously been killed by the same person, and it seemed they had nothing in common *except* PSYCHICs. Tony had been the owner of three small restaurants in New Jersey, had had business problems, and might or might not have been involved with certain unsavory people. Sandra had been a quiet woman, a writer of children's books, who lived in solitude in Connecticut. They hadn't been having an affair, there wasn't a connection there; Oscar thought he would have sensed it if so, and besides, he had always suspected that Sandra preferred members of her own sex.

Then why? Why?

What Oscar found most painful to deal with was his own sense of implication. The group was his; he had brought Tony and Sandra together, brought them all together. The possibility that he might be responsible, however innocently, was lodged like a splinter in his mind.

Gloria said abruptly, "Where are Leslie and Jo? It's five past six already; they should be here by now."

"They'll be along," Oscar said. "Be patient."

"Oscar, you know what I think of this whole monstrous idea of yours. I only agreed to come as a favor to you. I have to get back to the playhouse tonight; we're opening *Desire Under the Elms* next week and O'Neill is *difficult*. I haven't finished—"

"Painting the sets," Oscar said. "Yes, I know. Just be patient, Gloria. This is an important meeting, believe me."

"You bet it's important," Neal agreed in his piping voice. "I think Oscar's right. I think some maniac is deliberately murdering PSYCHICs."

"You're both making me nervous," Gloria said, and shuddered in a theatrical way. "All this talk about murder, one of us being next—it makes my flesh crawl."

"Think about Tony's and Sandra's flesh."

Frowning, Oscar said, "Son, you're not helping matters."

"You can't run away from the truth. That's why we're here."

The boy—Oscar always thought of him as a boy—seemed excited, even more intense than usual; his eyes bulged brightly behind his glasses. But the intensity and the excitement were those of someone caught up in a thrilling adventure instead of in a life-and-death crisis. Oscar wondered if Neal fully understood the danger, if he had any real compassion for Tony and Sandra, or if he could only see himself in a child's game, so absorbed in an imagined role that he was beyond normal emotion toward others, incapable of a mature outlook on anything. Sad, if so. But Oscar was the first to admit that, for a clairvoyant, he was not terribly insightful.

"I have a theory, you know," the boy said.

"What theory?"

"On why this maniac is killing PSYCHICs. I think—"

He stopped speaking because there were the sounds of footfalls on the wooden floor. It was Harmon Colebrook, the inn's spare, middle-aged owner, approaching from the dining room. Colebrook's wife, Myrna, had checked them in, and the youth who worked here, Buddy Quint, had served them their drinks; this was Colebrook's first appearance.

"Hello, Mr. Colebrook," Neal said. "How are you? I'll bet you're glad to have us back up here in the middle of winter like this when you don't have many customers."

"That so?" Colebrook said stiffly. His voice and his inflection told you he was a native Vermonter, but there was none of the so-called Vermont friendliness in his eyes as he stood looking down at them. He looked, Oscar thought, even less pleased than he had last October, just after Leslie moved to Whitehall from New York City and the PSYCHICs had held a weekend meeting here at the inn.

"Sure," Neal said. "There's nothing like paying customers, right?"

"Mrs. Colebrook would like to know if you'll want dinner."

Oscar said, "Perhaps later. We're planning to have a meeting and it will probably take some time."

"We don't serve after nine o'clock."

"Yes, I remember that."

Colebrook seemed reluctant to leave. "You folks planning to stay awhile?"

"At least until tomorrow."

"Wife says Mr. Iverson here come in with two suitcases."

"Oh, that's because I always travel with extra clothes," Neal said. "You need lots of warm clothing in the winter, so you won't catch cold or the flu—" He broke off and blinked behind his glasses, then looked down at the floor beside his chair, looked over into the reception foyer. "My suitcases," he said. "Where are my suitcases?"

"Mrs. Colebrook took them up to your room, son," Oscar said. "Remember?"

"She did? Oh, sure, that's right. For a minute there, I was afraid something had happened to them."

Colebrook's eyes narrowed. "That so?"

"Mr. Iverson is always misplacing things," Oscar said. "That's what he meant."

"Yes, that's what I meant." Neal looked at the innkeeper. "It's kind of funny, isn't it, Mr. Colebrook?"

"What is?"

"The way I misplace things, like an absentminded professor. I mean, I'm a psychic and you'd think I could just concentrate and I'd *see* where the things are."

"Psychic," Colebrook said. His mouth worked as if he wanted to spit.

"But it doesn't work that way. You can't control clairvoyant visions, particularly the ones about yourself. Sometimes, though, when I'm wearing my vision cap like I am now, I can touch things that belong to *other* people and I'll have an experience. That's called psychometrics, you know."

"Yeah," Colebrook said.

"And sometimes, all I have to do is *study* other people and I'll have an experience. If I concentrate hard enough, that is." He stared at Colebrook intently.

The innkeeper glared back at him. "Don't try that occult stuff on me. I don't truck with it."

"It's not occult, it's clairvoyance." Neal closed his eyes, touched his cap, and frowned in concentration. "Yes, I can sense something about you. An argument with your wife that's going to take place in your bedroom. Right, now I've got it. There's something you want to do and she doesn't—"

Warningly Oscar said, "Son, that's enough."

Neal didn't seem to hear him. "But you persist," he said to Colebrook. "I see you reaching out, touching her, and I see her pulling away—"

"For heaven's sake, Neal!" Gloria said.

Colebrook's face was congested; he spun around, stalked away from them without speaking, and disappeared into the bar.

Neal opened his eyes, blinked several times, and said, "Now what's the matter with him?"

"What do you think is the matter with him?" Gloria said.

"How would *you* like it if a stranger, a psychic, started talking about *your* sex life?"

An expression of genuine wonderment spread across Neal's face. "Is that what the vision was about? His *sex* life?"

The boy was impossible sometimes, Oscar thought. He had none of the control and responsibility that his gift demanded; he couldn't resist parlor trickery, the kind that could get him into serious trouble someday. If Oscar had felt that it would do any good, he'd have had a talk with him long ago; but Neal lived in his own world and seldom listened to anyone other than himself.

The antique Simon Willard clock chimed the quarter-hour: 6:15. Gloria glanced over to it, then back at Oscar nervously. She started to say something—and there was a sudden draft of chill air, a sharpening of the sound of the wind, as the inn's front door opened.

They all turned. A moment later the door closed and Oscar saw Leslie and Jo appear together, wrapped in coats and mufflers and mittens, their cheeks flushed from the cold.

"Good," Neal said happily, "everybody's here now. Just in time to hear my theory about the murders."

6:25 P.M.

Brad Saxon shifted position again, uncomfortably, on the passenger seat of the gray Bureau sedan. It had been an interminable drive up from Hartford. He had never been able to sleep or even to doze in moving vehicles, and his field partner for this investigation, Stan Walker, was a poor conversationalist, chewed gum with a noisy, grinding precision, and kept trying to turn the inside of the car into a furnace. There was nothing outside, either, to occupy his attention. Hadn't been anything to look at since they passed through western Massachusetts. Just darkness for the last hour and a half, just mountains and birch and pine forests and endless fields of snow. Even the cleared two-lane state highway they were on now was deserted, running between windrows like a frozen black river speckled with ice.

The bleak landscape depressed him. Snow and emptiness, a small town or hamlet, then more miles of snow and emptiness. Endless repetition. This was Saxon's first trip to Vermont, and with any luck it would be his last. He had never cared for snow and ice and winter, particularly not after the year in Billings, Montana; he was too much an urbanite, and maybe too much a cynic, to appreciate the work of that old mother, Nature.

The pun made him smile in a wry way, but then fresh waves of too-warm air began to buffet him through the vents: Walker had turned the damned heater up again. The heat made Saxon's head ache; he shifted his body and looked with irritation at Walker's big, stolid frame behind the wheel.

"Stan, how many times do I have to ask you not to put the heater on full blast? Christ, I'm suffocating in here."

"Sorry," Walker said. He reached over to reset the dash lever. "It's just that it feels chilly to me and I can't stand being cold. I guess my metabolism's different from most people's."

Saxon watched Walker's jaws work on the wad of gum. "You have to make so much noise when you chew?"

"Noise?"

"Can't you hear yourself?"

"No. But if it bothers you—"

"It bothers me."

"Okay," Walker said in mild tones, and took the gum out of his mouth and dropped it into the ashtray.

Perversely, that annoyed Saxon, too. The mildness, the passive compliance. You couldn't offend Walker and you couldn't provoke him. Maybe that was because thirty years in the Bureau taught you self-control and infinite patience. But more likely it was because thirty years in the Bureau, thirty years of conformity and pressure and inflexibility, robbed you of the ability to care. Saxon knew a lot of older, small-city resident agents like Walker: plodders doing what they were programmed to do without question or will. When Washington sent out a field agent in charge of an investigation, their job was to give him 100-percent cooperation. And in their minds that meant 100-percent cooperation in *everything*. It didn't matter if the field agent was twenty years younger and inclined to be something of a shit; whatever Saxon wanted, important or trivial, why, then, he got it. Unquestioningly. Passively. Mildly.

If I stay in for thirty years, Saxon thought, will I be just like Walker is right now?

But it was an old fear, an old question that didn't have an answer. The seed had been sown by his ex-wife a long time ago, and it sprouted every once in a while, like now, but it never quite matured enough to make him resign. Or maybe *he* had never quite matured enough. The truth was, the Bureau was only part of the problem. The other part was himself. He was thirty-two years old and he didn't know what the hell he wanted out of life, what it would take to fulfill him and give him peace. Once he had thought it was Evelyn, but it hadn't been her at all.

He massaged his temples with sweating fingertips, ran his hands through his longish black hair. The Bureau let you wear your hair long now that Hoover was gone; Walker, of course, wore his in a neat graying crew cut. Saxon looked over at him again.

"How much further to Whitehall?" he asked.

"Just another fifteen miles or so."

"Good."

Walker cleared his throat. "You really think anyone in this psychic group can help us?"

"Your guess is as good as mine," Saxon said. "Sandra Harris was part of the group; somebody might know something that'll give us a lead. There's another angle, too."

"What's that?"

"Some clairvoyants can visit the scene of a violent crime and get strong enough emanations to trigger a vision. It's happened before. There are a couple of Dutchmen, Dykshoorn and Peter Hurkos, who specialize in that sort of thing."

Walker shrugged. "I've heard of that."

"But you don't believe it, right?"

"Let's just say I'm skeptical."

"I used to be skeptical, too," Saxon said. "But I've seen too much firsthand evidence in the past couple of years."

"You worked on many cases involving psychics?"

"A few. The Bureau keeps assigning me to them." Saxon's smile was humorless. "I did a lot of research the first time—read the books by J. B. Rhine and Gardner Murphy, talked to some parapsychologists. So now I'm the resident expert on clairvoyance."

"I once read about some ESP tests at Duke University," Walker said thoughtfully. "There were random demonstrations, but none of them were duplicated in front of scientific witnesses."

"There are a hell of a lot of things that science hasn't been able to explain. The Resurrection hasn't been duplicated, has it? Besides, psychics find it hard to produce on demand."

Walker was silent, and the silence was eloquent: He was thinking, plainly, that it was all horseshit. Well, let him think it. It was the same as religion: You either believed or you didn't believe, and no amount of debate was going to make you change your mind.

"Anyhow," Walker said at length, "psychic visions or not, it would probably turn out to be a waste of time. Taking somebody from this group down to the Harris farmhouse, I mean."

"Not if it helps solve the murder."

"But that's not our job; Morris Evers is. Unless the murder is connected with Evers's disappearance, and that seems like a pretty thin possibility. Don't you think?"

"Pretty thin," Saxon agreed. "But it's worth checking out. Don't *you* think?"

"Sure," Walker said. Mildly. "We've got to cover all the angles."

Morris Evers was a middle-rank AEC administrator who had vanished from Washington ten days ago. None of his friends, family, or government associates had any idea why; he had simply left his office at 6:00 one evening and disappeared. Evers was involved in classified work and there was always the possibility of foreign agents being responsible. The director had assigned a number of Bureau agents to the investigation, none of whom had as yet uncovered anything worthwhile.

It was only after the discovery of Sandra Harris's body yesterday morning that Saxon had been called in. The Harris woman was a distant cousin of Evers's, and Walker, as the Hartford resident, had checked her out shortly after Evers's disappearance. She had claimed to have no knowledge of his whereabouts, to have had no communication with him in several years, and Walker had been satisfied that she was telling the truth. Except now she had turned up dead—murdered. Which opened up the possibility that the two incidents in Washington and Connecticut were somehow related.

During the course of their check on the woman's friends and relatives, Saxon and Walker had found out, earlier today, about the PSYCHICs group to which she had belonged. They hadn't been able to contact any of the surviving four members of the group, who lived in Connecticut and New York, but had learned that they were all gathering for the weekend in Whitehall, Vermont, where a fifth member lived. Apparently, because Sandra Harris was the second of their number to die violently within a month, they were concerned that someone had targeted the group. If that were the case, there wouldn't seem to be any connection with Evers, and it would be wholly a matter for local and state law enforcement agencies. But until Saxon was satisfied, the death of Sandra Harris had to be considered a matter of Bureau interest.

Thin flakes of snow began to spatter against the windshield; the night, the winter-barren countryside, seemed even darker now. Walker switched on the wiper blades and then began to gnaw the inside of his cheek with the same grinding precision with which he chewed the wad of gum if with less noise.

Saxon moved lower on the seat, laid his head against the back. He closed his eyes and thought about the upcoming session with PSYCHICs. The idea of meeting five clairvoyants at once was vaguely intriguing, even under these circumstances. He had always gotten along well with people who had the gift, no doubt because he was a believer. And because he understood what it must be like for them, the pain and the loneliness and the uncertainty.

What would a whole group of them be like? he wondered. Individually they were sometimes defensive and withdrawn, sometimes open and defiant, sometimes deliberately mysterious. Multiply that by five and what did you have?

6:25 P.M.

As soon as Leslie and Jo Turner had shed their coats and hats in the foyer cloakroom and, dispensing with the amenities, taken seats in front of the lobby fireplace, Neal Iverson said, "I've got a theory about the murders, about why Tony and Sandra were killed."

"I'm sure you do, dear," Jo said wearily.

"It's a good theory, too. I think it might be the answer."

"We can hardly wait to hear it," Jo said, and turned her head to give Leslie a small ironic smile. "Can we, love?"

Leslie held her hands out to the fire to warm them. "I suppose not," she said.

"The way I see it," Neal began, "the person who killed them is a psychotic who has a really insane hatred for clairvoyants. Maybe he had a bad experience with a psychic at one time and it kept festering inside his head and finally turned into a homicidal compulsion—to kill as many clairvoyants as he could. You know, like at random. Nothing personal in it." He looked around at them expectantly, his eyes glittering. "Well? What do you think?"

"I think it's utter nonsense," Jo said. She reached over and patted his knee. "But there's nothing personal in that either, sweetheart."

"I think it's nonsense too," Gloria said. "I mean, *really*."

Neal began to look defensive and a little petulant. "It's a sound theory," he said. "It's a very sound theory."

"How would this person know about our group?" Oscar asked him. "We don't exactly advertise our existence, son."

"There are ways," Neal said. "You can find out anything if you want to badly enough."

Jo lit a cigarette, brushed a strand of shag-cut blond hair off her forehead. She was a thin, angular woman, rather striking for someone in her late forties, Leslie thought; the angularity of her features was somehow sensual in a rough sort of way, and her gray eyes were brash and cynically wise. Wearing one of the black pantsuits she seemed to prefer, holding her cigarette at a careless angle, she looked more Lauren Bacall than Tallulah Bankhead.

"If you're right, angel," she said to Neal, "then our lives are in danger, too. And I simply refuse to believe that."

"Well, *I* believe it."

"I don't," Gloria said. "I agree with Jo. It's nonsense; what happened to Tony and Sandra just *can't* have anything to do with us."

"I'm afraid it can," Oscar said, "and I'm afraid it does." His eyes were sorrowful and he looked unhappy for the first time since Leslie had known him. "Neal may be right about that much."

"I think I'm right, period," Neal said. "What about you, Leslie? Don't you think I'm right?"

"I don't know what's right," she said. "None of us does. All I know is Tony and Sandra are dead because someone murdered them."

"Exactly," Jo said. She waved her cigarette. "And let's assume that Neal and Oscar *are* right and someone is after the rest of us, too. Well, then, isn't it a mistake to be meeting here like this? Meeting at all, at any time?"

Oscar frowned. "What are you getting at, Jo?"

"The point, sweetheart. We ought to consider disbanding."

"What?"

"You heard me. Disbanding the group."

He looked at her aghast.

Neal said, "That's not a good idea at all. For one thing, there's safety in numbers. And for another, we might be able to find out who this psychotic is if we work together."

"How can we possibly do that, darling?"

"By concentrating in a body, trying for a fusion of our powers. I mean, recently I've been having a series of intimations and cloudy symbols. I don't know what they mean yet, but I'm pretty sure they're connected with the murders. If we can create enough psychic energy among the five of us, I might be able to have a clear vision—"

"Balls," Jo said. Which was another of her less-than-endearing traits: using coarse language at odd moments, as if for intentional shock value. "Clairvoyance doesn't work that way and you know it as well as we do."

"It's worth a try," Neal said. He tapped the spot between his eyebrows. "I feel that I'm sensitive to the murders. I feel that I can help solve them with the power of my gift."

Nobody said anything to that. But Leslie wondered if Neal really was sensitive to the murders. She had felt, illogically, that she must be the only one of them who was, but that didn't have to be the case at all. Any of the others could have been affected, too.

She looked around at each of them. Oscar with his dull, wistful personality and his overenthusiasm for PSYCHICs; Gloria with her giddy nature and her annoying habit of saying everything as if it were an actress's lines in a bad play; Jo with *her* annoying habits and her brash manner that may or may not have concealed insecurity or unhappiness; Neal with his tendency to be offensive, his petulance, his childish self-importance, and the rest of a long list of negative qualities. She didn't know any of them beyond those superficial points and she didn't really like any of them either. She wished they hadn't come to Whitehall tonight. She wished she hadn't let Oscar talk her into joining the group in the first place. From the time of her first psychic experience at the age of eight, the gift—the curse—had been an ugly private thing that hurt her and kept on hurting her. Oscar had convinced her that associating with others who shared it would bring her a sense of peace and kinship. Instead, as she should have known it would, it was only bringing her more misery.

Oscar leaned forward on his chair, hands clasping his plump knees. "We can't disband PSYCHICs," he said to Jo. "I won't hear of it."

"It makes sense, darling."

"No, it doesn't. We're a group, Jo, we're almost a *family*. We have to see this through together."

"Right," Neal said. "We have to join hearts and minds for the common good."

"Don't be dramatic, love," Jo told him. "And why don't you take off that silly cap, you look like a teen-age Sherlock Holmes."

"Sherlock Holmes wore a deerstalker hat," Neal said. "This isn't anything like that, it's unique. I had it made especially for—"

"Oh, shut up about your hat," Gloria said. "I'm *tired* of hearing about your idiotic vision hat."

"It's not idiotic—"

"It *is* and I don't want to hear about it anymore. I don't want to hear about Tony and Sandra anymore either; I just want to go back to Storm Junction and paint *sets*." She took a breath. "Disbanding the group is the best idea anyone's had so far, it really is."

Imploringly, Oscar turned to Leslie. "You don't feel that way, do you?"

"Yes," she said. "I'm sorry, Oscar, but I do."

"But it would be a terrible mistake. We have to think of each other, our mutual safety."

"We also have to think of our peace of mind," Jo said. "If we stay together, darling, we're only going to get on each other's nerves. And sooner or later that would lead to all sorts of nasty suspicions."

Leslie stiffened.

"Suspicions?" Oscar said. "What suspicions?"

"Of each other, naturally."

"I don't understand what you mean."

"I do," Neal said suddenly. His eyes glittered again; the thick lenses of his glasses made the pupils look enormous. "Jo's saying that one of us might be the murderer."

Oscar paled. Gloria put a hand to her mouth and said in a horrified voice, "My God!"

Jo said, "That is *not* what I'm saying, Neal. Don't put words in my mouth. None of us is a murderer. I'm only pointing out what paranoia can do—"

Leslie stood up. She didn't care much for alcohol, with the exception of wine with meals, but if she was going to stay here and face this much longer, she needed something to settle her nerves. "I'm going to get a drink. Do any of you want anything?"

"God, yes," Jo said. "A double manhattan, love."

Leslie nodded and turned away. Behind her as she crossed the lobby she could hear Gloria saying in shrill tones, "I won't *listen* to any more of this wild talk. I simply *won't*. . . ."

When she entered the bar, five pairs of eyes swung around to watch her. Harmon Colebrook was sitting on a wooden stool at the far end, across the bartop from where the antique dealer, Ephraim Buell, and young Buddy Quint sat on padded chairs. The other two men were elderly year-round residents whose names she knew but couldn't remember, playing cribbage at one of four tables.

"A straight vodka and ice, please," she said to Colebrook. "And a double manhattan."

He nodded, stood without enthusiasm.

Buddy Quint turned his head away from her and covered the nearest of his acne-blotched cheeks with his hand; he was a lanky youth with red hair and the same dour expression as his father, Tom, who owned Quint's Country Store. Buell watched her with his body tilted slightly to one side. His eyes were dark, guarded, faintly glassy; she thought he might be a little drunk. He was a small, shrunken man in his late fifties and he had a bullet-shaped head spotted with hair the color of dust; in this light it looked like moss on a gray rock. Not only was he as taciturn and provincial as the Quints, as Harmon Colebrook, but he was odd in a way that Leslie couldn't quite define. She always felt uncomfortable in his presence, had not exchanged twenty words with him in the four months she had lived in Whitehall.

Colebrook scooped ice into a glass, tipped a bottle of vodka over it. "Should have told us your friends were coming up for the weekend," he said to her.

"I didn't know it until last night."

"Don't care for any of them much, you want the truth. Particularly that young man of yours."

"What?"

"Smart-mouthed one in the cap. Iverson."

She winced. "He's not my young man. He's married."

"Too bad for his wife," Colebrook said, and one of the old cribbage players cackled as if he thought that was a fine joke.

Leslie said nothing. Colebrook didn't care for the group for the same reason he and the rest of Whitehall didn't care for her. Clairvoyance, in the minds of some rural New Englanders, was a dark power akin to witchcraft. The old Puritan beliefs died hard up here, if they ever died at all. *Bad enough having one living in your village; a bunch of them under your own roof at one time was real cause for alarm. No telling what they were capable of, what they might do to you.*

Oh, yes, she knew all about that kind of attitude. She had grown up in a rural Vermont town not much larger than Whitehall, upstate, and she had had to deal with it all through her adolescence. So she hadn't told anyone that she was psychic when she moved here. Only then, despite her objections, Oscar had gotten the group up here for a meeting in October; and silly, loud-mouthed Neal had let out the truth. Before that weekend, Colebrook and the other villagers had accepted her in their aloof way; after that weekend, they had turned distant and mistrustful. And the anonymous phone calls had started. The only people who had shown any real friendliness toward her were the Johnsons, a young couple who lived a mile from her on Green Rock Farm and who admitted to being ex-hippies and born-again Christians. But she had discovered early on that their only interest in her was religious conversion, as if she were someone who had to be exorcised of demons, and she avoided them now as she more or less avoided everyone else here.

If this was the year 1650, she thought bitterly, they would have burned me at the stake by this time. And Colebrook and Buell would have read the depositions over the flames.

"They all going to stay until Sunday?" Colebrook asked her as he set two filled glasses on the bar.

"I don't think so."

"Fat one with the white hair said they might."

"Then maybe they are. You'll have to ask them."

She took two dollar bills from her purse, laid them down, and picked up the glasses. Buell was still watching her with his veiled eyes; his mouth was puckered as if he were tasting something sour. She met his gaze for a moment, because she had learned long ago not to show vulnerability to men like him, and then turned and went out into the lobby again.

The first thing she noticed as she emerged into the lobby was that Gloria's chair was empty. Neal and Jo seemed to be arguing; Oscar was sitting with his shoulders slumped and a look of dismay on his round elf's face. Leslie crossed to them, handed the manhattan to Jo.

"Thanks, darling. I do need this."

Leslie sat down. "Where's Gloria?"

"Gone back to Storm Junction. To paint her sets, I suppose."

"I tried to keep her from leaving," Neal said. He was frowning and he sounded hurt. "She told me to go to hell and walked out."

"It's your fault, Jo," Oscar said. "If you hadn't suggested it was one of us who killed poor Tony and Sandra—"

"Oscar, love, how many times do I have to tell you I suggested no such thing?"

"It's an interesting theory," Neal said, brightening. "But I like my theory better. About the psychotic stranger who hates clairvoyants and wants to kill them at random. Us at random. No, all clairvoyants at random."

"Our lives may be in danger," Oscar said plaintively. "Why can't anyone except Neal understand that?"

"Oh, we understand it, dear. We just don't believe it."

"We can't disband PSYCHICs. We need each other."

"Right," Neal said. "Absolutely right." He stroked his checkered cap. "You know, I'm *sure* I'm sensitive to the murders. Maybe all of us don't need to work together; maybe I can use my vision hat and my tarot cards to solve the case myself."

"Bullshit," Jo said. "No offense, angel."

Neal didn't seem to hear her. He blinked rapidly several times, as if struck by a sudden insight. "Hey," he said, "do you know what that would mean? It would mean that I'd bring a homicidal maniac to justice with my psychic gift. My name would be in all the newspapers, I'd be famous. Jo, think what that would do for my career as a psychic entertainer!"

"For the thousandth time, darling, I don't handle psychic entertainers," Jo said. "Kazoo players are my bottom line."

"The Prince of Psychics," Neal said. "Boy!"

Leslie raised her glass and took a long swallow of vodka. Neal was saying something else, but she didn't listen to it. Instead she stared into the fireplace, watched the flames lick up around the birch logs on the grate.

She had never felt more alone.

7:05 P.M.

Harmon Colebrook watched the Abbott woman walk out of the bar into the lobby, and then shook his head and sat down again on his stool. She was just like the rest of those damned psychics out there, maybe worse because she'd brought them here in the first place. All her damned fault, when you got right down to it.

One of the cribagge players, Seth Adams, called to him, "Hey, Harmon, you think that missy can really tell the future?"

"No," Colebrook said.

"Too bad. I'd like to know when George here is going to beat me at a game of cribbage."

"Old fool," George Parsons said. "Ain't nothing funny about them people."

Adams cackled. Everything was funny to him; he hadn't been entirely right in the head since his stroke four years back.

Buell said, "Do me again, Harmon," and pushed his empty glass across the bar.

"You got something to celebrate tonight, Eph?"

"Celebrate, hell. Man works hard all day, he's entitled to a little relaxation. If he can get it with bunch of crazy city people around that claim to have ESP and psychic visions."

Colebrook stood again and poured three fingers of rye into Buell's glass. It was his suspicion that Buell was an alcoholic. Did too much drinking for it to be purely social. But he had himself under control, if so—at least in public. Colebrook had never seen him more than just a little unsteady on his feet in the two years since Buell opened his antique shop down the road. At any rate, he wasn't a bad sort. Native, came from up Burlington way, he said. And he'd given Colebrook a good deal on a few antiques for the inn, including that Simon Willard tall clock out in the lobby and the pillar-and-scroll on the wall in here. If Buell cared to get tighter than usual tonight, what the hell, that was his privilege. Who could blame him?

Buell took a bite of his drink, wiped his mouth with the back of one hand. "How come you let those people stay here again, Harmon?" he said.

"Myrna checked 'em in," Colebrook said. "I was doing chores."

"It's your property. You don't have to let 'em stay."

"No, and maybe I won't past tonight."

"I thought we'd seen the last of 'em in October," Buddy

Quint said. "Now here they are again. What for, in the middle of winter?"

"Wish I knew," Colebrook said. "There's something going on, all right. You can feel it. Only four of 'em this time, besides Leslie Abbott, and they been arguing ever since they came. Caught bits and pieces of what they been saying—that smart young bastard's got a loud voice. But not enough to make much sense of it."

"None of 'em said anything to you or Myrna?"

"Just that they're having a meeting."

"Come all the way to Vermont to have a meeting?"

"Account of Leslie, maybe."

"That girl," Buell said. "She hadn't moved here, we wouldn't be troubled like this. Be better for all of us if she went somewhere else."

"Not much we can do about that. Just now, anyway."

"Maybe not," Buell said. He put away the last of his rye. "She's scared about something, Harmon."

"Think so?"

"Damn right. Saw it in her face a minute ago. What's she got to be scared of in Whitehall except those damned friends of hers, tell me that?"

"Why would she be afraid of 'em?"

"Don't ask me. Seems you're the one to find out just what the hell's going on."

"Well, I intend to do just that."

"Sooner the better."

"In time, Eph."

"Time's now," Buell said sullenly, and pushed his empty glass across the bartop. "Might as well set me up again. One for Buddy, too. I'm not fixing to go back and sit around alone tonight."

Colebrook poured the drinks. As he was putting the rye bottle away, Myrna came through the lobby entrance and beckoned to him.

Christ, now what? He went down to her. He'd thought her a decent-looking woman when they got married sixteen years ago, and maybe she had been. Wasn't now, for a fact. Forty-five and getting fat, and the shine and softness long gone out of her hair; half the time it looked like strands of frayed black string. She didn't like it in bed anymore either, if she ever had in the first place. Virgin when he married her, by God. Hadn't had a man because she'd spent all her time teaching grade school and tending to her teched old mother. Woman like that, never with a man until she was almost thirty, what could you expect? Still, it was a hell of a thing when your wife wouldn't let you touch her but once a month, and then under protest. What that young snot had said before, about them having another bedroom argument . . .

Hell with it.

He said, "What this time?"

Her face was all pinched up, the way it got when she was peeved at something, and her back was straight as a stick. "Two strangers just came in," she said. "They want rooms."

"Good. Regular guests we can do with."

"These aren't regular guests."

He grimaced. "Meaning what?"

"You'll see when you talk to them."

"Why didn't you take care of it?"

"You'll see," Myrna said again, flatly. "They want dinner; I'll tend to that." She went down to the dining-room entrance and disappeared through it.

Damned woman, Colebrook thought. He stepped out from behind the bar, crossed into the lobby and then into the reception foyer. The two men standing in front of the desk were wearing overcoats over dark business suits, wearing snow-flecked hats, and carrying small overnight bags. One of them was in his thirties, lean and dark-featured, with eyes that were steady and alert and didn't blink much; the other one was maybe twenty years older, Colebrook's age, and was big and blocky and had a gray crew cut under his hat.

Still frowning, he said, "Help you?"

"Yes," the young one said. "We'd like rooms."

"Just for tonight?"

"Probably."

"Passing through, are you?"

"Not exactly. We're here to see some of your guests."

Colebrook's mouth tightened. "What guests?"

"Members of a group called PSYCHICs."

Well, god*damn* it. "You more of the same?"

"More of the same what?"

"Psychics, clairvoyants, whatever you call yourselves."

"No. Would those people in the lobby over there be members of the group?"

"They would. What do you want with 'em?"

"What we want with them is a private matter, Mr. Colebrook. You *are* Mr. Colebrook, I take it?"

"That's who I am. And if I'm going to let you stay under my roof, I got a right to know who *you* are."

"Sure you do," the older man said, and reached inside his suit coat and came out with a leather case. He flipped it open, held it out so Colebrook could see the identification card and photograph it contained, the blue and gold badge.

Federal Bureau of Investigation.

"Now then, Mr. Colebrook," the young one said, "do you want to let us register so we can get on with our business?"

I knew it, Colebrook thought. I knew there'd be trouble. The FBI. Jesus Christ, the FBI!

7:25 P.M.

The little group sitting before the lobby fireplace reacted with surprise and worried frowns when Saxon showed his credentials and told them he and Walker were there about the murder of Sandra Harris. Three of them reacted that way, anyhow. The fourth, the boyish-looking one in the cap and the thick glasses, Neal Iverson, seemed more excited than anything else; he kept squirming around on the sofa like a puppy about to pee on itself.

The other three seemed ordinary enough, at least on the surface. The elderly, white-haired man, Oscar Koskovich, looked like somebody's nice old grandfather; Jo Turner, the middle-aged blonde, looked—not unpleasantly—like a madam in a high-class whorehouse. Leslie Abbott, the slim brunette, was the most interesting of the four, though, and Saxon found himself paying more attention to her than to any of the others. She was attractive, that was one thing: the sort of attractiveness that comes over you subtly and then lingers in your mind. You might have to look at her twice to notice it, but you'd never have to look a third time. But more than that, there was an odd combination of strength and vulnerability about her, of independence and suffering. It made him curious to know what she was like inside.

The fifth member of the group, Gloria Mason, had been there until twenty minutes ago, when she'd left for her home in Storm Junction, New York. Neal Iverson had volunteered that information.

It was Iverson who broke the silence now by saying, "The FBI! Wow! I never expected the FBI to be working on this case."

"What case is that, Mr. Iverson?"

"The murders, of course. Tony Murray and Sandra Harris. That's why you're here, right?"

"Yes and no," Saxon told him. "We're only concerned with the death of Sandra Harris. As it might relate to the disappearance of a government official named Morris Evers."

"Oh, sure, that was in all the papers. I read about that."

Oscar Koskovich said, "How could Sandra's murder be connected with a missing government official?"

"She and Evers were cousins. She never mentioned that fact to you?"

"No. No, she didn't."

"I didn't know about it either," Iverson said.

"How about you, Miss Abbott?"

"No." Soft voice, same mixture of strength and vulnerability.

"Miss Turner?"

"I'm afraid not."

"Did any of you talk to Sandra Harris recently?"

None of them said they had.

"When was the last time you saw her?"

"The week before Christmas," Iverson said. "Just after Tony Murray was killed. We had a meeting in New York City." He stroked his cap, nibbled his lower lip like a squirrel with a nut. "You know," he said abruptly, "maybe the Mafia is behind it all."

Saxon stared at him. Walker, who had been quietly taking notes, looked up and spoke for the first time: "Mafia?"

"Neal, dear," Jo Turner said, "don't be a horse's ass."

"Well, it's *possible*," Iverson said. "I mean, there was some talk that the Mafia supplied the money for Tony's restaurants in New Jersey. Maybe they killed him and then killed Sandra; maybe they killed Morris Evers, too."

"What on earth for?"

"I don't know. The Mafia murders people all the time."

"They don't murder government officials," Jo Turner said. "At least not Atomic Energy officials. And they don't go around strangling clairvoyants and hanging them afterward."

"Tony Murray wasn't mixed up with the Mafia," Koskovich said. "There wasn't any truth to that rumor."

Iverson said, "Well, I don't *really* think the Mafia is behind it. It was just an idea. I think my original theory is much better."

"What original theory?" Saxon asked him.

"That it's a psychotic who's murdering clairvoyants at random because he had a bad experience with one once and it turned into a homicidal obsession. Random obsession. Don't you think that's a good theory?"

Saxon wondered if the man was playing with a full deck. "What we're interested in is facts, Mr. Iverson, not theories."

Iverson looked aggrieved. "My theory *is* fact. I know it is, I can feel it like birds fluttering in my consciousness."

Saxon decided to ignore him. He asked several more questions about Sandra Harris—her habits, her friends, whether or not she had strong political leanings. The answers were all negative in the way of useful information. He questioned them about her psychic abilities, which had apparently been limited and which she had apparently been reluctant to discuss. Nothing there either.

Koskovich said, "You seem to know quite a bit about clairvoyance, Mr. Saxon."

"I've worked with clairvoyants in the past," he said.

"Really?" Iverson asked. "To help you solve a case?"

"On two occasions, yes."

"I'd like to help you solve *this* case. See, I've been having these cloudy intimations and I'm convinced I'm sensitive to the murders. With my vision hat I know I can bring them into focus and identify the killer."

Walker said, "Vision hat?"

"This cap I'm wearing. I call it my vision hat because it allows me to have clearer and stronger visions."

Walker watched him warily.

"Maybe if I visited the scenes of the murders. You know, like Peter Hurkos does. Then maybe that would—"

"Neal, for God's sake," Leslie Abbott said, "can't you please shut up?"

"Shut up? But I'm trying to—"

Saxon said, "Mr. Iverson, if we decide we can utilize your psychic ability, we'll let you know. Right now you can cooperate by keeping still."

Iverson's expression turned sullen and pouting; he folded his arms across his chest like a kid and stared into the fireplace.

Maybe the man *was* sensitive to Sandra Harris's murder, but Saxon doubted it. Iverson was a buffoon, and that made everything he said or believed suspect.

Saxon was aware of Walker's eyes on him, didn't meet them because he knew what he would see: *I knew these people were weird.* Instead he put his own gaze on Leslie Abbott.

"Miss Abbott," he said, "may I speak to you privately?"

"Privately?"

"Would you mind?"

"No, I guess not."

He led her across the lobby to where two armchairs were turned toward each other. They sat down. Her eyes were steady on his, but in her lap her hands moved together and apart in an agitated way. Strength and vulnerability. She was an intriguing woman, all right. The kind of woman who attracted him; the kind of woman his ex-wife, Evelyn, had been when he first met her in Billings. Maybe that was because he had always had a good deal of empathy—too much empathy, Walker would probably say, for a man in his position.

Screw Walker.

He said, "Have you ever done any cooperative work with law enforcement agencies, Miss Abbott?"

"Cooperative work?"

"Using your gift to help on criminal investigations."

"No," she said uneasily, "I've never done anything like that."

"Have any of the others?"

"Not that I know of." She took a breath. "You're going to ask me to go down to Sandra Harris's house, aren't you? That's what you're leading up to."

"Yes. But it's your decision. I won't insist if you say no."

She shook her head, and Saxon thought that she was on the point of saying just that: no.

"You can trust me, Miss Abbott," he said, and wasn't sure why he had put it just that way. "I don't want you to be hurt."

There was a subtle change in her expression, something that he couldn't quite read. She was silent for several seconds; then she took another breath and said, "All right. I don't know how much good it will do, but I'll go down there with you."

He nodded and thought: Good, I'm glad.

Because as much as anything else, it would give him a chance to know her.

MIDNIGHT

Leslie couldn't sleep.

She lay in bed with her eyes closed, listening to the faint whisper of wind-hurled snow against the windowpanes, and tried to will herself into unconsciousness. But her mind refused to shut down. It was restless, hyperactive; thoughts came and went and came again: Oscar and Neal and Jo and Gloria, Brad Saxon and the FBI, the visions, the murders, the painting, the feeling of predestination, the trip tomorrow to Sandra's farmhouse in Connecticut.

Part of her wanted to make the trip, and part of her dreaded it. She was already sensitive to the murders, and scenes of violent death were often fraught with triggering emanations. Maybe she would be able to identify the dark shape; she owed it to Sandra and Tony, to the others, to herself, to at least enter into a situation where it could happen. Free will in that, at least. But maybe, if she did have an experience, it would be nothing more than a repeat of the other two visions—the colors, the terror, the screams, the smell of excrement, the dark figure that had no face for her to see.

Ambivalence. Uncertainty. It was good that Brad Saxon had asked her to go, and good that she had agreed; but she had been on the verge of refusing him, would have refused if he hadn't asked her to trust him. Strange thing for him to say. No one had ever said that to her before, and the last person she would have expected it from was an FBI agent who had known her for fifteen minutes.

But he wasn't anything like what she had imagined an FBI agent to be. He seemed to understand, as well as anyone could who didn't have the curse himself, what it was like to be clairvoyant; and he seemed to be a man who had known pain and recognized and responded to it in others. At this point she needed someone like that, someone to trust, even if it were only for a little while.

She turned on her side, wrapped her arms around the pillow.

He's coming at nine o'clock, she thought. You've got to get some rest. Stop thinking. Just sleep. Sleep—

Out in the kitchen the telephone bell went off.

The sudden noise was shrill in the quiet darkness, like a distant shriek. She sat up in bed, blinking. It came again, and a third time, and a fourth. She rubbed at her eyes, stared at the luminous dial of her clock radio. Who would be calling her at this hour?

Unless—

Oh, God, she thought, not again. Not again.

Five rings. Six.

Don't answer it.

Seven rings. Eight. Nine . . .

The sound began to grate on her nerves. She couldn't let it go on; it was liable to keep up for minutes. She fumbled for the switch on the bedside lamp, turned it, and swung out of bed.

Ringing. Ringing.

Leslie threw her robe around her, slid her feet into her slippers. Went out of the bedroom and through the hallway into the kitchen.

Ringing.

She ran the last few steps to the wall extension, ripped the receiver off its hook. Silence again, except for the wind outside and the rapid murmur of her breathing. She brought the receiver slowly to her ear and mouth.

"Yes? What is it?"

"How many times you have to be told?" the voice said. The same voice as all the other times—muffled, genderless, threatening. "You're not wanted in Whitehall, we don't want *any* of your kind here."

Angrily she said, "Who is this? Who are you?"

"You'll find out who I am, you stay around here. You'll find out. Those paintings of yours'd make a nice fire, miss bitch, you ever think about that? A nice hot fire on a cold winter night."

Leslie leaned forward and slammed the receiver back into its cradle, so hard the bell sounded a single sharp note. "God-damn you," she said aloud. "Goddamn you to hell."

For a time she stood there in the darkness, waiting for her respiration to slow. Then she unhooked the receiver again and laid it down on the drainboard nearby; she didn't want any more phone calls tonight. Or ever again: She'd have the damned number changed and unlisted first chance she had.

Back in the bedroom, she switched off the lamp and lay down on her stomach and pulled the blankets around her head. Buried her face in the pillow. But as soon as she did that, phantom echoes of the shrieking phone began to repeat themselves in her mind. Only to change into the haunting melody of a flute. And finally become a woman's voice, screaming.

Not Sandra Harris's voice. Someone else's.

A voice that might have been her own.

CHAPTER 3

Saturday, January 20

8:30 A.M.

With Walker for company, Saxon had breakfast in the inn's dining room: ham, griddle cakes and maple syrup, chickory-flavored coffee. Walker ate heavily and stolidly, as he had at their late supper last night, but he didn't seem to take any real enjoyment in the food. It was as if eating were a directive handed down by the Bureau and it was his duty to perform it to the fullest. Saxon liked the food but he wasn't hungry and ate sparingly; Leslie Abbott had been on his mind when he went to bed and she was on his mind now.

He hadn't invited Walker to accompany them down to Connecticut, and Walker hadn't asked to go along. It was obvious, though, that he didn't care for the idea of spending the day in Whitehall with Iverson and Koskovich and Jo Turner; and it was just as obvious that he felt the PSYCHICs group was a dead end as far as the Evers case went and that they should be on their way back to Hartford this morning. But Saxon knew Walker's Bureau training would hold: Never question a field agent-in-charge, just do what you're told. The Programmed Man.

When Saxon finished his coffee, he said, "I'll be going now. After we get to Twin Forks I'll check back with your office." They had called the Hartford office last night, before supper: nothing new on Evers there or in Washington either. "You might do the same."

"Right," Walker said. He unwrapped a stick of gum. "You want me to talk to those people again?"

Those people. As if they were freaks. "Yes. Stir up their memories, see if there's anything they might have overlooked or forgotten."

"I doubt if there will be."

"You can also get in touch with the woman who left last night before we got here. Gloria Mason."

Walker put the stick of gum into his mouth and began to chew noisily. "Whatever you say."

Saxon left him and went out through the lobby and through the foyer, onto the front terrace. The snowfall had stopped sometime during the night, the clouds had broken up and drifted on, and the morning was cold and clear and bright. There were a couple of inches of crusted snow on the ground. On the street a small snowplow that probably belonged to the village was chuffing along. The branches of nearby elm and evergreen trees were stiff and weighted with ice. Icicles hung from the eaves of the inn's weathered brick facade, glistening with prismatic colors in the sunlight.

The innkeeper, Colebrook, wearing gloves and a heavy mackinaw, was working on the terrace with a long-handled snow shovel. Saxon nodded to him, got a blank and sour-faced stare in return. Country hospitality, he thought sardonically, and went down the front walk to where Walker's Bureau sedan was parked.

There was not much to the village, he saw when he drove out onto Main Street past the snowplow. Just the inn, a general store and service station, an antique shop, a dozen scattered houses of which half looked to be closed up for the winter, and a lot of trees and open space. With the cold winter sun shining on it, it looked less bleak and oppressive than he had taken it to be last night. It even had a kind of picturesque beauty. But it also had an aura of emptiness and provincial and cultural isolation: a place on the edge of nowhere.

He wondered why Leslie Abbott had chosen to live here. Maybe it was just that she liked backcountry solitude. Or maybe it had something to do with her gift, something to do with running away. None of his affair, really; what *should* concern him about her was whether or not she could help on the Evers or at least the Harris case.

Except that cases had stopped being just cases to him in Syracuse in 1969. Except that his interest in Leslie Abbott went beyond the professional and he would have been deceiving himself if he didn't admit that. She was the first woman since Evelyn who had affected him quite this way.

Syracuse in 1969.

And Evelyn. Evelyn Kempner Saxon.

Ironic how everything that had happened to him in the last decade, everything he was or was not today, could be traced to one or the other. Until Syracuse he had been a twenty-four-year-old kid, a graduate of the FBI Academy with a lot of idealistic opinions about the Bureau and his own role in government work. The assignment there was only his second in the field: undercover work on the Syracuse University campus, investigating the so-called radical counterculture. Observer mostly, with just a bit of agent provocateur thrown in. No physical danger, but a lot of excitement and the added spice of meeting girls who believed in free love and plenty of it. That was how he'd thought in those days.

Only then there had been a demonstration one night that turned into a riot, and he had had to stand by and watch a score of young people hardly younger than himself—friends, some of them, in spite of the assignment—brutally beaten, one of them so badly that permanent brain damage was the result. Some of his own ideals, his own beliefs, had been clubbed away during that night.

The next day he had applied for a transfer, stating his reasons in Bureau jargon, and after several counseling sessions with senior agents, the transfer had come in. It had come in, all right: to Hoover's famous office in Billings, Montana, where all of the Bureau fuckups or recalcitrants or those who had been caught living out of wedlock with women were sent.

In Billings he had met Evelyn, then a graduate student in English at the state university. No grand passion at first, just a mutual attraction and a good deal of steamy sex. He had surprised himself after six months by asking her to marry him, and she had surprised him further and probably herself as well by agreeing. It was only after a year of marriage that he had come to understand that he was in love with her.

But there was no peace. They had little in common except the bedroom, and they fought constantly about any number of things, not the least of which was his work. She had never liked the fact that he worked for the FBI, and she grew to hate what the Bureau symbolized; she kept telling him it was rigid and dehumanizing and that it would someday turn him into a hardened fascist. What she wanted him to do was to go back to college and study criminal law, and it mattered not at all to her that he had no interest in doing either of those things, nor that it was the hardened fascist who was helping to finance her through the graduate year in English she wanted.

The fact was, he might have quit the Bureau eventually if only she had not kept nagging him about it. He was just not ready to make that decision without an alternative that appealed to him. They were living in Arlington, Virginia, then—apparently mollified by his work in Billings and his marriage, Hoover had called him back there after thirteen months—and he had been given interesting and inoffensive assignments, and the pain of Syracuse had more or less ebbed. So while Evelyn finished off her master's degree and then her doctorate, he found himself working twelve to fifteen hours a day. The distance between them continued to widen, until he came home one night to find Evelyn gone and a note on the table telling him it was over and to please call her lawyer about a divorce settlement.

He hadn't had any contact with her in over four years. He

didn't miss her, hadn't missed her even in the days after she left him; but he had never quite stopped loving her either. Just as he remained with the Bureau but never quite forgot Syracuse. Just as he thought about quitting but never quite got his mind around to doing it.

Ambivalence, that was the story of his life. The marginal man; the man in the middle.

He drove past the two-lane county road, went a quarter of a mile to where a lane branched off Main Street to the east. A sign there read Maplewood Road. He turned off onto the lane and stopped finally in front of the third house on the right, the one Leslie had told him was hers.

It sat in the middle of an elm-shaded yard, set back a hundred yards from the lane; a low rambling stone fence, half-hidden by snowdrifts, enclosed the property. Obviously it had once been a small country church; the steeple and bell tower were still intact. Just as he stepped out of the sedan, the front door of the house opened and Leslie appeared. He stood waiting as she came down the front walk, her booted feet making thin crunching sounds in the crusted snow.

"Morning, Miss Abbott."

"Good morning."

He hesitated. "You look tired."

"I didn't sleep very well."

"Look, if you'd rather call this off—"

"No," she said, "I want to go through with it." She glanced past him at the car. "Where's your partner?"

"He won't be coming with us."

"Because he doesn't believe in clairvoyance?"

"Something like that."

She was silent after they got into the sedan, and he left it that way until they were a mile out of the village on the county highway. Then, because the silence began to feel awkward, because he wanted to know her, he said, "Are you a native of this area, Leslie? You don't mind if I call you Leslie, do you?"

She looked over at him. "No, I don't mind." Pause. "I was born in Vermont, yes, but not around here. Upstate."

"You lived in New York for a while, didn't you?"

"Three years. How did you know that?"

"We did some checking."

A small smile. "Yes. The FBI has files on all of us, don't they?"

"Not really. The Bureau isn't quite the Big Brother people think it is. For one thing, there's the fact that *people* work for it."

"Mmm," she said.

"You're an artist, right?"

"Yes."

"Commercial art?"

"In New York, yes. Not anymore."

"How come? Good money in it, isn't there?"

"Not good enough to keep me in Manhattan."

"You didn't like it there?"

"I got tired of being put on display by my so-called friends," she said. "Greenwich Village loves freaks; the people there expect you to perform for them like a trained bear."

"Meaning your gift."

"Meaning my curse."

Saxon had heard psychics use that term before, and the bitterness in Leslie's voice as she said it gave him a certain insight into her. He let a half-dozen seconds pass before he said, "How did you happen to come to Whitehall?"

She shrugged. "The house I live in was listed in a real-estate ad in the Montpelier newspaper. I liked it and I like the area. There's a lot of subject matter around here."

"Subject matter?"

"For my work. I do landscape paintings."

"Oh, I see. Can you make a living from that?"

"I manage." She shifted position. "Look, Mr. Saxon, do you mind if—"

"Brad," he said. "Short for Bradley, but forget that."

"All right. Brad. Do you mind if we talk about something else besides me?"

"If you want. But you're an interesting topic."

"Why? Because I'm clairvoyant?"

"I've known clairvoyants before. It's not that."

"Then why?"

"Because I'm attracted to you," he said.

The admission surprised him as much as it did her, but in the silence that followed he was glad that he had brought it out into the open. You had to be honest, particularly with someone who reached you on a personal level. She looked at him for a long moment, and he thought he saw something in her eyes that might have been a responsiveness, a tentative interest of her own. Then she moved her gaze to the windshield and stared at the highway beyond.

He said, "Do you mind my saying that?"

"No, I don't mind. You can't help how you feel."

"How do *you* feel?"

"About you? I don't know. You're not anything like I imagined an FBI agent to be."

"How did you imagine one to be?"

"More like your partner."

Saxon smiled without irony. "Walker's typical, all right."

"And what are you?"

"Good question. Just a man trying to do a job, I guess."

"I don't think so," she said. "That's what Walker is. You're something else." She paused again. "Do you really think there's a connection between the case you're working on and the murders?"

"Well, it's a slim possibility."

"Then why are you taking me down to Sandra's?"

"The Bureau teaches you to be thorough," he said. "Besides, someone killed your two friends and maybe we can both help to find out who it is, FBI case or not. I'd like to know you're going to be safe."

Her eyes softened, and for the first time some of the tension in her seemed to ease. "Thank you."

"For what?"

"For being someone who cares," she said.

10:00 A.M.

Their breaths making vapor plumes on the cold air, Jo Turner and Oscar Koskovich walked along the middle of Broadelm Road, a narrow lane that wound away through birch woods east of the inn. The sun's warmth had softened sections of the ice-glaze on the roadbed, and the footing was slushy in some spots and slick in others. A thin breeze dislodged unfrozen snow from the tree branches, sifted it onto Jo's stocking cap and inside the collar of her coat.

She felt cold and uncomfortable and in an altogether unpleasant humor. She shouldn't have allowed Oscar to talk her into going for this damned trek through the countryside. But he had seemed so dismayed and pathetic at breakfast, and so in need of companionship, that she had finally given in. She had always been too softhearted, that was her problem—which was no doubt part of the reason why she was a third-rate theatrical agent with a client list dominated by specialty acts and smutty resort comedians. At least she didn't handle psychic entertainment acts, she thought, and thanks to Neal Iverson she would never be in the least tempted to.

And of course all Oscar wanted to talk about was the group. PSYCHICs. Such a silly acronym. "You've got to reconsider, Jo," he kept saying to her. "You can't leave us now—we need you, we all need each other."

She had tried again to point out the logic in disbanding, or at least in not gathering together for a while, but he wouldn't be reasoned with. So finally she had said, "All right, darling, I'll give it some more thought," just to placate him and keep him off her case, as the kids put it these days. She had no intention of reconsidering; she had made up her mind. As soon as those FBI agents gave her permission to leave Whitehall, she would get into her car and drive straight back to New York, where there were streets and buildings and a civilized lifestyle. Nature in the raw and quaint rural people bored her terribly. For that matter, so did Oscar and Neal and Gloria.

As the composer Maurice Ravel had once said of himself, she was a pretty artificial person at heart and the better for it.

Oscar said now, "You don't think *I'm* to blame for what's happened, do you, Jo?"

"Blame?"

"By bringing us all together in the first place. I thought it would be nice—the companionship, finally having others like ourselves to talk to and share our experiences with. I didn't imagine it would lead to anything like this. I couldn't bear it if I was in any way responsible for Tony and Sandra being murdered."

"Don't be foolish, Oscar," she said. "You're not to blame. How could you be, darling, if the murders have nothing whatsoever to do with the group?"

"But I'm afraid they do. I'm convinced they do."

She sighed inaudibly. "Have it your way, love."

A crow swooped out of the woods, chattering to itself, and she watched its black-winged flight until it disappeared. Then Oscar said, "I don't think it's an FBI case at all. But I'm glad they're investigating. I feel better having them around."

"I don't. The FBI is good at violating your civil rights, but that's about all."

"Those two agents seem very competent to me," Oscar said. "Particularly that young one, Saxon."

"He doesn't think we're strange, anyway, I'll give him that."

"The other one does, I'm afraid."

"No doubt. Neal and his bloody vision hat."

"Neal," Oscar said musingly. "Maybe Saxon should have taken him down to Twin Forks instead of Leslie. The boy did say he might be sensitive to the murders."

"Do you actually believe that, angel?"

"I don't know. I never know what to believe with Neal."

"He's a twit," Jo said. "Amusing sometimes, but still a twit."

Oscar hunched his shoulders inside his gray wool overcoat. "I just hope Leslie is able to help. She does seem to have a stronger gift than any of the rest of us."

"She's hardly a Dykshoorn, dear."

"Hope, Jo, we have to hope."

"So we do," she said.

They walked in silence for a time. When they neared the edge of the woods, a series of clear, partially webbed animal tracks appeared in the smooth snowbank paralleling the road. Oscar left her side immediately and hurried over to them, sat on his heels to examine them with interest. Animals and PSYCHICs, Jo thought: Those were his only passions now that his wife was dead. And some passions they were, too, poor man.

"Muskrat," he said at length, almost happily. "These are muskrat tracks, Jo."

"How interesting."

"They're fascinating animals, muskrats. Did you know they get their name because they have a pair of large glands in their groin that secrete a substance with a musky odor?"

"Balls," Jo said.

"What?"

"Nothing, darling. Nothing at all."

Beyond the woods there was a rumpled-looking meadowland and a series of hillocks that stretched away to another forest; the sun glistening off all the snow made it look like polished silver. The road curved at a sharp angle to the south, and at the opposite side of the bend it passed through an old-fashioned covered bridge that spanned a narrow stream. The bridge was painted a weathered brown color and had a peaked roof; gaps showed between its board siding, but it was in decent-enough repair considering its probable age.

She wasn't impressed by it, but Oscar clearly was. Probably because he thought there were muskrats or bats or some other nasty creatures living in it or under it. Not without reluctance, she let him lead her inside the bridge. Dark and damp and musty. Something made a scurrying noise in the shadows above, among the crossbeams. Outside, ice cracked in the stream like crockery breaking and there was the faint purling of water beneath the wooden floor. It all made Jo feel colder and more ill-humored.

"Oscar," she said, "I've had enough of Whitehall's darling little attractions for one morning. Suppose we go back now."

He nodded. "'I guess we'd better. I want to call Gloria later on. Maybe I can talk her into driving over from Storm Junction so we can all be together."

Jo said nothing. Oscar simply would not give up.

They went out through the far end of the bridge. A hundred yards further on, the outlines of a trail or cow track wound away in the direction of the village. Oscar took her along there; he had prowled this area in October and seemed to know where he was going. They passed through a long snowfield dotted with barren apple trees, through more birch woods, and eventually—and to Jo's relief—emerged on the north side of the village center, near the antique shop.

As they started past the shop she noticed a large sign behind the front-door glass that said OPEN. Jo collected antiques on a small scale—nothing very expensive; who could afford the prices for even junk nowadays?—and generally did a bit of antiquing whenever she was forced to come to New England. In October she had visited this same shop but hadn't bought anything because the owner was a surly man who had treated her as if she were a potential thief. Still, he had a rather large array of items for sale, and browsing through them for a while struck her as more appealing than sitting around the inn, listening to Oscar and Neal and answering more questions from the older FBI agent.

"I think I'll stop in here for a few minutes, darling," she said to Oscar. "You can toddle ahead to the inn if you want."

"No, I'll come in with you," he said. "Gloria never gets up before eleven and she sleeps so soundly she never hears the phone ring."

They went along the walk to the front porch. Behind a display window was the same litter Jo had seen in October: glassware, copperware, moustache cups, shaving mugs, sand shakers, a cheese press. The usual junk, except for a nice-looking coach lamp on a wooden pedestal in the middle of it all. She pushed open the front door and they stepped inside to the tinkling announcement of a bell.

The interior was a single long dark room with a high-beamed ceiling and a counter at the far end. Behind that was a closed door that probably led down to the cellar. The place was cluttered with more junk, but here and there were worth-while antiques: a cobbler's bench that looked to be over a hundred years old; a parlor stove with nickel trim; a silver-plate copper teakettle; a patchwork quilt made of calico and silk; several small table and wall clocks. There was no sign of the surly owner.

Jo went to one of the shelves and examined an Early American "occasional clock." And as she did so, she began to feel shadowy symbols moving inside her mind, the kind of symbols that usually forecast a vision. Damn! Of all times and places . . .

She backed away from the shelf, ran her gloved hands roughly over her cheeks. The symbols faded and were gone. She let out the breath she had been holding, relieved. In the past few years she had been able, sometimes, to retreat from a vision, force it away willfully. The older she got, it seemed, the less intense and more within her limited control her gift was. Which was a blessing because she didn't see any mark of distinction in it, nor was it central to her life. Until she'd joined PSYCHICs in another softhearted (or softheaded) yielding to Oscar, who had dredged up her name from a years-old newspaper account of a vision she'd had involving a neighbor's runaway daughter, she had had no contact whatsoever with other clairvoyants. And wouldn't again once she was free of the group. Her ability had always been painful; it was best dealt with in private ways.

Oscar said alertly, "Jo? Did you have an experience?"

"No, darling," she told him. "Absolutely not."

Footsteps sounded on the cellar stairs, and a moment later the door opened and Ephraim Buell's wizened form appeared. There was a thin professional smile on his mouth, but it disappeared the instant he saw who his customers were. His face darkened and his lips thinned to a line as puckered and white as a surgical scar; he hurried out to them with an air of belligerence and hostility.

"What do you want here?" he demanded.

"Antiques," Jo said. "What else would we want? Doughnuts?"

"I don't care for your business. I'm not open for you."

Oscar frowned. "But we're only—"

"Maybe the Colebrooks'll put up with you over to the inn," Buell said, "but I don't have to. I don't want you in my store."

Jo said, "Now look, Mr. Bool—"

"Name's *Buell*. Buell, you hear? Now get on out of here. Go on, get out. And don't come back!"

Oscar retreated to the door, looking bewildered. Jo glared at the antique dealer and then followed Oscar out to the porch, down onto the front walk. She stopped a dozen paces along and looked back at the doorway. Buell was standing there, staring out at them with his baleful eyes.

In a deliberate gesture, Jo raised the middle finger of her right hand, and mouthed the words that went with it: *Fuck you.* Then she swung around again, took Oscar's arm.

"And these rural people think *we're* strange," she said bitterly.

10:20 A.M.

"Your partner's making a real mistake," Neal Iverson said to the FBI man, Walker. "You know that? He should have asked *me* to go down to Sandra's place, not Leslie. I'm the one who's been having cloudy intimations about the murders; I'm the one who's sensitive to them."

Walker watched him, his face solemn, his jaws moving steadily around a wad of gum. They were sitting alone in the lobby, facing each other across a chess table with carved wooden chessmen arranged on it. The black pieces were on Neal's side, which bothered him vaguely. He wondered if

Walker, who had sat down first, had chosen the white side because he thought it gave him some sort of psychological advantage.

"Well," Walker said, "he's in charge. He makes the decisions."

"Leslie won't be able to help him," Neal said positively. "He'll just have to make another trip with me, that's all."

"These intimations of yours, Mr. Iverson. What do you see in them, exactly?"

"I don't see anything in them. They're *intimations*."

"You mind explaining that to me?"

"What I've been having are strong feelings, full of symbols that I can't quite decipher. With my vision hat and maybe even with psychometrics, if I could go down to Sandra's place, eventually I'll have a psychic experience with shape and form and inner substance."

"Inner substance," Walker said. "Uh-huh."

"Normal people have intimations all the time—intuition, you know?—but they don't always have significance. With a psychic, these intimations are usually linked to outcome. Clairvoyant intimations are always projective."

"Always projective," Walker said.

Neal scowled at him. Walker was a nonbeliever, there was no doubt about that, and the skepticism was plain in his voice. A hint of mockery, too. Oh, he knew mockery when he heard it; he'd had to put up with a lot of that, not to mention abuse, from his relatives and peers when he was growing up on Flatbush Avenue in Brooklyn. His mother had even taken him to a psychiatrist once, when he was fifteen, and *that* charlatan had mocked him, too, said he was emotionally immature and that his clairvoyance was nothing more than regressive fantasy projections designed to call attention to himself. Regressive fantasy projections! Crap. He not only had the gift, he was, by God, the most mature man he knew.

But there was just no use in trying to convert skeptics like Walker and his mother's shrink. They didn't want to hear the truth. Even when you showed it to them, as he would when he solved the murders with his gift and his vision hat, they would make up explanations to suit their own beliefs. But truth was truth, that was all that mattered. Truth and becoming a famous mentalist like the Amazing Kreskin and going on concert tours as the Prince of Psychics. Which would happen, all right, it was only a matter of time. He had intimations about that, too—about appearing on *television* someday.

He said, "Is there anything else you want to ask me?"

"A couple of things. How well did you know Sandra Harris?"

"Not too well. She didn't talk about herself much."

"Why not?"

"She was shy. She thought her psychic experiences were too personal to share with anyone, even us. What I think, a lot of them had to do with sex."

"Why do you think that?"

"I just do. I'm pretty sure she was gay."

"Uh-huh."

"Was she? Gay, I mean? You probably investigated her private life pretty thoroughly."

"Whatever we might have found out, Mr. Iverson, is privileged information."

Neal nodded. "Check," he said. "But that's okay, you don't have to tell me. She was gay, all right."

"Did you ever see her socially?"

"No. Why would I see a gay person socially?"

"Do you know if she socialized with anyone else in the group?"

"None of our other women are gay," Neal said.

"Mr. Iverson, I'm not talking about personal relationships here. I'm trying to find out if she knew anyone in PSYCHICs well enough to confide in."

"Well—Gloria, maybe. She'd be the only one."

"Gloria Mason?"

"Sure. That's the only Gloria in PSYCHICs."

Walker sighed. "Were Gloria and Sandra Harris intimates?"

"No. I told you, Gloria's not gay."

Walker sighed again. "Let me rephrase the question. Why do you think Sandra Harris might have known Gloria Mason well enough to confide in her?"

"I don't really think that," Neal said. "I just meant Gloria's the only one who saw Sandra outside our meetings."

"For any particular reason?"

"Well, they only lived about ninety miles apart, and Sandra wrote some publicity releases for Gloria's last production. It was Shakespeare, I think. One of the comedies. Is *King Lear* a comedy? Gloria manages a playhouse in Storm Junction. But I guess Sandra wrote the publicity releases at her place in Connecticut. No, it wasn't *King Lear*, that's one of the tragedies. A *Midsummer Night's Tempest*, that was it."

"I see," Walker said, but he didn't sound as if he saw anything. In fact he sounded confused. And FBI agents were supposed to be so clearheaded at all times, Neal thought. Another myth exploded.

"Why don't you ask Gloria about all that?" he said. "She can tell you a lot more than I can."

"Yes. I'm sure of that." Walker stood, so abruptly that his knee jostled the chess table and toppled some of the pieces. Most of the fallen chessmen, Neal noticed with vague satisfaction, were white.

"I don't have any more questions. You're free to go about your business."

"I don't have any business to go about," Neal said. "Not until your partner and Leslie get back from Sandra's place. Except to call my wife, I guess. I forgot to do that last night."

Walker started away toward the foyer; he seemed to be shaking his head as he went.

Myrna Colebrook came in from the dining room wearing a heavy mackinaw and carrying an armful of kindling and birch logs. Her chubby face was pink from the cold outside. She passed near where Neal was sitting without acknowledging his presence, went to one knee on the fireplace stones, and laid down the load of firewood.

"Mrs. Colebrook," he called to her. "Mrs. Colebrook?"

She glanced up reluctantly. "What is it?"

"When you're done there I'd like to have a Coke, please."

"Dining room's closed and we don't open the bar until noon."

"But I just want a *Coke*—"

"Quint's Country Store right next to here," she said. "They have plenty of Coke." She went back to placing logs and kindling on the grate.

Damn it, Neal thought irritably. None of them showed any respect for him. Not the FBI and not even Oscar and the others. That just wasn't right. He was entitled to a little respect, wasn't he? Not because he was special, though he *was*, but because he was a human being and the Prince of Psychics.

He glared at Myrna Colebrook's back for a moment and then stood and went upstairs to his room. It was a nice room, he had to admit that. Done in Vermont farmhouse style, with big bed and chairs upholstered in calico print. His wife, Tina, would have liked it. . . .

Damn! He had almost forgotten to call her again. He pulled the telephone toward him, then had to wait almost three minutes before Buddy Quint came on the switchboard and got him long distance. Tina answered on the third ring.

"This is me," he said.

"Hello, lover. Why didn't you call last night?"

"I forgot. We had a lot of important discussions, and two FBI agents showed up and questioned all of us."

"Really? Tell me all about it, honey."

He told her all about it.

"It sounds wonderful," Tina said. "You solving the murders and everything, I mean. How long do you think it'll take you?"

"I don't know. Those things are hard to judge."

"Well, I hope it doesn't take *too* long. I mean, I miss you a lot when you're away. I wish you were home right now. You know why?"

"Why?"

"So I could play with your pecker."

"Tina, this is very serious business here—"

"I think your pecker is very serious business," Tina said. "I've got to go now. I'll call you again later."

Neal hung up and sat brooding at the phone. Tina was a very intelligent woman—almost as intelligent as he was—but she certainly did like to screw a lot. Not that there was anything wrong with screwing, but you had to keep it in perspective. The *least* important thing right now was sex; the *most* important thing was solving the murders so he could finally get his career as the Prince of Psychics off the ground.

He lay back on the bed and took off his vision hat and held it tightly in his hands. But he couldn't seem to concentrate. Damn his wife, anyway. He shouldn't have called her; he definitely should not have done it.

All he could seem to visualize was Tina playing with his pecker.

TWIN FORKS, CONNECTICUT—11:55 A.M.

When they came around a bend in the country road and the farmhouse appeared ahead of them, Leslie felt herself beginning to tighten up inside. The day was cold and heavily overcast here, threatening snow, and the house seemed dark and forbidding in the gray light. Behind it she saw muddy fields pocked with dirty gray snow and desolate marshland that stretched away into shadow. The phrase "a perfect place for a murder" came to her, and she suppressed a shiver. Stop it, she thought, don't make it any worse than it is. But *murder* remained in her consciousness, *murder* billowing like a sheet in gusts of wind.

"Leslie?" Brad Saxon said. He was watching her with one eye, and there was concern in his voice; he seemed to understand exactly what was happening inside her. "You going to be okay?"

"Yes. I'll be all right."

He braked and turned slowly onto the access road that

wound in to the farmhouse. Parked near the front porch. When he shut off the engine, she could hear the sound of the wind, thin and whispery, blowing in over the marsh. She sat motionless, staring at the house. There was an old-fashioned swing on the porch, and around to the side the winter-barren remains of a vegetable garden; all the windows were shuttered, like dead eyes. She had never been here before, but it was all terribly familiar: just as she had seen it three nights ago in the kitchen of her house, in the vision.

Murder.

I don't want to go in there, she thought.

Murder. Murder.

She took a deep breath, got a tight grip on her control, and stepped out of the car. Brad came around beside her. The wind was cold against her face; she drew her coat tightly around her shoulders as they crossed the muddy ground to the porch.

On the door was a new hasp and padlock, a police barrier. Brad took a key from his pocket and opened the lock. With his hand on the doorknob, he looked at her searchingly.

"Ready?" he said.

Or not. "Yes." Here I come.

He opened the door and they stepped inside.

Darkness. A room filled with crouching shadows. He reached out to the wall, found a light switch, and flicked it. The shapes of furniture seemed to leap at her: sofa, chairs, tables, a highboy, a china cabinet, a music stand near the fireplace. Familiar, too, some of it. She began to feel, strangely, as if she were shrinking inside herself, as if her consciousness were narrowing to a tight circle.

Murder.

But nothing clairvoyant happened.

Dimly she heard Brad shut the door, heard him say, "She was found on the rear porch but she may not have been attacked there. The local authorities weren't sure."

She had nothing to say.

"Do you want to go from room to room?"

She managed a nod.

His hand grasped her arm. Walking then. Hallway. Bathroom. Bedroom. Small study. Kitchen.

Nothing. All unfamiliar.

Rear porch.

Brad pushed open a swinging door, held it for her. She took a step—and came to an abrupt, rigid stop. The shrinking sensation deepened; there was a metallic taste in her mouth.

The porch was foul with the odor of death.

She backed away from it, wheeled around, and half-ran across the kitchen. Behind her Brad's voice called her name and she heard him coming after her. But she didn't answer, didn't stop again until she was back in the front parlor.

"Leslie?"

The death smell was in here now.

Her gaze went from wall to wall. The music stand: She found herself staring at it, fixating on it.

Sounds.

Music. Shrill, piping.

Flute.

And it began, coming from the center of her with the same sudden intensity as before. The colors appeared in her psychic eye, the blues and blacks, the reds and whites. The music stopped and the terror came, the choking pressure at her throat, the pain, the inability to breathe for several seconds. The screaming.

Her legs wobbled; hands caught her, held her. She heard a voice saying words a long way off—

The screams stopped. The stench of excrement made her gag.

And the colors shifted, faded, became an image: Sandra lying on the floor near the silver tube of a flute. Crumpled, dead. Legs, the tails of an overcoat. A hand holding a blue velvet cord.

Blue and black, red and white.

Image: the rear porch, the dark figure standing there, Sandra hanging from one of the rafters with her eyes bulging and her tongue like something wet and unspeakable crawling out of her mouth.

Blue and black, red and white.

Image: a face, shadowed beneath a hat, half-seen, a subliminal perception of eyes, nose, mouth, jawline.

I know that face—it's someone I know.

Part of her was drawn toward the figure, compelled to seek its identity; part of her was repelled by the horror of what she had seen and what she might yet see. Fragmentation. And the image collapsed into the colors and then into the outlines of the parlor. The visual, auditory, and olfactory impressions vanished one by one, leaving only the terror.

External awareness, then. Chills on her back, sweat on her face, body trembling. Brad Saxon beside her, his face pale, holding her with one arm tight over her shoulders. The music stand, the furniture, the walls, the floor: inanimate things so charged with psychic energy that they seemed sentient, malevolent.

Words came from her in a thick whisper. "Take me out of here. Take me *out* of here."

Immediately he led her to the door, hurried her down off the porch and across to the car. He opened the passenger door, eased her inside. Then ran around to the opposite side and got in beside her and started the engine and put the heater on.

The trembling stopped right away, but it was minutes before the warmth of the air blowing through the heater vents took away her chill; before the last of the terror vanished and her thoughts settled into patterns that were wholly normal.

"Leslie?" he said.

"Yes. I'm okay."

His eyes were grave. "It must have been bad," he said. "You looked—" He shook his head.

"It was bad," she said.

"Can you talk about it yet?"

"I have to, don't I?"

"Not until you're ready."

She looked through the windshield at the farmhouse, at the threatening sky and the marshland beyond.

"We'll go now," he said.

"Yes. I don't think it would do any good to try again."

"I wouldn't ask you to."

He left the car and went back up to the porch. She watched him shut off the parlor light, relock the door. When he came back, he put the transmission into gear and took them away from there.

Her cheeks felt greasy; she picked up her purse, found a tissue, and scrubbed at them. "What I saw won't help much," she said.

"Tell me when you're ready."

"I'm ready. Sandra was killed in the parlor. She was playing the flute and someone, a dark shape, came in and strangled her with a blue velvet cord. Then he—hung her body on the rear porch."

"Did you see all of that happen?"

"No. Just fragments of it. Brief images."

"You're sure it was a blue velvet cord?"

"Yes. Blue velvet."

"Did you hear anything?"

"Screams. Just screams."

"Any other impressions?"

"Yes." She explained the experience in detail: everything she had seen, everything she had heard, felt, smelled.

Grimly he said, "Was there anything significant about the dark shape?"

"He was just a figure wearing a hat and an overcoat. But his face . . ."

"What about it?"

"It seemed familiar."

Brad frowned. "Someone you know?"

"Yes."

"In what way was it familiar?"

"No specific way. It was just a feeling of recognition." She paused. "Brad . . ."

He looked over at her.

"This isn't the first vision I've had of Sandra's murder," she said. "I had a similar one the night she died. The same colors and sounds, everything. And I had one the night Tony Murray died, too, though not as strong. I wish to God I wasn't but I'm sensitive to them."

There was a troubled look on his face. He didn't say anything.

"I can still feel the psychic impulses," she said, "and I'm afraid of them. I'm afraid something else is going to happen. To one of the others. To me."

"Nothing's going to happen to you, Leslie."

"It could," she said. "It might."

"But it won't." He put his right hand on her arm. "Nothing is going to happen to you," he said again.

She took his hand after a moment, allowed his fingers to twine with hers. But she was thinking about the painting now, the unfinished winterscape of her house with the faceless figure on the snow outside. She had been able to tell him about the visions, about her sensitivity, but the controlling forces wouldn't let her say anything about the painting.

Why? What did it mean? What role was it going to play?

Nothing's going to happen to you, Leslie.

It could. It might.

And if it was supposed to, it would. There was just nothing she or Brad or anyone could do to change it.

WHITEHALL, VERMONT—1:20 P.M.

Gas pains drove Stan Walker out of the inn, through slushy snow to Quint's Country Store. He had eaten too much breakfast and then too much lunch: two thick ham sandwiches and a double helping of Indian pudding. He was a compulsive eater, had been all his life. The price he paid for that could have been much higher than chronic gas pains, like thirty or forty extra pounds of lard, but he had the kind of metabolism that kept weight from being a problem. Just as he had the kind of metabolism that made him hypersensitive to cold.

And it was *damned* cold here in Whitehall. The sun had been obliterated by a thick grayish haze, and the wind was up and there was the kind of snow bite in the air that forecast a coming storm. New England winters were his only regret about the Hartford residency. When he finally retired in a few more years, the first thing he and his wife, Beth, would do would be to pull up stakes and head south to the Florida Gold Coast and all that hot muggy sunshine.

His feet were chilled by the time he reached the store, although the distance was only a couple of hundred yards. He went inside and bought two rolls of Rolaids and a package of gum from a bearish man with the thickest red moustache Walker had ever seen. The man—Quint, he supposed—said nothing to him, just waited on him mechanically and watched him out of unfriendly eyes.

And a nice day to you, too, Walker thought.

Outside again, he opened one of the Rolaids and ate three tablets. Then headed quickly back to the inn. There was nothing to do now except wait for Saxon and the Abbott woman to return from Connecticut, and try again to get through to Gloria Mason over in New York State; he had already called her home and the playhouse three times without getting a response. He had also had second sessions with Iverson and Koskovich and Jo Turner. And he had checked in twice with his office in Hartford. Young Phillips had told him the second time that Washington had turned up a possible lead there on Evers. Phillips hadn't been informed as to what the lead was; word would come up if and when it panned out.

It couldn't be any more of a dead end than this PSYCHICs angle. All they were doing here was spinning their wheels and wasting time. Saxon would have to accept that too, before much longer—maybe soon enough for them to leave when he got back from Connecticut. Senseless shot in the dark, that trip. But Saxon was too emotional and inclined to go off on tangents, inclined to get personally involved. Like with the

Abbott woman: It had been obvious last night that Saxon was interested in her.

Not that it was Walker's place to say anything. Besides, he had a pretty good idea what Saxon thought of *him*. Plodding, impersonal, humorless, deferential to authority—the Bureau stereotype. Well, Walker had learned long ago, under Hoover, that you had to follow the book or you'd get it thrown at you.

Walker belched sourly as he came up onto the front terrace and paused to unwrap another Rolaids tablet. When he stepped inside the foyer, he saw the innkeeper, Colebrook, standing in front of the reception desk, glaring over at the cloakroom. Someone was making a lot of noise in there, clomping around and rattling hangers.

The rattling stopped as Walker shut the door, and Iverson came out of the cloakroom looking agitated. For the first time he was without his checkered cap; he kept clapping one hand to his rumpled straw-colored hair as if feeling for it.

Colebrook said to him, "You break anything around here, you'll pay for it. I'm warning you again, mister."

Iverson ignored him. Took a couple of long strides over to where Walker stood and blocked his way to the stairs. "Mr. Walker," he said, "have you seen my vision cap? I can't remember what I did with it. I've looked all over and it's just not anywhere."

"Sorry, no."

"Damn!" Iverson said. "I've got to find it. I *need* it."

Walker had had enough of him. He said with mild sarcasm, "Why don't you go look under your bed?"

Iverson blinked at him behind his glasses. Then his expression brightened unexpectedly and he said, "Hey! Under my bed! Sure, I never thought of that." He spun around and ran up the stairs.

Nut case, all right, Walker thought. Crazy as a loon.

Colebrook came over beside him. "Mr. Walker. Ask you a question?"

"Go right ahead."

"How long you planning to stay on here?"

"That depends."

"On what?"

"On when we decide to leave."

Colebrook pursed his lips. "Haven't seen your partner around since breakfast," he said. "He out on FBI business or something?"

"Or something."

"Be back pretty soon, will he?"

"Soon enough. Anything more you'd like to know?"

"Seems a man ought to be told what's going on inside his own hotel," Colebrook said stiffly. "Particular when there's government agents and murder involved."

"What do you know about murder, Mr. Colebrook?"

A vague look of alarm came into the innkeeper's eyes. "I don't know nothing about it."

"Then why don't we just keep it that way?" Walker said, and went away from him and up to the second floor.

Iverson was coming out of his room down the corridor. He had the checkered cap pulled down over his head and was smiling with evident relief. "You were right, Mr. Walker," he said. "My vision hat was under the bed. I guess it must have fallen off onto the floor and I kicked it under there by accident."

Christ. Walker unlocked the door to his room without saying anything, went inside, and shut it after him.

He sat on the bed, opened his notebook to the numbers he had copied down for Gloria Mason's home and for the Storm Junction Playhouse. He tried the home number first. No answer. There was no answer after six rings at the playhouse either, but just as he was about to hang up, the line clicked open and a woman's breathless voice said, "Yes? Hello?"

"Is this Miss Gloria Mason?"

Silence.

"Hello?" Walker said.

"Yes, I'm here. Are you a Mr. Walker?"

He was surprised. "That's right."

"Oh, dear," the woman said. "An FBI person."

"How did you know that?"

"Well, I just knew it, that's all."

"Miss Mason—you *are* Miss Mason?"

"*Mrs.* Mason." She sounded flustered, distracted. "You're calling from the inn in Whitehall, aren't you? Then you must be investigating what happened to Tony and Sandra. But why would the FBI be involved?"

Walker was frowning now. "We're investigating the disappearance of an official named Morris Evers," he said. "Sandra Harris was his cousin."

"Oh, yes, I know. She told me about him."

"When was that? Recently?"

"I don't seem to remember."

"I'd appreciate it if you'd try."

A ten-second pause. "I'm sorry, Mr. Walker. I'm so busy I can't think straight right now. It's been a terribly hectic day —I had to drive all the way to Parkton to pick up a special costume for the play we're doing and I *still* haven't finished painting all the sets for it."

"Mrs. Mason—"

"Is it really important about Sandra and Morris Evers?"

"It may be. We're not sure."

"If it will help find out who killed that poor woman, then of course I'll *try* to remember. Could I call you back later on, or better yet tomorrow?"

"Mrs. Mason, we'd prefer to get this—"

"Oh, *damn*! I think one of the sets is going to collapse!" There was a thin crashing sound in the background. "Yes," she said, "it collapsed." And she hung up.

Annoyed, Walker replaced the handset. Damn these people. Trying to hold a reasonable conversation with them was like trying to hold mercury in your hands.

He undressed and went into the bathroom to take a hot shower. Her claim to know who he was and what he was before he identified himself nagged at his mind. Clairvoyance? Hell, he couldn't accept that. He was a practical man, and there was no place in a practical outlook on life for a belief in parapsychology. The Mason woman had probably talked to one of the other PSYCHICs last night or earlier today; that was how she knew his name, knew he was with the FBI, knew he was in Whitehall staying at the inn. She'd seemed surprised by it all, but maybe that was just an act. Maybe she did have information about Evers and Sandra Harris and was reluctant to talk about it for some reason. It might be a good idea to talk to her in person, just in case; Storm Junction wasn't that far away, and he and Saxon could detour by there on the way back to Hartford later today.

Clairvoyance.

People like Saxon could believe in it if they wanted to; that was their privilege. As far as he was concerned, it was a combination of abnormal minds, stage-magic trickery, and a little bit of bullshit.

2:45 P.M.

Inside his house on Broadelm Road, Colebrook finished changing into a pair of slacks and a new Pendleton shirt. He checked his wallet to make sure he had enough money. Then he pulled on his mackinaw, went out through the rear door, and started for the detached garage.

Myrna was stalking toward him from the inn.

Damn. He stopped next to the half-dead apple tree that he'd probably have to cut down come spring and waited for her, hunching against the sting of the wind. Another storm coming in, the radio said; be here late tonight or early tomorrow. And a nor'easter right on its heels, which meant blizzard by tomorrow night. Sky was already dark and restless; the gray half-light made everything look shadowed, made the frozen surface of the pond behind the inn look like slate. Made Myrna's dumpy face and stringy hair look like slate, too. Hell, she might as well have *been* slate for all the warmth and comfort she gave him these days.

When she neared him, he saw she had that peeved look again. She said, "You were just going to run off without saying anything, I suppose."

"Wasn't anything to say. I told you this morning I was going to Rutland."

"You told me you weren't sure you'd go or not."

"Ben Purdy's got twenty-six cases of dented goods laid away for us," Colebrook said. "He won't hold 'em past six tonight and they'd be gone in five minutes at the price. We can't afford to pass up a hundred-dollar savings."

"Hundred-dollar savings mean more to you than what's going on around here?"

"What kind of talk is that?"

"Plain talk," she said. "We got an inn chuck-a-block full of psychics and government agents and you're running off to Rutland for canned goods."

That made him angry. "Goddamn it, Myrna, it don't matter if I'm here or not the next few hours. I can't change anything, it's out of my hands."

"Well, Ephraim Buell doesn't think so. He rang up a little while ago and *he* thinks it's our place to do something."

"Oh, he does, does he?"

"They're all under our roof, Harmon."

"And just what the hell're we supposed to do? Tell the government to get out of our lives? Force the FBI and the rest of 'em out of Whitehall? Use your head, woman. And tell Ephraim to use his, next time you talk to him."

"Two of that bunch have been killed," Myrna said uneasily. "That's a fact—we both heard Iverson say so after dinner. Well, who's to say there won't be another of them done away with? Or somebody else—one of *us*. I could be murdered in my bed while you're gone, how would you like that?"

I guess I wouldn't mind it, Colebrook thought. But he didn't really mean that. He didn't hate Myrna; just didn't like her much anymore. He said, "Nothing's going to happen to you or anybody else here. That's the only good thing about the FBI sucking around."

"You sure of that?"

He wasn't, but he said, "Sure enough."

"Well, I'm not."

After a moment, reluctantly, he said, "All right then, come with me to Rutland, you're so worried."

"Then who'll cook supper and tend to chores? No, thank you. Besides, there's my mother to look after."

Her mother. Drooling old woman in her seventies, lived alone over on Moss Oak Farm. Had spells where she'd sit in a chair and stare at nothing for hours, grinning to herself and rocking her arms like she was holding a kid. Teched, that's what she was. Teched ever since her only son died a long time ago. If *she* was murdered in her bed, he wasn't sure he'd mind at all.

"Have it your way," he said. "I'd better be leaving if I'm going to get there by six."

"You go right along, Mr. Colebrook," Myrna said. "Stay the night if you like." She swung around and stalked back toward the inn.

Mr. Colebrook. When she called him that, it meant she was going to harbor a grudge. Wouldn't let him touch her for a couple of months, probably. By God, maybe he ought to spend the night in Rutland. Find some willing tramp in a bar, like he'd done a couple of times before when Myrna was in one of her moods, and put it to her good and proper. Man had a right to a little loving, didn't he? Man had a cold wife, he had a right to get it where he could, didn't he?

But he knew he wouldn't stay in Rutland tonight, not the way things were here. Too much on his mind to get it up anyway. Psychics. FBI. Murder. How could you get it up with all that worrying around inside your head?

He trudged over to the garage, decided to take the pickup instead of the station wagon because of its load capacity, and drove away into the darkening afternoon.

3:25 P.M.

Saxon brought the Bureau sedan to a stop beside Leslie's house, set the emergency brake but left the engine running. She stirred next to him, arched her body to ease stiffened muscles, and said, "Do you want to come in for coffee?"

"I'd like that, but I've got to check in with Walker. I can come back a little later, if you want me to."

"I want you to. We can have dinner; I'm a pretty fair cook."

"Sounds good."

She was silent for a moment. "How long will you be here in Whitehall?"

"I don't know," he said. "Another day or so."

"But you weren't planning to stay, were you? Before what happened at Sandra's house, I mean."

"Does that make a difference?"

"It might. I don't want you to get into trouble over me. With your superiors."

"I won't get into trouble."

"What I'm trying to say is that I appreciate your concern and I'm glad you're here, but I won't fall apart when you leave. I've done a lot of coping in my life; I know how to take care of myself."

"I never thought you didn't."

"Just so you understand."

"I understand. I also understand that I like you and I don't want to see you hurt. Okay?"

A wan smile. "Okay."

She got out of the car and came around the front of it. He watched her walk through the snow to the house, waited until she was inside and the door had closed before backing the sedan out to Maplewood Road.

How did he feel about her? he asked himself. He didn't know how he felt about her. She affected him differently from any woman he had known, including Evelyn. She brought out a tenderness in him, a capacity for feeling that had long been buried. When she had had her vision inside the Harris farmhouse, when he had seen the agony of her face and heard the sounds she made, he had felt a wrenching inside him that seemed somehow beyond simple empathy and compassion.

He knew her a little now, knew some of the sources of her strength and her vulnerability, and that only made him want to know her more. And to protect her. That was something else she brought out in him: a feeling of protectiveness. But there was nothing macho in it; it was just a desire to keep someone he'd begun to care for from harm. He couldn't just walk out of her life today, and it didn't matter worth a damn whether or not Walker and the Bureau approved his decision.

The night-lights at the inn were on, in deference to the encroaching dusk; they made the brick structure look cheerily rustic against the backdrop of snowfields and white-mantled woods. Saxon left the sedan in the lot, went up onto the terrace and inside. Warm air and the smell of woodsmoke greeted him, along with a guarded stare from the pimply youth—Buddy something—behind the reception desk.

He crossed to the desk. "Do you know where Agent Walker is?" he asked.

"No, sir. Up in his room, maybe."

Saxon nodded to him, started to turn for the stairs. But Oscar Koskovich had appeared in the lobby entranceway, looking hopeful, and was gesturing to him. "Mr. Saxon? Could we see you for a minute?"

What the man wanted, obviously, was a report on what had happened in Connecticut. But there wasn't going to be any report. He had already decided not to say anything about Leslie's psychic experience. She hadn't told them she was sensitive to the murders, and what she'd seen amounted to little they didn't already know; he didn't want them bothering her with pointless questions.

He went over to Koskovich, who retreated with him into the lobby. Jo Turner was sitting in a chair near the fireplace, holding a half-filled Manhattan glass in one hand and a half-smoked cigarette in the other. Fortunately there was no sign of Iverson; Saxon wasn't in any frame of mind to deal with buffoonery.

Koskovich said, "Is there any news, Mr. Saxon?"

"No, I'm afraid there isn't."

Disappointment clouded the man's round face. "Are you planning to try again with someone else?"

"I don't think it would accomplish much."

"Neither do I," Jo Turner said. "You'll pardon me for saying so, but I don't think any of us is accomplishing much in these quaint rural surroundings. May I ask when we'll be free to leave?"

"Jo—" Koskovich began.

"Darling, it's a reasonable question. Mr. Saxon?"

"I'd prefer that you stayed until tomorrow."

"I was afraid of that." She shrugged philosophically, drained the last of her drink, and extended the glass to Koskovich. "Oscar, be a love and get me another Manhattan—where I wish I was," she added wryly.

Koskovich trundled toward the bar and Saxon went back into the foyer, upstairs to the second floor. He knocked on the door to Walker's room. Walker opened it after a moment, jaws grinding away on another wad of gum, and stepped aside to let him enter.

"How'd it go? The Abbott woman have a psychic vision?"

"Would you believe it if I said yes?"

Walker shrugged. "Did she?"

"She did. But there wasn't much conclusive in it."

"Uh-huh."

The skepticism in Walker's voice made it pointless to go into detail. Saxon asked him, "Anything new on Evers?"

"Washington's got some sort of fresh lead, they didn't say what. They'll let us know if it pans out."

"You get anything more from the other PSYCHICs?"

"No."

"What about Gloria Mason?"

"Well, I talked to her briefly on the phone, strange conversation, and she said Harris mentioned Evers to her."

"Oh? In what context?"

"She claimed she couldn't remember. But she acted a little odd, like she might be withholding something. We probably ought to see her on our way back to Hartford."

"We're not going back to Hartford just yet. We're staying here tonight. And maybe tomorrow night, too."

Walker studied him for a moment; his face revealed nothing of what he might have been thinking. "Mind if I ask why?"

"I'm not satisfied there's nothing here for us, that's why. Call it a gut feeling. You ever have gut feelings, Stan?"

"Sometimes. But we've already covered this angle pretty thoroughly."

"Leslie Abbott is sensitive to the murders, that's one thing," Saxon said. "And you said yourself Gloria Mason might be withholding information about Evers and Sandra Harris."

"So I did," Walker admitted.

"You can drive over to Storm Junction and interview her tonight if you don't feel like sitting around here."

"All right. What'll you be doing?"

"I've got things to do, don't worry."

"Like seeing Leslie Abbott again?"

Is it that obvious I'm attracted to her? Saxon thought. Well, maybe it was—and the hell with it. It was none of Walker's business.

"That's right," he said. "Like seeing Leslie Abbott again."

"Okay," Walker said compliantly. "It's your case and I guess you know what you're doing."

"I know what I'm doing, all right."

But after he left the room and started down the corridor, Saxon wondered if he really did know. Or if he had ever really known what he was doing since the days of Evelyn Kempner Saxon.

6:25 P.M.

Oscar was resting on the bed in his room when the animal vision came to him.

He had come upstairs immediately after an early dinner. Jo had been a little drunk and disinclined to talk, and Neal had kept prattling on incessantly about his intimations and his desire to be taken to Sandra's farmhouse. And when Oscar had telephoned Leslie, to ask her to come to the inn for another meeting, she had sounded preoccupied and told him she had other plans for the evening. Oscar had begun to feel depressed; it seemed more and more certain the Parapsychological Society of Yankee Clairvoyants was doomed by murder and apathy and fear, and there just wasn't anything he could do to hold together what was left of it. In a way it was like watching his wife, Susan, die. Not as tragic and intensely personal, of course, but still like witnessing the destruction of a family, the only family he'd had since Susan's death. If his family died too, what would be left for him? His job and his love for animals weren't enough to give full meaning and purpose to his life.

Animals . . .

The vision came slowly, forming in his mind like a film clip: soft focus at first, gradual sharpening until it was distinct and vivid. An apple orchard in spring, all the trees bright with blossoms; a wooden fence on which a small freckle-faced boy sat holding an old baseball wrapped in black tape; a large English sheepdog and a smaller, brown-and-white spaniel romping in the grass near the boy's feet, tails wagging with excitement. Oscar could hear the dogs barking, could hear the boy telling them to get ready, get ready, he was going to throw a long one this time.

Oscar smiled sadly. Dogs. They had always been his favorite animals. He had thought about getting one for companionship after Susan passed on, but ever since the little terrier they'd bought after they were married was run over by a car and died licking his hand, he'd vowed never to have another. He couldn't bear the death of an animal any more than he could bear the death of a human being; the possibility of losing yet another loved one kept him not only petless but from even thinking about remarriage.

With his psychic eye he watched the boy draw back his arm, the dogs poise and then dart away as the ball sailed out into the orchard, bounced off the trunk of one of the apple trees, and disappeared into the high grass. The sheepdog reached it first; the great shaggy head dipped down, came up again with the ball in its mouth. The spaniel frisked around the larger animal, barking, making a playful effort to take the ball away. Then the sheepdog raced back to the boy, the boy reached out a hand to retrieve the ball—

Sudden stench: urine, feces, corruption.

—and the boy and the dogs faded, the orchard dissolved—

Creaking sound. Creaking. Creaking.

—and he was in a dark place, looking up at a body hanging from a rafter, turning there at the end of a rope, creaking there in the darkness, its face just starting to come out of shadow—

Fear. Unreasoning terror.

—and the face came half into view and he knew it without knowing, recognized who it was without being able to put a name to it. The rope creaked and the body turned again, the face went into shadow again; the body turned, the face came half out of shadow; the body turned—

Something happened inside his mind: a jarring, then flickers and pulses of pain. His consciousness seemed to retreat toward the center of him, crouching, shriveling. The terror flooded him. He came up off the bed in convulsive movements, turned around and around again in confused circles. He felt as though he were suffocating. And half-blind: The shapes of furniture were blurred, as if he were seeing them through a thin curtain on which the vision remained superimposed. He heard himself gasping, making little whimpering noises.

Disjointed thought: Oh my God awful awful never anything like this

Another: Unbalanced my mind I'm losing my mind

Another: Air I can't breathe

He groped at the latch on the window, tried desperately to raise the sash. It was stuck, it wouldn't budge. He swung around . . . and there was a blank period . . . and he found himself on the back stairs, going down the stairs while he struggled into his coat . . . and another blank period . . . and he was outside, standing in the snow at the rear of the inn, looking in confusion at the writhing black shapes of trees.

Icy wind harsh against his face; flecks of snow, stinging. A tremor racked him. But he could breathe now, the feeling of suffocation was gone. And his sight was no longer blurred. And the hanging body and the face that he knew but couldn't name had faded into ethereal shapes like ghosts haunting the cavern of his mind.

Another disjointed thought: I've got to go there

He began to run.

7:10 P.M.

They sat on the old corduroy couch in front of the fireplace, sipping the last of the wine from dinner and listening to the magic of Louis Armstrong. The choice of music was Brad's; he had glanced idly through her collection of records and when he'd noticed her affinity for jazz he seemed genuinely pleased. It was an affinity they shared, he said; in fact he even played a little trumpet himself. In his teens he had put in some time with a neighborhood band and even now he occasionally went to after-hours jazz clubs in the Washington area and sat in when he could.

"Only on Dixieland, though," he said. "Everything after Teagarden is a wasteland to me. Gaps in my soul, I suppose."

"Then we've got the same gaps. I don't care for modern either," Leslie said. "I'd like to hear you play sometime."

"Well, I'm not very good. Unimaginative improvisation and

a forced upper register. I would have starved to death as a professional."

"You enjoy it, that's the main thing."

"I guess it is." He paused to listen as Armstrong began his four-measure solo in "Muggles." When it was finished, he said, "He was a remarkable man, old Satchmo. An artist. There wasn't anyone better in his time."

She nodded, tasted her wine again. She felt warm and relaxed with him. What had happened this afternoon, all the fears and uncertainties and the sense of inevitability, had receded into the back of her mind; her psychic eye was tightly shut. It had been a long time since she'd felt quite so at ease with a man. Not for seven years, since her brief engagement to Jim Parker in Montpelier. But Jim had been a shallow person, an egotist, and Brad Saxon was neither of those things. What he was was sensitive, honest, caring, and very much in control of himself. Even the sense of torment he seemed to have over his job and his ex-wife—he had opened himself up to her over dinner—seemed controlled and in perspective.

She had been candid with him about her own life, too. The early discovery that she was psychic and the loneliness of her childhood; the little girl who had cried hysterically in her room the night she had seen, hours before it happened, the death of her father from a heart attack while he was on business in Burlington. The college years in Middlebury, the commercial art jobs in Montpelier and later in New York, Jim Parker, the whole truth about why she had left Manhattan and moved back here to Vermont: "It wasn't just being treated like a freak; it was all the pain I could feel around me—so many people, so much distress." Putting it all into words had been good for her. She had had it all locked away inside her much too long.

He had his head tilted back now, eyes closed, listening to Armstrong do "St. James Infirmary." Leslie studied his face in the firelight. He hadn't struck her as a handsome man last night or even earlier today; he wasn't homely, but he didn't have conventional good looks. But he seemed attractive at this moment. Very attractive. She felt a vague tingling sensation in her groin. It was almost six months since she had been to bed with a man, and that a casual encounter in Greenwich Village. She wasn't exactly the horny type, or so Jim Parker had told her once; but she was a little horny now. She wondered if Brad felt that way too. He hadn't made any overtures so far, hadn't even touched her hand as he had in the car today. He wasn't a grabber, that was another point in his favor. No need for either of them to force it; they would go to bed or they wouldn't. Just let it happen.

When "St. James Infirmary" ended, the machine shut off automatically because it was the last piece on the record. Brad's eyes were still closed. "There's really nothing to say after that, is there?"

"He said it all."

"Yes, I think he did."

"Would you like some coffee?"

He opened his eyes and raised his head. "If you want some. Don't make any just for me."

"I've only got Sanka."

"Fine."

She went out into the kitchen and filled the teakettle with tap water. She was just setting it on the stove when the telephone rang.

Oscar again, she thought immediately. He had already called once tonight, to try coaxing her into another PSYCHICs meeting, and he could be persistent sometimes. She put down the teakettle, turned on the gas flame, and then crossed to the extension and cut off the bell on its third ring.

"Hello?"

"This is your last warning," the muffled, anonymous voice said. "You and all those other psychics don't get out of Whitehall pretty soon, I'll fix you good. You understand, miss bitch?"

A rush of helpless anger took away the warm, relaxed feeling inside her. "You again! Damn you to hell!"

"You're the one who's damned to hell, you and your filthy kind. Now you get out of Whitehall while you can. Otherwise I'll fix you good and—"

Furiously she slammed the handset into its cradle with enough force to make the bell ring.

"Leslie? What's going on?"

She turned, saw Brad come through the kitchen doorway. He was frowning, and the frown deepened when he saw her face. "You're upset. Who was that on the phone?"

"I don't know who it was."

"Anonymous? For God's sake, an obscene call?"

"No. Not exactly, not that kind of obscene."

"Then what?"

"The people around here don't like the idea of a clairvoyant living in their midst," she said. The fury had begun to drain out of her; she had herself under control again. "Somebody doesn't like it so much he started calling last November and threatening all sorts of things if I didn't leave."

His lips thinned angrily. "Death threats?"

"No. Property threats. My paintings. The calls stopped last month, but I had one last night and now this one. The same person."

"You have any idea who it is?"

She shook her head. "It could be anybody."

"A man?"

"I'm not sure. It's just a muffled voice."

"Why didn't you tell me about this before?"

"I didn't think it mattered. I've had to deal with cranks all my life, everywhere I've lived; there's nothing to be done about them."

"Cranks can be dangerous," he said.

"Not this one. He'd have done something by this time if he was going to."

"Maybe. And maybe he already has."

A coldness brushed her neck. "You don't mean Tony and Sandra?"

"That's just what I mean."

"I can't believe that, Brad. The first call was four months ago; if it was the same person, why wouldn't he have killed me by now? Killed me first? Why Tony and Sandra instead? It doesn't make sense."

"None of this business seems to make sense," he said. "Which means that just about anything is possible." He stepped forward, took her arms. "Look, it might be a good idea if you did leave Whitehall, at least for a while."

"Where would I go? There are people like that in every city and town. And if whoever murdered Tony and Sandra *is* after the rest of us, he could find me anywhere I went. He's already been to New Jersey and Connecticut, hasn't he? No, Brad. Whatever happens, good or bad, is going to happen whether I'm here or someplace else."

"Do you really believe that?"

At least I was able to say that much, she thought. "Yes. I really do."

He seemed to want to argue with her, changed his mind, and silence resettled between them. His eyes probed her face, showing concern at first, then something else. She felt the silence change subtly. His hands moved up her arms to her shoulders, and she knew what was in his eyes then and came in against him, fitted her body to his. His arms tightened across her back.

Desire welled through her. Yes. Her initiative after all. She drew her head back and kissed him. First kiss: soft, clinging.

"Come to bed," she said.

He touched her cheek with his fingertips. "If it's what you want, Leslie."

"It's what we both want," she said. "Come to bed."

7:45 P.M.

Leslie was already in bed when Saxon finished undressing in the darkness of her bedroom; and when he joined her, her body was cold and covered with gooseflesh. He held her, just held her, letting his warmth and the warmth of the blankets flow into her, and after a time her skin smoothed and lost its chill. She stirred against him, began to stroke his back.

He kissed her gently at first, then with increasing passion as her tongue probed his lips, met with his tongue. The full touch of her body became electric; he could feel himself beginning to harden.

God, it had been a long time since he had felt this way with a woman. His affairs after Evelyn had been so glancing, so peripheral: a bed partner here, a bed partner there, just sex and nothing more. But with Leslie it was different, more than just physical—the way it had been with Evelyn in the good early years.

The need, so long suppressed, a buried part of himself, began to uncoil slowly like something let out into the light of day after a long, long night. He caressed her breasts, the smooth skin of her stomach, the moistness of her vulva; kissed her nipples and the hollow of her throat. When she touched his erection it became as rigid as stone. The need grew, spiraled, became urgent and demanding; he moved over her, entered her—and it was as much a stunning collision as a coupling. He had expected willingness, complete acceptance, but what he had not expected was that the hard grinding force of her need would be even greater than his.

In response he found himself plunging into her violently. And was suddenly afraid of hurting her. He stopped moving for an instant, began again in a gentler rhythm. But she said against his ear, "No, it's all right, I want it that way, do it that way, hard," and because it was what she wanted, he let everything that had been trapped inside him come out in a controlled ferocity that she matched with an equal ferocity of her own.

They rolled on the bed, kicking off blankets, and found a new and better position. Too soon he felt himself nearing orgasm, eased his motion again, but she made a small protesting cry, clutching at him, and he realized that she was approaching her own climax. "Don't hold back," she whispered, "not this time. Come. Come. Come."

The words were a sensual litany in his ears—and he came, crying out, hearing her cry out, feeling her shudder beneath him.

When their bodies were still and they lay quietly, breaths mingling, he made a move to withdraw from her; but she held him, saying, "No, no," and he remained joined with her—the first time in his life he had not diminished after release. There was a period of resting, of soft caresses without words, and then they began as one to make love a second time: much more slowly, much less violently, the need more emotional than physical; not colliding but embracing, bound and fused on every level. For him there was no sense of time or place, there was only Leslie.

She climaxed again, and a third time, and when his own orgasm overtook him it was exquisite, a sensation beyond pleasure, a sweet, lingering pain that left him utterly satiated.

She held him inside her still, would not release him. They were both slick with perspiration, both exhausted; he could feel a deepening languor seep through him. Leslie kissed his eyelids, caressed his face in gentle massaging strokes.

"Sleep now," she said. "We'll both sleep now."

He slept.

STORM JUNCTION, NEW YORK—8:10 P.M.

Alone on the small stage inside the Storm Junction Playhouse, Gloria Mason stood working on the last of the flats for *Desire Under the Elms.* The trees were already completed, but she wasn't quite satisfied with the detail work; she wanted a few more leaves, a studied branch or two just for color and effect. She had a clear mental picture of what the flats should look like when they were ready, and it was that picture which she felt compelled to match. Someone less thorough and painstaking than she, she thought, wouldn't have bothered with the detail work for what was, after all, a minor local production, but that just showed the difference between professionalism and amateurism.

Except for the pale yellow stage lights, the interior of the playhouse was shrouded in darkness. The stage lighting was really not very good at all, but estimates from several electricians for improving it had been exorbitant, far too much for the playhouse's limited budget. Shutting off the house lights saved money.

The place had been a barn before some enterprising patron of the arts had converted it for theatrical productions in the 1950s. The stage was at the far end, and the rest of the cavernous space was given over to seating on a series of raised platforms. Two hundred seats altogether, and more than half of them yet to be filled at any single performance since Gloria had taken over as manager six years ago.

Not that that worried her; you couldn't expect much better in a place like Storm Junction. The important thing was that they drew enough people so that she could maintain a year-round production schedule. If they had been forced to close down during the winter months, she wouldn't have known what to do with herself. The playhouse was her whole life, now that her husband was gone.

Gloria stepped back and squinted critically at the leaf she had just painted. Too drab, she decided. It needed more color. She switched brushes and began to add green in careful strokes.

As she worked she remembered the FBI agent, Walker. He had called her again at 6:00 and said he wanted to interview her in person and would she mind if he drove over from Whitehall tonight. Well, she certainly did mind. She had all this work to do, and no one in the cast willing or able to help her; they had all gone home after this afternoon's rehearsal. She had tried to explain that to Walker, and tried to explain, too, that she just didn't know anything about poor Sandra's murder and still couldn't recall what Sandra had told her about her cousin, Morris Evers. But he had insisted on seeing her, and of course she'd had to relent. You couldn't very well say no to the FBI, even these days.

It was all so pointless and upsetting. What had happened to Tony and Sandra was terrible, *terrible*, but it simply did not have anything to do with her. She'd had enough tragedy in her own life, hadn't she? She was entitled to a little peace of mind, wasn't she? Particularly when she had so much work to do here.

Well, she had only herself to blame for last night. She should have known better than to drive over to Whitehall for Oscar's damned meeting. Oscar talking incessantly about banding together for protection, Neal making all sorts of wild speculations about a homicidal maniac who hated clairvoyants, and Jo suggesting that it might even be one of *them* who had killed Tony and Sandra. It had upset her no end, that was what it had done, and she hadn't slept very well after she got home.

Then today, getting that first call from Walker and having a psychic experience about him as soon as he spoke to her. After which Oscar had called and tried to talk her into returning to Whitehall. After which came Walker's second call, and now his arrival here any minute for more talk about murder and death. It was enough to give a person as sensitive and overworked as she a nervous breakdown. It really was.

And no one seemed to understand how she felt. Oscar least of all. He was a dear man, and he cared for her in his own way, just as she cared for him in hers; but when it came to PSYCHICs he simply lost all perspective. She wished she could take him seriously, but how could she? How could you take seriously a man who thought a clairvoyant social group was the most important thing in life? How could you take seriously a man who worked for a pet magazine and who had told her once that he spent half his mornings calling local pet shops at random from the phone book and asking questions like, "Do your birds break down more quickly when caged in large groups or when caged alone or in pairs?" *Break down.* That was the phrase pet dealers had for birds and animals dying before they could be sold, and what an awful phrase it was. What awful people to look on their little pets as just so much merchandise—

Somewhere inside the playhouse there was an abrupt clumping sound.

Gloria straightened from the flat, blinking. She had been so absorbed in her work, in her thoughts, that the sound had penetrated but not the direction from which it came. She listened. Silence, except for the faint keening of the wind outside. Turning, she looked out into the shadows that blanketed the tiers of seats. Nothing stirred there; the wide front doors were still closed. Perhaps it had been her imagination—

Clump.

She identified the location this time. Backstage, in the area where the dressing rooms and the side door were. It was probably either Walker or Dave Lyons, the director, who had told her earlier he would try to come back and help with the flats.

"Hello!" she called. "I'm out here on stage!"

No answer.

"I'm out here!"

Clump.

A shuffling noise.

Silence.

Oh, for heaven's sake, she thought, annoyed. It was certainly Walker, stumbling around back there in the dark, looking for the way out to the stage. He could have answered her, but that was the FBI for you. No manners and no sense of decency.

"All right," she called. "Just wait, I'll be right there."

Silence.

Gloria sighed, set her brush down on the work table, and wiped her hands on a paint-stained rag. Then she went across the stage to exit left, making her way carefully through the flats and props that formed an obstacle course on the dusty boards. *Damn* this lighting.

When she came around into the backstage area, the shadows were thick and concealing; she could barely make out the dressing room doors, the side door, the shapes of stacked folding chairs and extra props.

She paused, peering into the darkness—and a vague apprehension began to nibble at the edges of her mind. The shadows were motionless; there was no sound except for the flutter of her breathing. And yet she knew she was not alone. She could *feel* the presence of someone there among the forms and pockets of black.

"Who is it?" she said. "Where are you?"

Silence.

The apprehension climbed inside her, became shimmers of fear. She took a step backward, but at an angle that brought her buttocks up against the yielding surface of a small wing flat. It skittered, tilted, and fell over with a dusty echoing crash that startled her and spun her half-around. Confused, she caught her balance, saw the dull glow of the stage light—

A voice behind her said, "It's too late, Gloria Mason."

It was a voice she knew, and for an instant, recognition kept her from running. Her head twisted reflexively. Over her shoulder she saw movement in the darkness and she moved herself then, she tried to run. But gloved hands caught her, jerked her body backward with savage strength, and pinned her against a chest and an upthrust knee.

Terror engulfed her.

She screamed.

The sound of it ripped through the thick shadows, reverberated among the rafters, assaulted her own ears. Her lungs convulsed, dragging in air for another cry.

Something thin and soft bit into her throat, tightened around her throat, locked the scream inside. She couldn't breathe, she could only struggle futilely against the pressure, against the arms and body that held her. While the thing around her throat kept tightening, tightening, tightening.

Suffocating pain.

Sick wild terror.

The voice whispering in her ear, "I'm sorry, I'm sorry."

Black.

WHITEHALL, VERMONT—8:40 P.M.

In her dream, Leslie saw the colors again: blue and black, red and white.

And the terror came.

And a woman screamed—a single scream this time, a different voice from Sandra's, climbing higher and higher until it was beyond sound, until the blue velvet cord bit into the soft throat. The choking pressure came. Went. She smelled the corruption of death.

Image: body crumpled on a floor, light shining on it, flash beam shining on blue black red white death, on blue black red white Gloria Mason.

Image: dark shape behind the light, face behind the light, hidden, *but I know that face—*

Another scream. Out of her, her voice. And the dream dissolved into vision, and the vision dissolved into blurred reality: She was sitting up in bed, naked, shrieking, and Brad was beside her, holding her, saying frantically, "Leslie, Leslie!"

In the terror-lit corridors of her mind, the cries that came out of her and the cries that came out of the vision echoed and intermingled.

Screaming.

Screaming.

Screaming . . .

STORM JUNCTION, NEW YORK—8:40 P.M.

He found the coil of rope in a storage closet between two of the dressing rooms, exactly where he had known it would be. He draped it over his arm and, with the flashlight guiding him, made his way back to the body of Gloria Mason.

For the first time, then, because he had to, he put the flash beam on her. Lying crumpled and still, eyes staring up at him, blood in little ridges at the corners, distended—distended eyes, blue-purple skin color, protruding and blackened tongue, saliva coating the edges of her mouth.

The vision.

He moved the light away, switched it off. The smell of her death was sharp and foul in his nostrils; the sound of her scream still lingered, brittle and continuous, in his mind. But the sounds and the smells and the images would all be gone soon enough, when he gave control back to the host and sank deep inside, into the warmth and the darkness and the peace.

Until next time.

Only three days between the last two visions—one on Wednesday and one tonight. No doubt now that they were going to happen more and more often. He was afraid, so afraid. But what could he do? The visions were all-powerful; he and the host were helpless before them.

Obey or die.

Protect the secret or die.

He began to work quickly. Get to the warmth and the peace, get to the place where there was little pain and little fear. Her body was heavy, and he had difficulty hoisting it up off the floor, getting it suspended from one of the rafters. His hands inside their gloves were sore and slick with sweat when he finally managed to tie the rope to a dressing room doorknob. He switched on the flashlight again, centered the beam on the hanging thing. Yes. Yes.

The vision.

The memory of her scream was already beginning to fade when he opened the side door. The wind blew sworls of snow against his face, and the scent of it was clean, fresh, it took away the smell of death. He stepped out and shut the door, looking up the incline at the rear of the playhouse, anticipating the walk through the stand of spruce to where he had left the host's car.

Bright-hazed light appeared suddenly on the snowbanks to his right.

He jerked his head in that direction, and a pair of headlights like an animal's eyes arced toward him. Car swinging off the road out front, entering the playhouse parking lot. A rush of fear stiffened him; he threw an arm up to shield his face. This had not been part of the vision, the vision had ended with the dead thing hanging from the rafter inside—

The dead thing inside!

Get away, get away!

He wheeled in panic, ducked his head, and ran awkwardly up the drifted incline toward the trees.

8:55 P.M.

When Walker saw the dark bulky figure half-crouched in the snow ahead, one arm swinging up furtively to conceal his face, he knew that something was wrong. In the next second, before the sweep of the sedan's headlights reached him, the figure took sudden flight—and Walker's reaction was automatic. He brought the sedan to a sliding halt on the lot's slushy surface, reached with his right hand for the four-cell flashlight clipped under the dash, with his left hand for the door handle. He was out of the car, thumbing the switch on the flash, before the man had gone twenty yards upslope.

The long, powerful beam cut through eddies of falling snow, probed past the elongations of light from the sedan's headlamps. Walker could make out the tails of an overcoat flapping low around legs that kicked up puffs of loose snow, but he couldn't tell what color the coat was, and the head was pulled down and hidden by some kind of hat. He shouted, "You there—stop!" but the words were shredded and lost in the wind.

He glanced over at the barnlike playhouse looming in black silhouette against wind-driven clouds: no movement there, just a vague suggestion of light behind one of the side windows. Walker put his eyes back on the running figure. *Just a prowler, damn it.* But he kept on moving forward, onto the incline, his right hand resting on the butt of his service revolver. Without knowledge of whom he was after and exactly what the situation was here—and unless it became a matter of self-defense—he had no justification for drawing a weapon.

The drifts on the slope were deep and loose, and he couldn't seem to make much headway. It was like trying to run through sand. The other man wasn't faring much better, but he had a forty-yard lead and the impetus of panic; he ran wildly, in huge chopping, plowing steps. Falling snow mingled with dislodged crystals to form a haze around him, swirling and glistening in the light from the flash.

Walker was acutely aware of the cold now. The wind burned his cheeks and his exposed ears; snow packed inside his low-topped shoes and began to numb his feet. His lungs ached with each hard breath. The flash beam made erratic jumps with each hard clumsy stride.

The running man was fifteen yards from the front line of trees now, plunging through a clump of alder bushes.

Walker's right foot came down into some kind of hole or depression beneath the drifts, sending him sprawling forward in a graceless belly dive. He lost the flash, and for an instant he was struggling in freezing darkness. Particles of snow stung his eyes, poured inside the collar of his coat, caked in his nostrils.

Goddamn it to hell!

He fought upward, shivering, got his knees under him, and wiped his eyes clear of snow. The four-cell was lying tilted a foot away, illuminating a small strip of drift and making it look as though it were on fire. He caught it up, threw the beam upslope, and steadied it beyond the trampled alder bushes.

The dark figure was gone.

Grimacing, Walker swung the light back and forth across the close-packed trees. Heavy mobile shadows; boughs swaying like drunken dancers behind the curtain of eddying snow. By the time he could get up there and pick up the tracks, the man could be anywhere—he could be long gone if he knew the area.

A mixture of anger and frustration made him slap roughly at the snow clinging to his coat, his face, his hair. If there was one thing the Bureau had instilled in him, it was a hatred of failure. Even a probably meaningless failure like this one. If he had gotten here two minutes earlier, he'd have caught the man. And he *would* have gotten here earlier, a full forty minutes earlier, for Christ's sake, if he hadn't taken a wrong turn in the storm and gotten himself lost.

Nothing had gone right the past twenty-four hours; this whole damned trip with Saxon had turned into a fiasco. Well, maybe he had at least frightened off the prowler before any damage could be done. Gloria Mason would be able to tell him that, or she would if she was still down there in the playhouse.

The cold was beginning to pain him. He was still shivering, and his feet felt swollen and numb. Turning, he followed the light hurriedly downslope to the barnlike building. There was a door set into the wall there and he crossed to it, shut off the flash, and used it to knock loudly on the panel. While he waited, he stomped caked snow off his shoes and trouser cuffs, dried his hands on his handkerchief.

No answer. He knocked again, waited again, and finally tried the knob. It opened under his hand.

The feeling of wrongness came back to him. He pushed the door open a few inches, saw dim light off to his left; but the area beyond was massed with black. The back of his neck prickled, and for the first time he instinctively drew his .38. Then switched the four-cell back on and stepped inside.

The hanging body of a woman seemed to leap at him out of the darkness.

Jesus! The muscles in his stomach clenched; bile rose into his throat; another shiver racked him that had nothing to do with the cold. He shut the door, took a step forward. She was suspended a few inches off the floor, hanging at the end of a length of rope; the body turned slightly, making a creaking sound, the bluish face and the blackened tongue coming half out of shadow and then turning back into shadow—

She had died in agony. That was the first thing that struck him, the first thing that always struck him when he was confronted with a vicious homicide. Death *hurt*, violent death hurt *violently*. And it always seemed worse with a woman, an unspeakable violation of warm living flesh that was somehow personal.

That son of a bitch out there did this, he thought. He did this and I let him get away. If I hadn't gotten lost, I might have saved her life. . . .

He shook himself. No. No, damn it. Professional detachment. What's done is done.

All right. No point in going back outside, trying to pick up the man's tracks; it was too late for that, it had been too late when he fell on the slope. He listened for a moment, but the playhouse was silent, deserted; you could tell that by the hushed aura that pervaded it. He took the light off the body, played it around the backstage area. What he saw told him nothing. No sign of a telephone back here either, but there had to be one somewhere in the building.

The image of the woman's dead face was fixed in his mind as he moved toward the dim light coming from the stage. Gloria Mason, that seemed obvious. And it seemed obvious, too, that she had been killed by the same person who had murdered Sandra Harris; the method seemed to be the same. But was it an FBI matter or not? Had she been killed because she knew something about Evers and Harris, or had she been killed because some maniac was trying to eliminate members of the PSYCHICs group one by one?

He realized he was still shivering; the chill of the wind and the snow had penetrated to the marrow. He would have to get out of this damp clothing before long, or at least find a blanket. Pneumonia was a real threat for somebody his age, with his metabolism.

At the far end of the stage, he found a telephone with a long extension cord sitting on a stool. He held the light on it, started to holster his service revolver.

Backstage, the moaning sound of the storm was suddenly magnified.

An instant later there was the sound of a door slamming.

Walker tensed, turned off the flash, and took three silent strides into the shadow of a flat. Footsteps echoed faintly backstage. Then silence. No one appeared within the reach of the pale stage lights.

With his hand tight around the butt of his .38, Walker moved away from the flat and crossed the stage in slow, careful steps, weaving his way through the clutter of props and flats, using them to shield his approach. When he reached the perimeter of the overhead lighting, he stopped behind the folds of a stage curtain to listen. From over where the woman's body was he could hear someone breathing, a rapid rattling noise.

He stepped out in a crouch, the gun and the four-cell extended, and snapped on the beam.

The flood of light illuminated, in frozen relief, both the body and the rigid profile of a man standing near it. Walker said in a tight hard voice, "Don't move, hold it right there," but the man wasn't moving, didn't react at all to the glare of light or to the sound of Walker's voice. His eyes were fixated on the body; his neck was arched, cords straining, and on his round face was a distorted expression of grief and horror.

"Oh, my God," Oscar Koskovich said, "Gloria, Gloria!" And he began to cry.

CHAPTER 4

Sunday, January 21

STORM JUNCTION, NEW YORK—12:10 A.M.

It was snowing less heavily than on the drive from Whitehall when Saxon left Leslie at the Storm Junction Lodge and went looking for the police station. Beyond the wiper-cleared semicircles on the windshield of Leslie's Toyota, the buildings and the empty white streets had a fuzzy, distorted look, like images in an old photograph. Or maybe it was just the tension and fatigue in him that made them seem that way.

God, what a night. Between them, he and Leslie had run the gamut of emotions, top to bottom, sliding up and down like a pair of Yo-Yos: peace and rage and ecstasy and peace and terror and pain and rage. When she had awakened screaming with her vision . . . it had been like knives hacking away at his soul. Then the telephone call from Walker not long afterward, confirming the fact that Gloria Mason was dead. Leslie had just sat there in the living room when he told her, hanging on to her control and saying again in a whisper, "The killer is someone I know. Now, not in the past. I know him, but I can't see his damned face."

He hadn't had any trouble convincing her to come with

him to Storm Junction; they had both known she couldn't stay alone in that house tonight. In the car on the way here, she had been quiet and withdrawn. But after they crossed the state line, she'd started talking again, and that time she'd said, "He wants all of us dead, Brad. He wants *me* dead. It's just not going to end with Gloria."

Whoever it was wanted members of PSYCHICs dead, all right. That was clear now. But why? And why did he first garrote them and then hang their bodies from rafters? And why did he use a blue velvet cord? Lunatic, yes, but even lunatics had motives of some kind. Warped and evil, but still motives.

Why?

Someone she knows, he thought. Oscar Koskovich? Walker had told him that Koskovich had shown up at the playhouse just after his own discovery of the body; that the man seemed to be badly confused and claimed to have been compelled to come there by a vision. Walker hadn't had a chance to interrogate him fully before the call, but maybe by now he'd gotten a confession and the whole business was already finished. Except that Saxon doubted it. More likely, Koskovich *had* had a vision, was as psychically sensitive as Leslie, at least in the case of Gloria Mason. The question of motive again, too. What possible reason could Koskovich have for killing off people in his own clairvoyant group?

Same thing with Neal Iverson and Jo Turner. What possible reason could either of them have?

Someone in Whitehall, maybe. The same person who had been making those telephone threats to Leslie? Possible. Yet it didn't make sense that the murderer would harass her with anonymous calls and then go around killing off the other PSYCHICs one by one. Someone else in Whitehall, then. Yet it didn't make sense either that, with Leslie living right there, she would be passed over as a target in favor of individuals who lived in New Jersey, Connecticut, and upstate New York.

Round and round—and no answers and no leads anywhere because it all seemed to hinge on the fucking motive. . . .

A sign loomed ahead, shining a misty blood-red through the snowfall: POLICE. Saxon swung the Toyota over there, stopped in front of a brick building with half a dozen cars parked in side slots; one of them was Walker's sedan. He stepped out into the chill wind and hurried inside.

A uniformed desk sergeant looked at his credentials, then took him down a corridor, past a communications room, and into a large office. Walker was sitting on one side of a desk with his coat on and a blanket over his knees, like an invalid, a cup of steaming coffee in both hands. Behind the desk was a short, solemn-looking man who turned out to be Adam Jensen, Storm Junction's chief of police.

When Saxon had shaken hands with him, Jensen gestured to where a hot plate sat on a table under one of two windows. "Help yourself to coffee." Then he excused himself deferentially, saying, "I'll be out front if you want me," and left them alone.

"Sorry I'm late," Saxon said. He didn't offer an explanation.

"Lousy night," Walker said. "I haven't been able to get warm; my feet are still numb."

Saxon poured himself a cup of coffee, brought it back to the desk, and cocked a hip against one corner.

Walker said, "How did Leslie Abbott take the news?"

"How do you think she took it? I brought her over here with me and put her up at the hotel. I didn't want her staying alone tonight." He said it challengingly, but there was no response. There were fatigue lines around Walker's eyes and he seemed subdued.

"Did you get anything from Koskovich?"

"No. He keeps telling the same story. He had this vision in Whitehall and it confused his mind and sent him away in his car. He says he can't remember much of the drive over here, says he wasn't even sure where he was going until he got near the playhouse."

"You don't believe him?"

"I'm not sure. His grief seems genuine, and it doesn't add up that, if he was the man I chased away, he'd have come back fifteen minutes later knowing I was there. But it's still a pretty wild story, even if the clairvoyant angle could be true."

"Did you have him arrested?"

"There wasn't anything to arrest him on. Jensen's men didn't find anything incriminating on him or in his car."

"Where is he now?"

"Here, in an office down the hall. Waiting for you."

Saxon sipped some of his coffee. "This man you chased. Was there anything distinctive about him?"

"No. It was snowing and he had a good jump on me. He was wrapped up in an overcoat and hat, but I couldn't tell what color or style they were."

"Size? Weight?"

Walker shook his head.

"What about evidence inside the playhouse?"

"There wasn't any. Lots of prints around, but the killer was wearing gloves outside and it figures he had them on inside, too. No clothing fibers, no traces of skin under Mason's fingernails, no marks on her except those on her throat."

"Did you go over her personal effects?"

"Yes. At the playhouse and at her home. There wasn't anything at all concerning Evers, or Sandra Harris either. A couple of letters from Koskovich, but they didn't tell us anything."

Saxon stood, paced away from the desk, paced back to where Walker was sitting. "You call Hartford yet with a report?"

"About an hour ago."

"Anything new on that Washington lead?"

"If there is, word hasn't gone out yet." Walker was silent for a moment; then he said, "If there's an Evers link to these murders, I just can't see it. The only common denominator seems to be the PSYCHICs group."

"Seems to be. We don't know anything for sure yet."

"Maybe not. So what do you plan on doing?"

"Talking to Koskovich, having a look at the body and the playhouse, and then trying to get some sleep."

"I meant tomorrow."

"We'll all go back to Whitehall and see what we can find out there. I want the survivors of PSYCHICs in one place."

"You going to take Leslie Abbott to the playhouse first?"

Saxon had already considered that, and his feelings were ambivalent. "I don't know," he said. "Maybe. Maybe."

Walker was silent. But his eyes said clearly that it would be another waste of time: There was no such thing as clairvoyance, so how could it help them find the answers?

He's wrong on both counts, Saxon thought. It was clairvoyants who were being killed, and it was Leslie and now maybe Oscar Koskovich who were sensitive to the murders. Clairvoyance was a major factor in this case; for all he knew, it might be the central factor. It would play a role in whatever happened from now on, just as it had played a role in what had gone before. He felt that with sudden conviction.

In one way or another, clairvoyance was or would be the key to everything.

12:50 A.M.

The room in which Oscar sat alone, slumped forward over a table with his head buried in his arms, was small and hot and smelled of disinfectant and of the cigar one of the policemen had been smoking. He felt light-headed, still nauseated even though he had already vomited twice—once at the playhouse and once here in the men's room. Tachycardia struck him at intervals, adding the vague fear of a heart attack to the darker fears that crowded his mind.

He kept his eyes open, focused on the buttons of his coat sleeve; every time he closed them he saw Gloria hanging there from the backstage rafter, turning and creaking, her face that hideous color mix of blue and black and white. In Whitehall the sudden vision of her death had been so powerful that it had thrown him into a disoriented state of shock. He understood that now. Subconsciously he had recognized her, and subconsciously he had been compelled to go to her.

Over and over he had asked himself why it had happened to him, a man whose gift almost always centered around animals. Was it because he had been Gloria's lover as well as her friend? Because her pain and terror were so great that the emanations had reached him through time as well as space?

There was no way he would ever know.

Gloria. Poor, sweet, theatrical Gloria. Dead. Strangled. Hung up like the remains of a butchered animal. What sort of monster could have done those things to her?

The sickness churned inside him. He wondered how much longer they would keep him here. There had been so many questions already, so much skepticism. They didn't believe in parapsychology—not Walker and not Chief Jensen and not any of the hard-voiced young officers. They kept asking him if he had ever had blackouts before. They kept asking about his relationship with Gloria. They kept treating him as if he were unbalanced, as if *he* could be the monster who had crushed the life from her. How could it have been him? He had tried and tried to tell them that, make them understand that he loved her as he loved all helpless living things. If they would only understand!

How could it have been him?

More time passed. Lost time, as Gloria was forever lost. Then there was the abrupt sound of the door opening across the room, and when he raised his head he saw the younger FBI agent, Saxon, enter and close the door behind him. Alone.

Oscar felt a vague relief. Saxon was at least a believer; he understood and accepted the truth of psychic experience. He straightened in his chair, tasted a salty wetness on his lips, and realized there were tears leaking from his eyes again, trickling down over his cheeks. He fumbled out his handkerchief and wiped his face as Saxon crossed to stand in front of him.

For a moment the young agent studied him gravely. "I'd like to ask you a few more questions, Mr. Koskovich," he said then.

"Yes," Oscar said. "But may I go somewhere then and lie down? I'm so tired, I don't feel well—"

"Do you want me to have a doctor brought in?"

"No. I just need to lie down. To sleep."

Saxon nodded, slid out a chair, and sat down. "Just tell me what happened to you tonight. Everything as you remember it."

Oscar told him.

"Have you ever had an experience like that before?"

"No, sir. Never."

"Any sort of vision about the other two murders?"

"No, sir."

"All right. And you saw nothing in the one tonight that might help identify the killer?"

Oscar shook his head miserably.

"When you got into your car and began driving, did you know you were coming to Storm Junction?"

"No. I felt there was someplace I had to go, something I had to see, but it was all vague and compulsive."

"Like driving when you're intoxicated?"

"Yes," Oscar said. "Just like that."

"Did you come straight to the playhouse from Whitehall?"

"I think so. I don't remember much of the trip."

"Do you remember if you saw anyone outside the playhouse?"

"No, sir. The first thing I remember clearly is standing there backstage, looking up at her in the darkness, and then a flashlight coming on and Mr. Walker talking to me."

Saxon said nothing; he seemed to be thinking.

"You do believe me, don't you?" Oscar said. "You don't think I could have done that awful thing to Gloria—"

"I believe you, Mr. Koskovich."

The words were a release that slackened him on the chair. "Then I'm not under arrest? They wouldn't tell me—"

"You're not under arrest. If you feel well enough in the morning, you can drive back to Whitehall." Saxon paused. "How long were you in the playhouse tonight with Agent Walker and the police?"

"I'm not sure," Oscar said. "It seemed like a terribly long time. They left Gloria hanging there and hanging there. . . ." He shuddered.

"Did you have any sort of psychic experience during that time?"

"No. God, no."

"Would you be willing to go back there tomorrow, when you've had a chance to rest?"

"Go back there?" Oscar blinked at him, and then understood. The sickness surged again; he swallowed against the rise of bile in his throat. "Oh. I see."

"It's up to you, Mr. Koskovich."

Up to me, he thought. PSYCHICs is my group, and three of us are dead already—Gloria is dead. Up to me?

"Yes," he said thickly. "I'll go there with you."

Saxon nodded, stood up. "I'll see to it you're taken to a hotel for the night. And I'll be in touch with you in the morning."

When he was gone, Oscar put his head on his arms again. More tears fled from his eyes; this time he made no move to wipe them away. As he sat waiting, he could hear the wind fretting around the weatherstripping on the windows, rising and falling like a voice in the night. A crying, accusing voice. Talking to him, saying the same things over and over.

Gloria, it said. Sandra. Tony.

Who's next? it said.

Who's next?

3:10 A.M.

Waiting alone in the hotel room, Leslie sat propped up in bed with the lights on and her eyes fixed on the door. Sleep was impossible. Every sound that disturbed the stillness scraped at her nerves. Every visual image that touched her mind seemed psychically charged.

She tried to focus her thoughts on Brad Saxon. On the closeness they had shared in Whitehall; on the poignancy, the combined savagery and tenderness of their lovemaking. But it was no good, no use. She kept seeing Gloria Mason's face, blue and black, red and white. She kept hearing Gloria's screams. She kept feeling Gloria's terror.

And she kept seeing, too, the dark figure with the face that she knew but couldn't see. Whose face?

Whose face?

Little girl alone in her room, she thought. Little girl who sees things and is sensitive to death. First her father when she was ten, then the boy she had dated casually in high school dying in a car accident, then Tony and Sandra and Gloria. How many others would there be in the future? How many more murders, more deaths?

What if I have a vision of my own death?

It could happen. It would happen if it was supposed to. Someday her psychic eye might open and the dead blue black red white face that stared up at her would be hers. . . .

Footsteps in the hallway outside. The sound of a key entering the lock, turning in the lock. Brad came inside, shut the door quietly, and crossed to the bed and sat down beside her.

"You should be asleep," he said.

"I couldn't sleep. What did you find out?"

He looked tired and grim. "Not much. No evidence, no real leads. At least, not as far as I'm concerned."

"What do you mean?"

"I didn't tell you this before," he said, "but Oscar Koskovich showed up at the playhouse just after Walker found the body."

"Oscar?"

"He claims to have had an experience of his own last night, around six-thirty. A precognition of Gloria Mason's death. Similar to yours, apparently, but intense enough to put him into a fuguelike state and bring him over here from Whitehall."

"My God!"

"Walker and the local police are skeptical; they think he might be the one who killed her."

Jo's words replayed in her mind: *It could be one of us*. Her skin crawled. "Could they be right?"

"I don't think so. I talked to Koskovich and he's in a pretty bad way; it's obvious he cared for the woman. It seems to me he's telling the truth."

"Then he's sensitive too."

"This time, yes; he says he wasn't affected by the Harris and Murray killings. I'm going to take him back to the playhouse later on. The murder scene didn't trigger him again last night, but that could be because of the state he was in."

"What if it still doesn't trigger him?"

He hesitated. "We'll cross that bridge if we come to it."

"Brad," she said, "there's no point in avoiding the issue. If Oscar can't help you psychically, we both know I'll have to try again myself."

"All right. We both know it. But I hate the idea of you suffering through another bad experience."

"I've spent most of my life suffering through bad experiences. I can survive another one because there's always another one to survive. That's what being clairvoyant is all about. Survival and pain."

"Maybe that's what life is all about, too," he said.

"Maybe. Except that there are other things that make it all bearable; it's the other things I need now."

He nodded and took her hand.

"Come to bed," she said. "I want to hold you. Not sex, I just want to hold you."

WHITEHALL, VERMONT—7:45 A.M.

The reception foyer and lobby were empty when Jo came downstairs. There was nobody in the dining room either. She took a chair at one of the set tables and lit her first cigarette of the day. It tasted absolutely foul, which suited her mood.

Beyond the rear windows, swirls of windblown snow whitened the gloomy morning. She could hear it against the glass: a sandlike whisper. It had been falling since last night, and according to the news broadcast she had watched after dinner on the lobby television, there was a full-fledged blizzard on the way. Lovely. If the storm was bad enough, she wouldn't be able to go back to Manhattan even when the FBI permitted it; they would all probably be snowbound for a day or two in this disgustingly rustic country inn. And her with two interviews scheduled for tomorrow, a desk full of work, and a contract dispute to settle between the manager of the Nevele Lounge and Mr. Magic, a fat fool who made more customers disappear than rabbits while he was on stage.

Except for the storm outside, the inn had a hushed, deserted atmosphere. Where *was* everybody, for God's sake? She hadn't seen Oscar or Neal since dinner, nor had she seen either of the two FBI agents. But then, she had gone to bed early because she'd had five manhattans, which, instead of getting her pleasantly smashed, had given her a monstrous headache. She hadn't slept very well either. Vague nightmares had disturbed her all night long, awakened her twice. Constant jabbering about murder and being detained by government agents, not to mention five manhattans, were enough to give anyone nightmares.

The innkeeper's wife came out of the kitchen—it was about time—and approached the table. "Good morning," she said curtly. "Breakfast?"

"Just coffee, dear."

"The name is Mrs. Colebrook."

"I know that, darling."

The woman made a grinding noise with her teeth and stalked back to the kitchen. Returned again a minute later and banged a cup and saucer down in front of Jo, spilling a little of the coffee.

Jo smiled at her. Bitch, she thought.

She finished her cigarette and had drunk most of her coffee before someone else finally entered the dining room. It was Neal, wearing his silly vision cap along with dove-colored slacks and a hideous blue-and-white ski sweater that had deer patterns all over it. He seemed excited as he hurried toward her; his face was flushed and his eyes bulged like a frog's behind his glasses.

"I knew it," he said as soon as he sat down. "I felt it during the night. Symbols, distinct intimations."

"How nice for you, sweetheart."

"They were like birds fluttering around my mind, the same as always," Neal said. "Pretty soon I'm going to catch them."

"What *are* you babbling about?"

"Gloria's dead," he said abruptly. "She was murdered last night in Storm Junction."

It didn't register for a second; then, when it did, the impact was stunning. She stared at him in disbelief.

"I just found out," Neal said. "I didn't know *who* it was, but I knew it had to be somebody. I guessed Gloria because she was the only one of us who wasn't here in Whitehall. And sure enough, when I called her house a policeman answered and said she'd been murdered. He wouldn't tell me very much, but I'll bet she was killed the same way Sandra and Tony were, by the same maniac who hates psychics. . . ."

There was more, but Jo didn't listen to it. Her head throbbed again; she felt cold and shaken. *Gloria was murdered last night.* A third coincidence? It didn't seem possible. Just as it hadn't seemed possible before that someone was actually killing off PSYCHICs. *Gloria was murdered last night.* Oscar and Neal, damn him, must have been right all along. Dear Christ!

She fumbled another cigarette out of her pack, lit it, and tried to compose herself. Neal's voice babbled on. He was still talking about the birds fluttering around in his mind, using his consciousness as a net to trap them so he could identify the maniac.

She cut through his monologue by saying, "Does Oscar know yet? Have you told him?"

"Oscar? No, he's gone," Neal said. "And so are the FBI agents. Maybe they're all over in Storm Junction, because that's where Gloria was murdered. Maybe they took Oscar over there." He scowled. "Or maybe Oscar found out about Gloria sometime during the night and went over to Storm Junction on his own. If that's it, he should have told us before he left, he should have asked us to go with him. What if the birds hadn't started fluttering around in my mind? We wouldn't have known about it for hours yet. I can't help solve the murders unless I—"

"Neal," Jo said savagely, "shut up!"

His eyelids flapped up and down. "What? What?"

"Gloria's dead, you say. Don't you *care?*"

"Of course I care. Why do you think I don't care?"

"You haven't expressed one single feeling of regret, that's why. All you can talk about are your bloody psychic birds."

He ran a hand across his forehead. "That's because they're important. I'm going to help bring her killer to justice, I'm going to help save *our* lives. I might even have been able to save Gloria's if Saxon had taken me down to Connecticut yesterday instead of Leslie." He paused for breath. "I feel terrible about her dying," he said.

Jo felt a sudden loathing for him. She stood, pushing her chair back sharply against the wall, and started away from him. She needed to be alone for a while. She needed time to think.

"I *do* care," Neal said behind her, "and I *am* going to solve the murders. You'll see, you'll all see. I am!"

8:00 A.M.

Colebrook eased his pickup through the snow at the rear of the inn and backed it to within five feet of the storeroom door. The wind blew cold dry flakes against his face as he stepped out. Temperature was below freezing now, and it would stay that way right up until nightfall. Radio said it was fifteen below up to Burlington, where the nor'easter had already fetched out eighteen inches of snow. Whole northern part of the state was the next thing to snowbound: roads closed, business and airports shut down.

Be the same around here before long, he thought sourly. Road to Pycott, eight miles away to the east, was already closed because the wind had blown over a dead tree during the night and knocked out the bridge across Pycott Creek. And the county road to the west wouldn't stay open long; snowslides in the hills and heavy drifts where it ran through bottomland always shut it down fast in weather like this. Happened every year. Nor'easter wouldn't pass them by until sometime tomorrow morning, and it'd be another day on top of that before the county got the roads passable.

If the FBI and those goddamned psychics didn't pack up and get out by early afternoon, the soonest he'd be rid of them was midday Tuesday. And the way it seemed, they weren't fixing to leave today. None of them had said anything to him or Myrna about checking out; and the cars that belonged to the FBI and the fat psychic, Koskovich, weren't out front in the lot. All three of them must have gone off somewhere last night or damned early this morning. Well, maybe they wouldn't make it back before the village got snowed in. He could hope for that much relief, at least.

He unlocked the storeroom door, untied the tarp across the pickup's bed, and began to transfer the twenty-six cases of canned goods he'd bought in Rutland. Every time he opened the door, the wind shoved it away from him, slammed it against the inside wall, and laid a fine sifting of snow on the floor. There was a thin carpet of it twenty feet long by the time he had unloaded all but the last two cases.

When he went out for those last two, a snow-blurred figure appeared around the south corner and slogged toward him. Ephraim Buell. Colebrook gestured him to the storeroom door, climbed up into the bed for the cases, then carried them down and inside.

Buell shut the door after him and stood slapping snow off his coat with his earflap hat. "Hell of a fine Sunday morning, Harmon," he said.

"Seen worse," Colebrook said as he set down the cases.

"I ain't talking about the weather."

Colebrook grimaced. "You come here to prod me again about those psychics? Hell, I don't like having 'em around any better than you, but it's out of my hands. FBI wants 'em to stay, and none of us is big enough to truck with the FBI."

"Why does the FBI want 'em to stay? That's my question."

"Because they're investigating about the two that got murdered. They think there's some sort of connection with that Washington bureaucrat that disappeared."

"Not what I mean," Buell said. "FBI wouldn't keep those people here unless they're on to something. Way I see it, they figure one of them done the murdering, maybe murdered that Washington bureaucrat, too. You like the idea of a murderer under your roof, Harmon?"

"Don't know that I got one under my roof, and neither do you."

"Possibility of it'd be enough for me."

"What would you have me do? Tell me that."

"Call up the state police and put in a complaint, that's what."

"Wouldn't do any good," Colebrook said. "You think the state police can tell the FBI what to do? Besides, we're in for a blizzard tonight, you know that as well as I do."

Buell ran his tongue loosely over his lips. "You should've put in a complaint first thing yesterday morning," he said. "Shit, you should've turned that bunch away when they showed up here Friday night."

"Maybe I should've, but I didn't and that's that." Colebrook's mood had shifted toward anger; he had enough on his mind without Buell whining at him. "You don't mind now, I got chores."

The sullen look faded from Buell's face; his expression turned abruptly apologetic. "Look, Harmon, maybe I spoke out of turn—"

"Maybe you did."

"But this situation is enough to make a saint edgy, ain't that right?"

"Right enough, I guess."

"Sure," Buell said. He ran his tongue over his lips again. "Ask you a favor?"

"What favor?"

"Sell me a fifth of rye?"

"Now? It's Sunday. No off-sale on Sunday."

"I know it. But we're friends, ain't we?"

"How come you want a bottle this early?"

"I can use a drink, that's all."

"Can't you wait for the bar to open?"

"Not likely. You know how it is, Harmon."

Colebrook took a closer look at him. Hangover, that's how it was. Buell's eyes were red-flecked, and his face, beneath its flush from the cold, was gray and mottled. Alcoholic, for a fact. Must have tied on a fine one last night. Well, what the hell, every man had to deal with things in his own fashion. He recalled Rutland and the tavern he had gone to after picking up the canned goods. Yes, sir. Every man dealt with things in his own fashion.

"All right," he said, "I'll sell you one. But I'll have to charge you extra for it."

"Sure," Buell said. "Sure enough, Harmon."

Colebrook started over to where he kept his supply of liquor for the bar. Just then the kitchen door opened and Myrna came traipsing in. Her face was all pinched up again, like somebody with constipation, and her eyes were nervous. She gave him a passing glare and walked over to where Buell was.

Still harboring her grudge about him going to Rutland, he thought. Harboring it fine, too. All she'd said to him this morning was how come he was so late getting back, and when he'd told her he'd gone out for dinner with Ben Purdy, she'd said, "Did you now? Well, I guess you both had your fun." *Had your fun.* That was the expression she used sometimes when she was talking about sex. He wondered if she suspected that he was bedding down with tramps in Rutland; wondered if he'd come home last night with the smell of the skinny young blonde on him. Didn't matter if she did suspect, though. She wanted a divorce; then, fine, he'd give it to her. Man was better off divorced than married to a cold woman, by God. Tramps, at least, were warm-blooded and showed a little feeling. And they helped you get it up even when you didn't think you could, so for a little while you could take your mind off the things biting on you.

Myrna said to Buell, but for his benefit too, "Something happened last night, over in Storm Juntion, New York."

"What happened?" Buell asked.

"What we've all been afraid of. Another murder."

Colebrook scowled and stepped over beside her. "Murder? What the hell're you talking about?"

She gave him a look and then fixed her eyes on Buell again. "Another one of the psychics was killed," she said in a fretted-up voice. "Gloria Mason, this time. Iverson and that Turner woman were discussing it in the dining room; I listened in from the kitchen."

"Jesus Christ!"

"I told you, Harmon," Buell said, and pointed a twitching finger at him. "Goddamn it, I *told* you."

"I told him too," Myrna said, "but Mr. Colebrook only listens to himself."

Colebrook's mouth tasted dry. "Settle down, both of you. It didn't happen here, did it? It wasn't one of *us* got killed, was it?"

They looked at him.

"Well, was it?"

"Not yet it wasn't," Myrna said.

STORM JUNCTION, NEW YORK—9:20 A.M.

Saxon spent fifteen minutes inside the playhouse with Oscar Koskovich. Stood with him in the backstage area where

Gloria Mason had died, watching sweat break out on his haggard face as he concentrated. Walked him around, made him touch things: the doorknob to which the hanging rope had been tied, the toppled wing flat, the knob on the side door, the worktable out on stage.

"I'm sorry, Mr. Saxon," he kept saying. "It's not happening. It's just not happening."

Saxon masked his own feeling of frustration. Finally took Koskovich outside again, to where Walker and Chief Jensen were waiting in the Bureau sedan. The wind had grown fierce and numbingly cold and snow eddied down in fat dry flakes that looked like soap chips; the sky was dark with low scudding clouds. Jensen had told him earlier that blizzard warnings were out all through New England. Some roads in central and southern Vermont were already closed, which meant that he couldn't spend much time here with Leslie if they intended to get back into Whitehall today.

Walker had the sedan's engine running and the heater up as far as it would go. The air in there, shimmering with heat waves, made Saxon's head pound. Man's like a damned spider, he thought—but he didn't say anything about it this time. They'd be back at the Storm Junction Lodge in ten minutes, and after that Walker could suffocate himself alone on the return drive.

"Anything?" Walker asked in his mild way.

"No."

Jensen said, "Looks like this clairvoyant business is a lot of hooey, all right. If you don't mind my saying so, Mr. Saxon."

"You're entitled to your opinion."

"More or less," Jensen said.

Which was a polite but pointed reference to Saxon's decision to release Koskovich. Jensen wasn't satisfied with the man's story, and if it had been up to him, Koskovich would have been held for more extensive questioning.

Koskovich was silent on the ride back to the hotel. He sat with his hands folded in his lap, eyes staring at nothing through the side window. He looked better this morning, if still a little shell-shocked, and he had been cooperative when Saxon questioned him again before they left for the playhouse.

The questions were more or less the same ones he'd put to Leslie earlier. Did any of the surviving PSYCHICs have cause to hate or even dislike the three victims? Did any of the survivors stand to benefit from their deaths, such as from individual or group insurance policies? Had PSYCHICs as a body ever been involved in a situation in which someone had been harmed or wronged in some way? Had Koskovich or Iverson or Jo Turner received threatening telephone calls or threatening letters? Had any of the three victims?

Koskovich's answers, like Leslie's, had all been negative.

When they arrived at the lodge and got out of the sedan, Saxon asked Koskovich, "You feel strong enough to drive over to Whitehall?"

"I think so, yes."

"All right. Agent Walker will follow you."

He took Walker aside. "When you get to Whitehall, talk to Iverson and Turner, find out what they were doing last night when Gloria Mason was killed."

Walker raised an eyebrow. "You think one of them did it?"

"I don't think anything. I just want to cover all the angles."

"Sure. How long before you'll be leaving?"

"Not long. An hour or two."

"You taking Leslie Abbott to the playhouse?"

"That's right."

"Uh-huh," Walker said. "Good luck."

"Yeah. Good luck."

Saxon went inside the hotel and upstairs to Leslie's room. She was sitting in a chair beside the window, looking out at the misty whiteness beyond; she turned as he entered, and her eyes questioned him and then read the answer immediately. A wan, humorless smile curved one corner of her mouth.

"Nothing," she said.

"No. He tried, but nothing triggered him."

She stood up. She had put on makeup from her overnight case, pinned her dark hair into a chignon; it made the strength and vulnerability in her face seem more pronounced, more compelling. He felt stirrings inside him as he looked at her, a kind of ache.

"I'm ready to go," she said.

He nodded. "The sooner we get it over with, the better."

They checked out at the desk downstairs, and in her Toyota he drove them to the playhouse. One of Jensen's uniformed officers was waiting in a cruiser out front; he unlocked the main entrance doors and let them inside, shut the doors again after them.

The house and stage lights were still on, but Saxon was aware of shadows crouching among the empty tiers of seats and in the corners above the rafters. Even to him, and as it had been when he was here with Koskovich, the stillness seemed charged with a sort of static electricity. He took Leslie's arm, watched her closely as her eyes roamed the barn-like interior. Nothing changed in her expression, but her body was stiff and tense. Like someone expecting to be struck.

He said, "Have you ever been here before?"

"No. Gloria invited me, but I never quite got around to it."

"Okay. We'll take it a section at a time."

He led her down the center aisle, along the low wall of the orchestra pit to where a set of stairs gave access to the stage. They mounted the stairs and crossed to the worktable and the flats on which Gloria Mason had evidently been working last night. Stood there for a time while Leslie stared at the brightly painted scenery, at the cans and brushes and rags on the table.

She shook her head: nothing yet.

He took her through the maze of props and flats at the rear of the stage. The faint mingled odors of paint and dust and winter damp dilated his nostrils; he could feel his stomach knotting.

When they entered the stage-left wings and approached the backstage area Leslie's stride turned balky, as it had at the rear porch of Sandra Harris's farmhouse. Under his hand, her muscles felt as tight as spring-steel bands. Her face had lost some of its color. But she didn't stop or make an effort to retreat as he led her out into the pale glow of the 100-watt bulbs backstage.

In the middle of the area she did stop, abruptly, and stood turning her head in slow quadrants, looking at the stacked folding chairs, the extra props and flats, the closed doors to the dressing rooms and the storage closet and the side exit. Then she stared at the floor; he heard her breath quicken and become irregular. Her eyes, unblinking, were dark and shiny as black opals.

She lifted her head, tilted it back, and peered up at the rafters. One side of her face spasmed, twisted. Her mouth came open, stayed open as if in a soundless scream.

He felt the wrenching inside him again, tightened his grip on her arm. She shivered once, just once; then, as if in release, her mouth clamped shut and some of the tautness in her relaxed. He turned her toward him.

"Leslie?"

Her eyes lost their fixity. "Yes. I'm fine."

"What happened? What did you see?"

"Colors. Colors and sounds. Screams."

"Gone now?"

"Gone," she said.

"Do you want to sit down?"

"No."

"Maybe we'd better go—"

"No, not yet. It may happen again."

But it didn't happen again.

They waited in silence for five minutes, ten, fifteen. Leslie stared at the floor, stared at the rafters, touched the same things Koskovich had earlier. Walked. Stood. Concentrated.

Nothing at all.

WHITEHALL, VERMONT—12:05 P.M.

Over the phone to his wife, Neal said, "So that's all I really know—just that Gloria was murdered last night in Storm Junction. I'll find out the details when the FBI gets back."

"It's just terrible," Tina said. "Another murder. Neal, honey, I'm so *worried* about you."

"Don't be. I can take care of myself."

"I know you can and you always could. But still, can't you leave there and come home right away?"

"Even if I wanted to," Neal said, "which I don't, I can't anyway, there's a blizzard up here. I wouldn't be able to make it all the way back to Massapequa in this kind of weather. I'd wind up snowbound somewhere on Route Nine."

"You'll have to miss work, then."

"Work? Who cares about that? My real work is right here, solving the murders so I can start being as famous as the Amazing Kreskin."

"But how long will you *be* up there?"

"I don't know. Tuesday or Wednesday. It all depends."

"Tuesday or Wednesday? Oh, Neal, I'll be frantic by then!"

"I'll call you a couple of times a day, don't worry."

"But that's not enough," Tina said. "I want you home, safe with me. Where I can touch you."

Uh-oh, he thought.

"Hold you in my arms. *Touch* you."

"Tina—"

"Naked. In bed."

"Damn it, Tina—"

"You know, do all those things with your pecker that you like so much."

"Screw my pecker!" Neal said with sudden anger.

"Oh, yes," Tina said, "that too. Definitely."

"Don't you understand what's happening here?" he shouted. "*Murder* is happening here, that's what. I'm going to solve three murders and save all our lives and become famous as the Prince of Psychics if I can just get a little co-operation!"

Tina sighed. "I'm only trying to make you feel better."

"You can make me feel better by hanging up now. I've got a lot of things to do, a lot of concentrating to do."

"Will you call me again tonight?"

"If you don't talk about my pecker anymore, I will."

"All right, I promise. Be careful, lover."

She made a kissing sound over the wire, and he grimaced and hung up. The woman just had no grasp of the situation at all. For that matter, nobody had a firm grasp of the situation except him. Ignoring him, mocking him, accusing him of not caring . . . why wouldn't they give him the credit he deserved, the cooperation he needed?

Well, they'd all change their tunes soon; they'd be sorry they treated the Prince of Psychics this way. They'd be sorry.

He stood and paced the room for a time, stroking his vision cap. He sat down again and shuffled his tarot cards. Nothing came to him. Then he pulled the phone to him, dialed Leslie's number for the third time today, and waited through a dozen rings. Still no answer. Was she over in Storm Junction, too, along with Oscar and the FBI? Damn. Practically everybody was in Storm Junction, it seemed, and here he was waiting all frustrated in Whitehall.

The need for some kind of activity drove him from the room finally and sent him downstairs. There wasn't anyone behind the reception desk or anybody in the lobby either; he wondered where Jo was and decided he didn't care after the way she'd treated him this morning. Whispery scraping sounds came from inside the bar, drew him to the doorway, and then stopped a couple of seconds before he entered.

The only person in there was the skinny pimple-faced guy who worked for the Colebrooks, who had been the bartender yesterday afternoon when Neal went in for a Coke. What was his name? Oh, sure: Quint, Buddy Quint. His father owned Quint's Country Store. Neal didn't like him very much because Quint glared at him a lot and had made him wait five minutes for change yesterday. Some of these rural people were pretty odd in a lot of ways.

Like in what Buddy Quint was doing right now. Which was standing next to the bar, leaning on a pushbroom, and picking a huge red-and-yellow pimple on his neck. No, not just picking it; working it around between his thumb and forefinger, getting a specialist's grip on it. Neal watched in fascination. He had never seen anyone squeeze such a big pimple before.

But he didn't get to see this one squeezed either, damn it. Quint seemed to sense at the last second that someone was there; he turned around. When he saw Neal, his face reddened and his eyes flashed with anger.

He said, "What the hell you doing, watching me?"

Neal shrugged. "Is the bar open? I'd like to get a Coke."

Quint glared at him and didn't say anything. Then he began to lash the floor with his broom.

"I said, I'd like to get a Coke."

"Bar's closed," Quint muttered. He shoved the broom across to the dining-room entrance and right on through it out of sight.

Neal shook his head, sighed, and went back into the lobby. Nearby, the grandfather clock chimed the half-hour, making a melodic counterpoint to the constant sound of the wind outside. He decided he might as well go out for some air. He liked snowstorms; they reminded him of the time when he was a boy and his mother locked him out of the house after one of his psychic experiences about her and Mr. Freedy, the grocer who lived next door on Flatbush Avenue. What had happened was that he had gotten lost, hadn't been found by the police until nightfall, caught pneumonia, and ended up in the hospital. The pneumonia hadn't been much fun, but what *had* been fun was the toboggan Mr. Freedy had given him as a get-well present. He still had it, still got it out and rode it down the hill behind his apartment building in Massapequa once or twice every winter. It was a terrific sled. He could understand why that guy in *Citizen Kane* had been in love with *his* sled; that was the way he felt, too.

Where was his coat, anyway? For a moment he couldn't remember; he tried the cloakroom first. And that was where it was, all right. He put it on—it was his favorite because it was a checkered black-and-white hunter's coat that matched his vision hat—and went out onto the front terrace.

Headlights appeared on Main Street a couple of seconds later: two sets of them, one following the other through the curtain of snow. Neal took off his glasses, wiped the lenses, and squinted through them again. The lead car approached the inn, tires spraying surface crystals, and he saw that it was Oscar's sturdy old Electra 225. The other car was the sedan belonging to the FBI.

Eager-eyed, Neal watched the cars turn into the parking lot, coast to tandem stops twenty yards away. He went down the steps to meet them, hurrying, not paying any attention to the icy surface of the bricks. His right foot slid out from under him on the bottom step, kicked up into the air, and he jarred down on his buttocks and skidded toward Oscar and Stan Walker through the snow, ending up in an awkward sprawl at their feet.

"Son of a bitch," Neal said.

Walker shook his head. "Hello, Mr. Iverson," he said wearily, and reached down to help him up.

1:20 P.M.

Snow was falling in thick eddies when Brad eased the Toyota into Leslie's driveway. "Do you want to come with me to the inn?" he asked her.

"No. I need something to eat and some time to rest. I'm in no mood to face the others yet."

He nodded. "I'll be back as soon as I can. A couple of hours, no more."

She squeezed his hand, got out, and hurried toward the

house. The front door was obscured by the snowfall; she didn't see it with any clarity until she reached it. And then she came to an abrupt standstill, staring. Her body stiffened; the flesh on her neck rippled.

One of the mullioned panes of glass was smashed, broken completely out except for serrated shards here and there like teeth in a shattered mouth.

Oh, my God, she thought.

She spun around, saw that Brad was just starting to back out of the driveway, and waved frantically at him. He saw her, stopped the car, and came running.

"What's the matter?" he said when he reached her, shouting above the wind. "What is it?"

Leslie pointed at the broken pane. "The storm didn't do that," she said. "Not that."

His face became tight and angry. He reached out, turned the doorknob. It was unlocked; the door popped open. Icy gusts rattled it in his grasp.

"You locked it when we left last night," she said. "I remember that you locked it."

"I locked it, all right." He let go of the knob and the door flew inward, made a cracking sound against the inner wall. On the floor in the entranceway was a thick fan of snow and a half-buried scatter of glass. A dull sense of dread came into her as she stared into the familiar gloom beyond.

Brad opened the front of his coat, slid one gloved hand inside, and brought it out again wrapped around the butt of his service revolver. She had noticed the weapon a number of times, but it had always been holstered: an abstraction. She had never thought about him having it in his hand, using it. She stared at it now, and it both repulsed and reassured her.

"You'd better stay out here," he said.

"No. Oh, no. It's my house, I've got to know what's happened in there."

He didn't argue. "All right. But stay behind me. Right behind me."

She nodded. And followed him inside.

The first thing he did was to close the door against the wind and snow. Then he stood listening. Silence. Empty silence? The shapes of her furniture grew more distinct as her eyes adjusted to the murky light. Nothing seemed to have been disturbed, at least not in the living room. Brad gestured finally for her to put on the lights, and she did that. Yes: everything in its place; no signs at all of an intruder.

But there was an aura of violation in the house; she could feel it now with her mind, a psychic shimmering. Not just intrusion. Violation. Something had happened here last night or earlier today; something had been done here.

There was a clenching sensation in her stomach as she trailed Brad through the living room. The rhythm of her pulse was loud and erratic in her ears.

The kitchen. Emptiness. Nothing disturbed.

The bedroom, the spare room she had outfitted as a den, the pantry, and the rear porch.

Emptiness.

Nothing disturbed.

The studio, she thought, and the sense of dread sharpened into fear. The winterscape, the *painting*.

Brad led her back to the loft stairs. Began to climb slowly, walking on the edges of the runners to keep them from creaking. Following him, Leslie found herself holding her breath as he neared the top of the stairs—

His body went rigid.

"Jesus," he said.

"What is it?"

"Leslie, you'd better not look at this—"

But she was already climbing up beside him, pushing past him. Then she saw—and the shock of it was almost physical. She took three faltering steps forward before he caught hold of her; she hardly felt the pressure of his hand.

The studio had been raped. Brutally, viciously raped.

All of her finished landscapes, all the fresh canvases, had been knife-slashed into shreds. They littered the floor, clung to broken frames like strips of flayed meat to bones. The easels were all torn apart, the catchall table had been smashed and overturned, the couch was a butchered corpse leaking stuffing like clots of blood. The walls and floor were covered with worms and daubs and streaks and smears of paint—a riot of intermingled colors, a wild nightmarish blending of blues and reds, yellows and whites and blacks.

Raped and turned into a madman's pop-art display.

Sickness welled inside her. She wrenched out of Brad's grasp, backed away to the stairs, turned, and half-ran down them. Away from all that carnage, away from what had once been hers but which now had been ripped away, stolen, ruined forever.

And away from the worst thing of all, the one thing in the studio which hadn't been destroyed or even moved, the one thing that still sat in the corner like a talisman beneath its draping of white cloth.

The winterscape and its figure without a face.

1:25 P.M.

Walker just could not get warm.

He'd spent ten minutes under a scalding shower, but it had had no more effect on the chill in him than the hot coffee last night at the Storm Junction police station, or the heavy blankets on his hotel bed, or the blasting heater in the sedan today. He didn't feel sick, yet it was as if the cold had lodged so deeply inside him that it couldn't be reached by external applications of heat.

He kept thinking about Gloria Mason, too. The way her body had looked hanging there, all twisted and discolored in the beam of his flashlight. It was one of the most terrible corpses he had ever seen, under some of the most bizarre circumstances, and he couldn't quite manage to keep it compartmentalized. The line between personal feeling and professional duty seemed to have blurred in this case, thinned out, so that for the first time in thirty years there was an unsettling overlap.

He wondered if it was that way for Saxon. Not only on this case, but in most of his drearier Bureau assignments: anger, frustration, flickers of pain. All the Bureau training could not change your emotions.

With his belly full of two sandwiches and three cups of coffee, Walker went back upstairs to tackle the questioning of Iverson and Jo Turner. He'd fended off their questions after his arrival, told them to wait in their rooms; the shower and food had been his first two orders of business. But when he knocked on the Turner woman's door, there was no response. Nor was there any response when he rapped on Iverson's door ten seconds later.

Walker sighed. These people just wouldn't listen to anybody. He moved down the corridor to Koskovich's room. The door opened immediately to his knock and he was looking at Iverson's damp flushed face. Past him, inside the room, he could see Koskovich slumped on the bed and Jo Turner occupying one of the two chairs.

Iverson started to say something, but Walker pushed past him. The room was hazy with smoke; Jo Turner had a cigarette in one hand and there was another smoldering among a dozen lipsticked butts in the ashtray beside her. She seemed nervous and a little haggard; some of the brash and brassy quality was gone. Koskovich had a withdrawn, shrunken look. His eyes, as they had been in Storm Junction, were clouded and moist with pain. Iverson was the only one of the three who showed any animation. He still appeared excited, and now there was a sort of pouting annoyance in his expression.

Walker said to him, "I thought I told you and Miss Turner to stay in your rooms."

"How could we do that, Mr. Walker? I mean, we already knew about Gloria being killed and we had to find out the details, didn't we?"

"You'd have found them out from me. Mr. Koskovich has had a rough time; you shouldn't have disturbed him."

"It's all right," Koskovich said in a dull voice. "I don't mind that they came."

"I just can't get over it," Iverson said. "About Oscar's vision, I mean. I thought I was the only one of us sensitive to the murders, and now I find out he had a precognition of Gloria's death. I'll bet Leslie's been having intimations, too."

Jo Turner flicked half an inch of ash from her cigarette into the tray; flakes of it fluttered onto the table. "If Leslie was sensitive, she would have told us, Neal."

"Would she? I don't know about that. Why else was she over in Storm Junction and going to the playhouse today with Saxon?" Neal turned to Walker. "That's why, isn't it? Because she's been having intimations just like me?"

"I don't know anything about that," Walker said.

"Well, it doesn't matter even if she has been. When is your partner coming back with her?"

"Pretty soon."

"I hope so. I've got to talk to him as soon as possible. It's not Leslie or anybody else who's going to solve the murders. It's *me*. I know it, I can feel these psychic birds—"

"For God's sake, shut up," Jo Turner said angrily. "I've had just about enough of you, I really have."

"Now what's the matter with *you*, Jo? Why won't you understand—"

"I understand too bloody much," she said. "I may have been a fool for doubting someone is out to kill all of us, but you—"

"You can say that again," Iverson muttered.

She glared at him. "Go fuck yourself, sweetheart."

"What? What?"

"Stop it!" Koskovich said. "Why do you have to go on like this? Gloria's dead, three of us are dead, isn't that terrible enough?"

"It's terrible enough, all right," Walker said. "Mr. Iverson, suppose you go sit down over there. I've got some questions for you."

"Questions? What questions?"

"About last night. What you did after dinner."

"Why do you want to know that?"

Jo Turner said, "Because we're suspects, why do you think?"

"Suspects? Mr. Walker, you don't believe it's one of *us*—"

"Facts are what I'm interested in right now," Walker said with more patience than he felt. "Factual answers to factual questions."

Iverson's lips moved as if he were mumbling something to himself. But he sat in the vacant chair and splayed out his legs and folded his arms across his chest. In that posture, with that damned checkered cap on his head, he looked to Walker like a lunatic in a mental-hospital dayroom. A docile lunatic, well controlled by drugs, but still a lunatic. Christ.

"What did you do after dinner, Mr. Iverson?"

"I went up to my room," Iverson said sulkily.

"For how long?"

"All night."

"You didn't go downstairs for any reason?"

"No."

"What were you doing alone in your room?"

"Concentrating. Working with my vision cap and my tarot cards."

"You and your vision hat and tarot cards," Jo Turner said sarcastically.

"What's wrong with tarot? It's a legitimate means of uncovering the unconscious."

Walker cleared his throat pointedly, and both of them shut up. He said to Iverson, "Did you see Miss Turner at any time?"

"No," she said.

"No," Iverson said.

Walker turned to the woman. "What about you, Miss Turner?"

"I spent the evening in my room, too. I had a filthy headache and I went to bed early."

"You didn't go downstairs either?"

"No."

"Or see anyone?"

"No."

"Or talk to anyone on the phone?"

"No."

Walker paced to the window, stood for a moment looking out at the flurries of snow. So neither Iverson nor Turner had an alibi for the time of Gloria Mason's death. One of them *could* have driven to Storm Junction and then driven back undetected. But so could anybody within a radius of a few hundred miles. This wasn't getting him anywhere. And what the hell could it have to do with Evers in the first place?

Looking out at the storm made him feel even colder. He turned from the window, reached into his pocket for a stick of gum.

The telephone on the nightstand rang shrilly.

Koskovich jumped, Iverson blinked, and Jo Turner dropped her cigarette on her pantsuit, flailed away ash, and then picked the butt off the floor. They all stared at the phone. When it rang again and none of them made a move to answer, Walker went over and caught up the handset himself.

"Yes?"

Pause. Then Colebrook's voice asked, "That you, Mr. Walker?"

"Yes. What is it?"

"Been trying to locate you. Long-distance call."

"From whom?"

"Man named Phillips in Hartford. Says it's important. You want to take it on that line?"

"No. Put it through to my room."

Colebrook broke the connection without saying anything else.

Walker put the receiver down. Koskovich and Iverson and Jo Turner were all looking at him. "Suppose we break this up for now," he said. "Miss Turner, you and Iverson go on back to your own rooms. Let Mr. Koskovich get some rest."

He herded them out of there and went back to his room to take the call from Hartford.

1:55 P.M.

There was a tight knot of rage inside Saxon as he drove from Leslie's house to the inn. He was alone in the Toyota: She had refused to leave with him. Nothing he'd said to her would change her mind; she'd just stood in the living room shaking her head, saying, "I don't want to see anyone now and I've got to clean up the studio. I'll be all right here, don't worry."

So there had been nothing he could do short of carrying her out of there bodily. She was stubborn, he was finding that out, and maybe too independent for her own good. He hadn't wanted to leave her alone, and yet he couldn't stay there with her any more than he could force her to leave against her will. There were things to be done. At least some of the answers *were* here in Whitehall, he was convinced of that now. Leslie would be safe enough in the house, with him and Walker close by; he kept telling himself that. And he wouldn't leave her alone for very long.

The small village snowplow was moving along Main Street near the county road intersection, spraying and pushing snow into windrows. He had seen dozens of them on the state and country roads coming over from Storm Junction: an army of machines like giant beetles, fighting a losing battle against the elements.

He had mixed feelings about being snowed into Whitehall for a day or two. On the one hand, it would give him time to find those answers without having to worry about the Bureau; on the other hand, he didn't like the idea of isolation in a place where there was at least a savage vandal and maybe a psychopath running around loose. But he didn't have any choice in the matter now. The nearest town was eight miles away and the road to it had been closed since last night; the car radio had told him that on the way in. And to the west, toward Storm Junction, there had only been one lane open in two different places. A state trooper at the first of those spots had told him that he expected the road to be closed entirely by two o'clock.

Saxon drove past the snowplow and down into the parking lot at the inn. Left the Toyota next to Walker's sedan. When he entered, Colebrook gave him a flat stare from behind the reception desk. Saxon didn't say anything to him until he had stomped snow off his shoes, stripped off his gloves, and crossed the foyer to stand in front of him.

Then he said, "How many adults live in Whitehall?"

The question took Colebrook by surprise. "How many adults?"

"That's right. Inside the village and nearby."

"Twenty-five, maybe. But I don't—"

"Think about it. I want the exact number."

Colebrook thought about it, looking puzzled and wary. While he was doing that, there were footfalls on the stairs, and at the edge of his vision Saxon saw Walker appear. But he kept his eyes on the innkeeper's face.

"Well?"

"Twenty-one," Colebrook said.

"All right. Most of them have phones?"

"They do."

"Good. You call them up and tell them all to be here in one hour. All of them."

"Here? What the hell for?"

"Because I want to talk to them."

"Why?"

"You'll find out when they do."

"Folks ain't going to like being called out in a storm like this, not without good reason."

"I've got plenty of good reason," Saxon said, "and I don't give a damn whether they like it or not. Or whether *you* like it or not. Do what I told you, Mr. Colebrook. Now."

Tight-lipped, Colebrook turned away to the small switchboard behind him.

Walker came the rest of the way downstairs, jaws working on more of his damned gum. Before he could say anything, Saxon gestured him into the lobby. It was deserted. They crossed to stand in front of the fireplace.

"What was that all about?" Walker asked then.

In clipped sentences, Saxon told him about the threatening calls Leslie had been receiving, the destruction of her studio.

Walker's expression was inscrutable. "Rough," he said. "But why get the whole village together? These are pretty closemouthed types; they're not likely to admit anything about themselves or their neighbors."

"I want the son of a bitch responsible to know I'm after him," Saxon said. "I want him to know I'm going to nail his ass." He paused. "Did you talk to Iverson and Jo Turner?"

"I did. Neither of them has an alibi for last night."

"Did you question anybody else? Colebrook, for one."

"No. I didn't think it was necessary."

"Well, I do. The same person who's been terrorizing Leslie could have murdered those other three PSYCHICs."

Walker gave him a probing look. "You've gotten pretty involved in this business, haven't you?"

"What if I have? Three people are dead. Maybe that doesn't affect you a hell of a lot, but it affects me. You bet it does."

"Who says it doesn't affect me?"

"If it were up to you, we'd have gone back to Hartford long ago. Admit it. You don't see any connection with Evers's disappearance; you don't think these killings are a Bureau case—"

"They're not a Bureau case," Walker said, "and there isn't any Evers connection. That's confirmed now."

"What?"

"I just talked to Phillips. Evers has been found."

Saxon's stomach tightened. "Where?"

"In Maryland. Dead. He's been dead ever since the night he vanished."

"How did he die?"

"He was stabbed to death by a thirty-year-old architect named Richard Varney who lives on a farm outside Landover. It seems Evers was a closet homosexual, leading a double life; he'd been having a secret affair with Varney for more than a year. Evidently he'd decided to break it off for one reason or another and they had a row. Varney lost his head and used a kitchen knife on Evers and then buried the body in a field. Seems he was pretty broken up afterward, so he took to the bottle. Yesterday he made a drunken confession to another of his playmates and word got back to the Bureau. They made the arrest and dug up Evers this morning."

"So that's that," Saxon said. "I suppose Washington wants me home as soon as possible."

"That's right."

"Well, we're not going anywhere for a day or two. Not with a blizzard and the road situation the way it is."

"Yeah, I know it," Walker said. "I told Phillips we were probably stuck here; he'll relay word to Washington."

"You'd better know something else, Stan," Saxon said heavily. "I'm not leaving when the blizzard's over and the roads open up—not unless I've gotten to the bottom of what's been happening to Leslie and the PSYCHICs group."

Walker was quiet for a time. Then, in his mild way: "The Bureau wouldn't like that."

"Screw the Bureau."

"It could mean your career—"

"Screw my career, too." Saxon made a frustrated gesture. "Ah, Christ, I don't expect you to understand. Forget it. Just forget it. The responsibility and the consequences are mine; you don't have to do anything now except stay out of it until the roads are open."

"Is that what you want? For me to stay out of it?"

"Isn't it what *you* want?"

"No. You really believe I'd take myself out of this while

we're here just because it's no longer a Bureau assignment? Well, you're wrong. I'm a law officer, same as you, and I don't like murder and terrorism any more than you do." He gave Saxon a faint mobile smile around his wad of gum. "You don't know me as well as you think you do, my friend," he said, and pivoted away and headed back into the foyer.

Saxon stared after him for a moment before following. I'll be damned, he thought. Maybe I don't at that.

2:40 P.M.

The vision came to Neal while he was urinating.

One instant he was in the bathroom adjoining his room, making merry splashes in the toilet bowl, and in the next his third eye popped open and he saw himself inside a dark cellar workshop, holding a lighted match aloft. The cellar was cluttered with furniture, the gutted case of a grandfather clock, lumber and hardware, tables and chairs and other antiques; a tool-littered workbench took up most of its back wall. He had never been there before, never seen any of these things before, and yet he seemed to *know* where he was.

The antique shop down the street.

The cellar workshop of Buell's Antiques.

He saw himself moving forward to the bench. Something dark and coiled lying on one corner of it began to take shape in the flickering glow of the match: rope, a coil of rope. He saw himself move closer, saw something else appear beside the rope, ribbons of something in a loose row. Leather. Old leather cut into long, thin strips—

They were all strangled with something thin and cordlike.

They were all hung from rafters with rope.

Excitement gushed through him. But as it did, the vision faded—turned frail as an autumn leaf and finally crumbled and dissolved; his psychic eye squeezed shut. He was staring at the bathroom wall again, squirming, sweat trickling warmly over his cheeks.

Thoughts hung in his mind, as glittering and sharp as icicles.

The cellar workshop of Buell's Antiques. Was Ephraim Buell the psychotic who had an obsessive hatred for clairvoyants? Had the murderer been right here in Whitehall all along?

It sure seemed that way. It seemed the fluttering psychic birds had finally come together into a true vision, just as he'd known they would. His great gift was leading him to the solution, all right, and where the solution appeared to be was right there in Buell's cellar.

Ephraim Buell. Why, Neal hardly knew the man, had never even spoken to him. But Buell had struck him as pretty odd, though, with funny eyes and a sour expression. Murderer's eyes and a murderer's scowl, now that he thought about it.

Son of a bitch—Ephraim Buell.

Neal wiped some of the wetness off his face, realized then that there was more warm wetness on his trouser leg. He blinked and looked down; his penis was still hanging out of his fly. Grimacing, he zipped up and scrubbed at his pants with a towel. Then he flushed the toilet and went out of there.

His vision hat was lying on the bed.

He stopped and peered at it. The vision had come to him without the aid of his vision hat, by golly—the first time anything like that had happened in almost two years. Now why was that? Maybe he had been trying too hard before with the cap and the tarot cards; maybe that was it. Well, it didn't matter. Vision hat or not, he was right on the verge of solving the murders. Neal Iverson was, the Prince of Psychics was. *That* was what mattered.

He sat on the bed. What he had to do now, he thought, was to go to the antique shop. He'd been there in the vision, and that meant he would be there sooner or later. You couldn't deny a precognition; you could get into trouble that way, trying to change what you were destined to do. So he would go there, and, once he managed to find a way inside, he would search the workshop for more evidence. Then he'd take whatever he found, along with the rope and the strips of leather, to the FBI. They'd listen to him then. They couldn't ignore evidence.

Right now was the time to do it, under cover of the storm. The antique shop would be closed in this weather and Buell wouldn't be working there on a Sunday—

There was a knock on the door.

Damn. Now what? Neal curbed his excitement; he didn't want whoever it was to know he was on to the truth, not yet. Then he arranged his face into what he felt was a nonchalant expression, and crossed to the door and opened it.

"My partner wants everyone downstairs," Walker said.

"Agent Saxon? Is he back?"

"Yes, he's back."

"Why didn't someone tell me?"

"I'm telling you now, Mr. Iverson."

"But I can't see him now. I've got something to do."

"Whatever you have to do can wait."

"No, it can't. It—"

He broke off because Walker was staring at the front of his trousers. Neal looked down at himself, felt a flush creep out of his collar; he had forgotten about the pee stain like a Rorschach blot on his pantleg.

"You have an accident, Mr. Iverson?"

"It's just water," Neal said fiercely. "I was washing my face and I splashed water on my leg."

"Uh-huh," Walker said. "Well, maybe you'd like to change your pants before you come downstairs."

"But I told you, I've got something *important* to do."

"It's not as important as what's going to happen downstairs."

"What's going to happen?" Neal asked. He felt a whisper of apprehension. "The murders haven't been solved, have they? Leslie hasn't helped solve them, has she?"

"Nobody's solved anything yet."

Neal relaxed. "Oh. Good."

"What?"

"I mean, that's too bad. I mean, why does Agent Saxon want to see us?"

"You'll find out in due time."

"I've already told you where I was last night—"

"Change your pants," Walker said with sudden harshness, "and come with me."

Neal changed his pants and went with him.

After all, what was another few minutes when you were fated to become a hero?

3:00 P.M.

From where he sat, next to Myrna, Harmon Colebrook watched the last two villagers—the Christers, Amanda and Bob Johnson—enter the inn and then join the rest of them scattered around the lobby. They were all here now, rounded up under his roof like sheep for the slaughter. Nazi Germany, by God, that was what this Sunday in Whitehall reminded him of. Village people herded together by a goddamned Gestapo agent named Saxon, standing over by the fireplace now and checking off names on the list he'd ordered Colebrook to make out for him.

What the hell for? Saxon wouldn't tell him, refused to say anything about it. Just asked him a lot of questions about where he'd been last night and how did he feel about Leslie Abbott. Asked Myrna and Buddy Quint the same questions, too, and was probably going to ask them of everybody else. Like *they* were criminals. Like it was them and not those psychics who were guilty of murder and crazy occult bullshit.

Leslie Abbott. She was the only one in Whitehall who wasn't here, except for Myrna's teched old mother.

Colebrook shifted uneasily on his chair and peered around at the other villagers. They all looked the way he felt: tensed-up, wary. Myrna so stiff beside him she might have had a stick rammed up her behind, face so pinched it made him think of a fat white prune. Ephraim Buell slouched in one of the dining-room chairs Colebrook had had to carry in to accommodate everybody; Buell was leaking little fumes of rye like air from a punctured tire, half-drunk again, skin as gray as a squirrel's ass. Buddy Quint fingering his pimples and Tom Quint biting down on the stem of his pipe so hard there were ridges of white muscle along his jaw. Miss Henrietta Daniels over in a corner, crocheting and running her tongue back and forth over her loose dentures. Seth Adams fiddling with the pieces on the chess table with one hand, scratching his crotch with the other. The Jesus freaks holding hands on top of an old gilt-edged Bible. George Parsons and his wife, Ed Docker and his wife, Zeke Coombs and his wife, all sitting in a row like scarecrows in a cornfield.

And none of them or the rest saying anything to each other, just sitting and fidgeting, looking at Saxon and his stony-faced partner, looking at the three psychics. Psychics weren't talking either: no sounds at all except people breathing and the birch logs crackling on the hearth and the faint soughing of the wind outside. Lull in the storm, Colebrook thought bitterly. Lull in here, too. And both ready to bust wide open before too much longer.

Saxon made them wait another minute. Then he said, "All right, now we'll get down to it," and the sound of it seemed to come so suddenly in the hush that half of them jerked in their chairs. Colebrook leaned forward, gripping his knees.

"You're all here because there's something going on in Whitehall that we're going to put a stop to," Saxon said. He stepped forward a pace and held the list of names out toward them as if it were a goddamn scarlet letter. "And I don't just mean Agent Walker and myself. I mean the Federal Bureau of Investigation. Let's get that understood right away."

He paused to scan the faces staring back at him. There was a kind of fearful expectancy in the air now; Colebrook could feel it. Felt it inside himself, too.

"One of you has been terrorizing Leslie Abbott," Saxon said. "One of you has been making threatening phone calls to her since she moved here, telling her to get out of Whitehall or something would happen to her paintings. Last night or this morning, that same person broke into her house and carried out his threat: He destroyed her paintings and made a wreckage of her studio. I want that person's name and I intend to have it."

Christ, Colebrook thought, so that's what this is all about. The others were murmuring, shifting toward one another, exchanging uneasy glances. Even the three psychics seemed surprised.

Saxon said, "Any of you have anything to say?"

Silence. Until Amanda Johnson, a washed-out young blonde with a funny glow in her eyes, said in her passionate monotone, " 'Put on the whole armor of God, that ye may be able to stand against the wiles of the devil.' "

Saxon stared at her. "What was that?"

"The devil has found unholy sanctuary among us," she said. "He has possessed Leslie Abbott and her friends with demons; he has possessed her tormentor with demons. Look to Jesus for the answer and the salvation; his word will cast them out."

"Amanda," her bearded husband said, "I don't think this is the time—"

"Jesus loves you all," she said. "Praise Jesus."

"Either of you know anything about these threatening calls?" Saxon asked Bob Johnson. "About the vandalism?"

"No, brother. No."

Buell cleared his throat. "What makes you think it's one of us?" he asked thickly. "Tell us that."

"You'd be Buell? Ephraim Buell?"

"That's who I am. Maybe it's an outsider, you consider that? Maybe it's one of her occult cronies over there."

Jo Turner glared at him as if he were something that had crawled out from under a woodpile. Koskovich shook his head and kept on shaking it.

Iverson said indignantly, "We're *clairvoyants*."

Nobody paid any attention to him.

"It's not an outsider," Saxon said. "It's somebody who

lives in Whitehall, somebody who doesn't want a psychic living here because he's afraid of something he doesn't understand."

"Ain't *none* of us want her kind living here," George Parsons said, "and that's a fact. But that don't mean any of us'd take to deviling her the way you say."

Buell said, "How come you're investigating this business, anyhow? Vandalism ain't an FBI matter."

"No. But murder is."

"You bet it is," Buell said. "Three of that bunch been killed already—we all know about that. One of us could be next, goddamn it."

Amanda Johnson slid around to look at him. "Blasphemers will never enter the Kingdom of Heaven nor sit with Jesus at the Father's side."

Old Seth Adams laughed out loud.

Buell said, "We got the right to feel safe in our beds, ain't we? We got the right to live our lives without seers and crazy occult worshipers in our midst."

"You sound pretty upset, Mr. Buell," Saxon said. "Upset enough to have already done something about it, maybe?"

Buell's face got grayer. "You accusing me?"

"I'm asking you. What do you know about these acts against Leslie Abbott?"

"Nothing. I don't know nothing about 'em."

"What about the rest of you people?"

Silence.

Saxon nodded darkly. "Okay," he said. "Okay then. We're all going to be stranded here for the next day or two by the storm; there's nothing we can do about that. But I'm warning you right now. Nothing else had better happen to Miss Abbott. She'd better not be bothered or harmed in any way. The same thing goes for Oscar Koskovich and Jo Turner and Neal Iverson. None of them had better be bothered or harmed either. Is that clear?"

Colebrook remembered the questions they'd asked him earlier, where he was last night and what he'd been doing, and a connection fused in his mind. A feeling of outrage came into him, made him blurt, "Hold on just a minute, now. You trying to say we're suspects in more than just devilment? You trying to say one of *us* could of murdered those other three psychics?"

"Somebody murdered them, Mr. Colebrook. And somebody's been terrorizing Leslie Abbott. Maybe it's the same person, maybe it isn't. I'm not ruling out any possibilities yet."

Stirrings, shocked whispers.

Buell said, "Ain't none of us a killer. You got no cause to be suspecting us."

"*I* think Agent Saxon is right," Iverson said. His left eyelid twitched as if he were winking at Buell. "The murderer is somebody in Whitehall, all right."

Buell stabbed a finger in Iverson's direction. "Listen, you—"

"That's enough." Saxon said it quiet, but there was something in his tone that made it seem like he'd yelled. His face was set tight and his eyes were hot and dangerous. Tough one, Colebrook thought grudgingly. You didn't want to cross a man like that; he'd be liable to fix you up good with the government if you did.

It got still in there again. Saxon let a few more seconds pass; then he said, "Understand this: We're not making any accusations of murder. We're conducting an investigation, that's all. And we're trying to keep anyone else from being hurt or killed, including all of you. That means questions and more questions until we get some answers. So what we're going to do now is talk to each of you individually in the dining room. After that, you're free to go about your business." He paused. "Anybody have anything to say before we get started?"

"Yes," Amanda Johnson said.

They all looked at her.

"Let the light of Jesus's truth spiral forth," she said. "Seek the spirit of Jesus Christ before it's too late. Seek the Holy Spirit."

Buell leaned over to Colebrook. The whites of his eyes looked bloody. "That's just what I'm going to do, all right," he muttered. "Open the bar, will you, Harmon? I need the holy spirit real bad."

3:40 P.M.

Leslie knelt on the floor of her studio and scrubbed at the multicolored streaks and blotches of paint. Her hands were encased in rubber gloves; a bucket of water and an almost empty can of turpentine stood beside her.

She had already cleaned up most of the wreckage. Swept up the flayed canvas strips and put them into cardboard boxes from the belfry; carried the boxes and the splintered pieces of frames and easels and furniture downstairs and burned them in the fireplace; righted what was left of the catchall table and draped it and the slashed couch in blankets. She hadn't been able to get all of the paint off the pinewood walls, no matter how hard she scrubbed or how much turpentine she used; it had gotten into the cracks and into the grain of the wood. Especially the blues and the reds. Those colors made the cracks look like veins and arteries leaking blood.

It was the same thing with the floor, but she kept on working anyway. Not because she had any hope of ever restoring the studio—it was a dead room now, as far as she was concerned; it had been raped and beaten and ravaged, and it was dead—but because cleaning it up gave her something to do, kept her from brooding too much. Kept her from dwelling on the pulses she could feel with her mind: intimations full of menace and evil.

She hadn't wanted to stay here alone. Even the inn, facing Oscar and the others, was better than being alone in a dead house. But the choice hadn't been hers to make. The controlling forces again, the sense of inevitability: She was here because she was supposed to be here. For whatever reason.

Pulses full of menace and evil.

For whatever reason.

Busy. Busy, busy. Brad would be back pretty soon; she had

called him at the inn an hour ago, as he had asked her to, just to let him know she was all right. It would be a little better when he got here. Maybe they could go to bed, make love the way they had last night. Yes. Make love.

She crawled forward, used the last of the turpentine to scrub up a thick orange-black smear. Then she stood and went across to the belfry door, up the narrow staircase inside. The dull afternoon light filtering in through the windows created shadows among the overhead supports where the church bell had once been mounted, more shadows among the clutter of storage boxes and unused canvases and odds and ends on the compact attic platform. Dusty up there, full of cobwebs that she'd never gotten around to clearing away. Quiet up there, too. Now that the storm had slackened, she could barely hear the voice of the wind shrieking under the eaves. She was glad of that. There were too many screams already echoing in the eaves of her mind.

She found another can of turpentine among her painting supplies, took it back down, and set it on the studio floor. And then straightened up and stood motionless; the back of her scalp prickled.

She felt as if she were being watched.

Twisting her head, she looked over at the stairs from the main floor. No one there—of course there was no one there. She hadn't heard anything, and the wood risers were old and creaked when weight was put on them. Then what . . . ?

The painting.

Leslie swung around and stared over at where it was propped against the wall near the belfry stairs. Her scalp prickled again. It *was* what made her feel watched: sitting there beneath its cloth cover like a giant eye, cataracted and milky.

She had a sudden desire—compulsion—to look at it for the first time in days. With hesitant steps, she went to it, squatted on her heels in front of it. Reached out and pulled the cloth away.

There was nothing different about it. She had almost expected that there would be, that it had been altered or transformed in some way. Just the house, the elm trees, and the woodshed along the north side. Snowdrifts like wavy sand dunes, snow falling from a dark night sky. And the figure in the shadow of one elm, looking toward the house—a blackish man-shape in a long coat, a winter hat with earflaps surrounding the upper half of a blank oval.

Whose face? she thought. The murderer's? Or does it belong to someone else I know?

The scene. Did it already happen, or is it scheduled to happen, or will it never happen at all because it's only a symbol?

Death, she thought. Death coming on pale snow instead of a pale horse, with a rope and a blue velvet cord instead of a scythe.

Coming for her?

3:55 P.M.

Neal left the inn by the rear entrance, circled the frozen pond, and plowed into the birch woods to the north. Most of the afternoon light was gone; the sky was the color of blackened metal. Shadows lay everywhere, expanding and contracting mistily beyond the veil of falling snow. Thin gusts of wind nipped at his ears beneath his vision cap, but he barely felt the cold. The excitement burbled like boiling water inside him; the race of his pulse was hot and rhythmic.

This was *adventure*, a heroic quest. The Prince making his way inexorably toward the solution to three murders, braving the bitter elements, risking his life and health for truth and justice. It was almost like something out of a television show: "The Adventures of the Prince of Psychics."

Except that this was serious business here. Deadly serious business. No mistake about that; he'd better keep that in mind every minute.

Lights flickered behind him and to his left, out in front of the inn. He wiped snow off his glasses and saw a white-shrouded car turn onto Main Street and come forward in the same direction he was heading. Seconds later it passed the murky shapes of Quint's Country Store and Buell's Antiques and then vanished except for the fading yellowish glow of its headlamps. Otherwise there was no one out in the storm except him.

That was because nearly everybody was still inside the inn, being interviewed by Saxon and Walker. Including Ephraim Buell. He had made absolutely sure of that before hurrying up to the second floor, donning his coat and muffler and gloves, and slipping down the back stairs. Nobody had seen him leave; nobody had paid any attention to him at all, just as usual. But this was one time he was glad to be ignored. While the FBI was asking a lot of pointless questions, he was out here solving the case for them.

He wondered if Buell was also the one who had been terrorizing Leslie. Probably. It all added up as far as he could see. A psychotic who hated clairvoyants was capable of anything, including threatening phone calls and vandalism. Buell was the one, all right. And on the other end of the spectrum, Neal Iverson was the one, too. Not Oscar and not Leslie. Just the Prince himself.

He left the birch wood directly behind the small dark cottage that sat at an angle to the rear of the antique shop. Pushed past the cottage, looking over again at the Country Store. Still empty. When he reached the shop, he climbed up the steps to the back door, licked snow off his lips, stamped it off his booted feet, and reached out eagerly to turn the doorknob.

It was locked.

Well, of *course* it's locked, he told himself. Psychotic murderers who keep guilty evidence in their cellar workshops *always* lock their doors. Which meant that the front door would be locked, too, and all the windows. So how was he going to get inside? Break a window? Kick in the door?

He turned the knob again, rattled the door. It didn't join into the jamb very well, and the lock seemed kind of old and loose. If it was a spring lock, he could try using one of his credit cards to open it, the way you saw private eyes do on television all the time.

He bent down and squinted at the latch. Damned if it didn't *look* like a spring lock. He fumbled inside his coat for his wallet, brought it out, slipped his Master Charge card from its plastic insert, and eased the card into the crack between the door and the jamb. Wiggled it around the lock. Wedged it against the bolt and wiggled it again.

Click. The door opened under his hand.

Son of a bitch, he thought. It really works, you can really pick a lock that way! That was amazing. He couldn't wait to tell Tina about it when he talked to her tonight on the phone.

Neal stepped inside and shut the door behind him, muffling the sound of the storm. It was dark in there, so dark that he couldn't see much of anything except lumpy masses of shadow. He took off his gloves and stuffed them into his right coat pocket. Then, from his left coat pocket, he fished out a packet of matches—he'd made sure to take a couple from the lobby ashtrays at the inn—and struck one.

Where he was, he saw then, was in a small corridor with another door at the far end and two rooms littered with stuff on either side. The cellar stairs weren't anywhere back here—a second match helped him conclude that. He moved ahead to the far door, his heart thudding, opened it, and peered through into the main shop.

Enough light penetrated through the front display window to let him see the outlines of shelves and tables and things hanging from the shadowy rafters. The hanging things made him blink nervously for a second, until he assured himself that they could only be lanterns and thunder mugs and brass warming pans suspended on twine.

Off to his right was a long counter with a cash register at one end; behind the counter was yet another closed door. He hurried over there and rotated the knob. Locked, too—not that that was surprising. He struck another match, and in its glow he saw that this lock was also of the spring type. So he took his Master Charge out again, worked it around until this lock said *click* and the door popped open.

There was nothing to that little trick, once you got the hang of it. He guessed he shouldn't have been amazed at all. It was how criminals got into places, wasn't it? He'd read about that. If it worked for private eyes and criminals, why shouldn't it work for the Prince?

Inside this door was a small landing and a set of stairs leading downward into blackness. Neal felt a little thrill of anticipation. Christ only knew what he might find down there; he might even find evidence that Buell was some kind of Bluebeard who had murdered a lot of other clairvoyants. He closed the door behind him, fired another match, and started down.

The flame cut a thin, wavering path through the darkness, made indistinct shapes and masses appear and disappear with each descending step. Odors wafted up out of the gloom: old wood, varnish, dust, and the overriding smell of damp decay. Neal's nose twitched. His breath came now in short fervid pants; he could feel sweat trickling out from under his vision cap.

When he was three-quarters of the way down, the match guttered and began to burn his fingers. He waved it out frantically and the shadows folded around him and made him feel like he was standing in the middle of an inkwell. He got a new match going, descended the rest of the way to a cracked concrete floor.

Ahead of him, he could see the workbench along the rear wall; around him, the vague outlines of tables and chairs and other antiques, the gutted case of the grandfather clock, the lumber and hardware that had appeared to him in his psychic eye. He started toward the bench.

The match went out. But instead of stopping this time to strike a fresh one, he took a step . . . another . . . a third—

Something seemed to clutch at his ankle.

He made a small bleating sound, lost his balance, and

toppled over sideways, dropping the matches as his hands spread out to break his fall. There was a jarring pain in his right knee when it struck the concrete, then a stinging pain in the palm of his right hand when it slid across the rough surface. He came to rest sprawled out on his stomach, one knee hooked under him, his glasses askew and hanging from one ear.

But he didn't stay that way for more than a second. He twisted around and hauled himself up. Straightened his glasses with his injured hand and used the other one to grope in his pocket for a second packet of matches.

The stillness in the cellar seemed breathless now, broken only by faint intermittent mutterings from the building's wooden joints. Neal's hands shook as he scraped another light, held it down toward the floor where the something had clutched at his ankle. But there wasn't anything there except for the curved frame of an antique handloom. Was that what had tripped him? Of course it was. It must have been. He was alone in here, wasn't he? There wasn't anything to be afraid of.

The pain in his knee dulled, but the sharp stinging in his right palm remained. Neal held the match flame close to it, shuddered when he saw the dark glistening moistness of blood. He shook out the light and rubbed at the blood with his thumb and felt a shallow gash beneath it. Superficial cut, that was all. He let out a sighing breath. What was a little cut, a little blood, to the Prince of Psychics? Blood spilled in the pursuit of knowledge was blood spilled in the light of truth. That was a good line, all right. Someday, maybe, after he became famous, he might even want to tackle the job of writing his memoirs.

He sleeved sweat off his forehead, struck another match, and moved forward carefully through the clutter. Then he was doing what he had seen himself do in the vision: approaching the workbench, seeing the dark coiled shape of the rope lying on one corner. Moving closer. Watching the loose row of old leather strips appear beside the rope.

He caught up two of the strips and thrust them into his coat pocket. Then he lifted the rope, looped it over his left arm and around his shoulder. He lit a fresh match. Now to search the rest of the workbench, the rest of the cellar for more evidence—

Thud.

The sound came suddenly from upstairs, and it was that of a door being slammed shut.

Neal froze. His heart seemed to want to climb into his throat. The matchlight began to dance erratically in his fingers, making little flaming smears on the darkness.

Footsteps on the floor above, rapid and heavy.

Buell? Oh, God, was it the *murderer?*

The cellar doorknob rattled.

Control deserted him. He staggered away from the bench, almost collided with the gutted clock casing; the match burned his fingertips and he hurled it away from him. Hide! Hide! He dropped to his knees, crawled behind the casing. Cowered there.

The door above jerked inward.

Someone started down the stairs.

Reality washed in on Neal in sickening waves: the reality of murder and death. Until this moment, what had happened to Tony and Sandra and Gloria had been an abstract; until this moment he hadn't been really afraid for his own life because at an essential level he had always believed that no harm could ever come to him. He had the gift, he was the Prince, and nothing terrible or painful had ever happened to him. But Buell was a psychotic killer, Buell had strangled and hung three people already, *Buell could kill Neal Iverson, too.* Murder. Not an abstraction, not an adventure, not a case.

Murder!

A black man-shape materialized halfway down the stairs. *Clump. Clump-clump-clump.* Coming closer, death coming closer.

Panic swelled inside him as the black shape reached the

bottom step. Then the darkness exploded in light from a bulb hanging overhead—

Neal screamed.

4:25 P.M.

In his room at the inn, Oscar sat with pad and pen, trying painfully to construct his lead story for the next issue of *The Pet Trader*. Deadline was Friday, and of the four articles he'd planned for the issue, he had completed only one back home in New York. Three PSYCHICs were dead, Whitehall was a place of fear and hostility, but you still had to pretend that mundane things like articles for a 10,000-circulation pet journal were important. Because if you didn't, if you failed to find something sane to occupy your time and your mind, you were just liable to come apart at the seams. He kept telling himself that as he struggled with the opening paragraph.

> The failure of routine cleaning processes to remove bird defecation and seed residue, what should be a simple matter of hygienic principle and a valuable tool for the maintenance of stock, is recognized by many progressive dealers in the metropolitan areas to be one of the frequent causes of birds breaking down. One owner, interviewed at length, stated that canary mortality in his store had dropped by forty percent since employees were instructed to empty trays at regular intervals and

He couldn't go on with it. He just couldn't. Writing this stuff with dedication to forget the death of his wife was bad enough; but this—this was insanity. Canary mortality. Bird breakdown. Dear God! Three people were dead. *Human* mortality, *human* breakdown; it was human beings who were being murdered—his friends, his PSYCHICs.

Oscar pushed the pad aside, laid down the pen, and

stood. Paced to the window. Encroaching darkness and flurries of snow formed an opaque screen beyond the glass, and the light from the lamp turned the panes into a mirror: He saw a gaunt-cheeked old man reflected there, with eyes like buttons embedded in white dough. A hazy face, distorted and strange.

A guilty face?

It's not my fault, he thought.

But I brought them together, I brought them *here*.

Whitehall, Vermont. Is Saxon right that the murderer is the same person who has been terrorizing Leslie? Does the killer live right here in the village? Not my fault. Leslie moved here on her own, I had nothing to do with that. But she didn't want me to bring the group to Whitehall; she didn't want anyone here to know she was clairvoyant. Not my fault. But would three of us be dead now if I hadn't insisted in October? Would Gloria be dead now if I hadn't insisted on this weekend?

Not my fault.

Maybe it isn't someone from Whitehall. Maybe there's no connection between the murders and what's been happening to Leslie. Maybe Neal is right: It's a psychotic who hates clairvoyants, a case of random homicide.

Or maybe it's one of us.

Neal? Jo? Even Leslie? Ridiculous, insane. But it's all insane, anything is possible—

The image of his face on the window glass dissolved suddenly and became an image of rabbits, rabbits, white and black rabbits tumbling with one another in a hutch, like puppies tumbling and playing, long ears flapping, pink little noses twitching, brains with their little sparks and gutters of light passing for thought

And the image of the rabbits dissolved into something else that was black and white, a dark place streaked and strewn with dull silver color, a place he knew, a place nearby—

Terror

Something hanging there in the black and white

Wind sound, creaking sound
Shapeless blob hanging, hair fluttering
Echoes of a scream dying in the creaking wind
A face he couldn't quite see, black and white and dead
And gone.

It all went through him in a stunning rush, like currents of electricity; his body jerked, his hands moved at convulsive angles, his legs carried him blindly back from the window. And it was last night again, last night all over: consciousness retreating, crouching, the terror flooding him and taking away reality. Suffocation. Blurred vision.

Thought: God not again not another one please

Ethereal voice, whispering: Go there . . . go there . . . go there . . .

Out of the room and standing in the hallway, coat in his hand. Putting on his coat and running for the stairs. No longer impelling his body, barely its observer.

Someone in front of him, coming out of another room. "Oh—Oscar." Jo's voice. "Where are you going, dear?"

Dead thing hanging.

Go there . . . go there . . .

Jo staring at him with widening eyes. "For God's sake, Oscar, what is it, what's the matter?"

No voice of his own, no words. Just her voice and the one in his mind, whispering urgently. Past her then, running on to the stairs. Jo calling after him. Tears in his eyes, pain like needles in his lungs.

On the stairs, down the stairs.

Outside.

Cold, cold. Snow, wind, black and white.

Not again please

Go there . . . hurry!

Running running running running running

Running

4:25 P.M.

As he eased Leslie's Toyota along Main Street, past Quint's Country Store, Saxon judged that there was better than six inches of new snow on the ground; the windrows snowplowed at the road shoulders were being transformed into smooth white drifts. If the blizzard turned into an all-nighter, there could be as much as twenty inches down by morning. And if there was another storm on the heels of this one . . .

The Toyota's engine labored coldly, misfiring every few seconds and causing the little car to buck and chatter around him. Gusts of wind dislodged clumps of snow from tree branches, sent them spattering against the already caked windshield. The wipers were sluggish, and despite the fact that he'd put the defroster on high, there was a film of condensation across the inside of the glass. Even with the headlamps on low beam, cutting through the gloom of dusk, he couldn't see more than a hundred yards ahead of him with any clarity.

He raised one gloved hand again and scrubbed at the moisture on the windshield. Outside, to his right, the dark contours of Ephraim Buell's antique shop appeared more distinctly; he was within a hundred feet of drawing parallel to it.

And in that moment, the front door of the shop burst open and someone—a blurred figure in coat and hat—came rushing out.

Saxon leaned closer to the glass, squinting. The figure staggered down off the porch steps, lost footing in the snow, and toppled over sideways. There was a great thrashing of arms and legs that sent up billows of loose flakes, then the figure rose up and lurched forward again.

Someone else ran out of the shop, waving what appeared to be a coil of rope over his head. As if, incongruously, he were about to try to lasso the first runner.

What the hell? Saxon had his foot on the brake by this time, and the Toyota skidded to a stop just as the lead figure, making frantic arm gestures, charged into the street. In the snowy gleam of the headlights, Saxon recognized the face, the checkered black-and-white cap above it.

Iverson.

He pulled on the emergency brake, shoved open the door, and swung out. Swept back his coat with his right hand and drew his service revolver. Behind Iverson, at the edge of the street, the second figure had slowed to a tentative walk; his arm and the coil of rope had come down to hang loosely at his side. But he was near enough for Saxon to recognize him, too.

Ephraim Buell.

Iverson ran headlong into the Toyota, hit the hood blindly, and bounced off it. He groped his way around to where Saxon was and pawed at him in a childish terrified way, as if he wanted to crawl into his pocket. Magnified by his thick glasses, Iverson's eyes were huge and bulging like detached eyeballs on stalks. His mouth hung open and his jaw wobbled up and down; he was trying to draw enough breath to make words.

With his left hand, Saxon pushed him away and against the car so he could keep the .38 free and poised. He had no idea what was going on here, but the fear in Iverson's expression and the rope in Buell's hand made the situation tense and potentially dangerous.

Thirty feet away on the street, Buell had come to a standstill. But he was half-turned and leaning in the opposite direction, back toward the antique shop, as if he were thinking about taking flight. Part of the rope had come uncoiled; it trailed down into the snow at his feet like a dead brown snake.

"Buell!" Saxon yelled at him. "Hold it right there!"

Buell kept leaning back toward the antique shop. Saxon couldn't even be sure that the man had heard him; he had barely been able to hear himself over the high wail of the storm. He held the revolver up and rocked it, and that got results: Buell straightened around and stood stiff and swaying like a tree in the wind. His face, visible in the headlamp glare, was twisted into a grimace of outrage and a fright of his own.

There was no sense in trying to talk out here. And the car would be too confining. Saxon reached out and caught Iverson's arm, steered him away along the street. When they neared Buell, he gestured with the .38. Buell licked his lips, then turned reluctantly and shambled ahead of them, looking back over his shoulder as he went. Iverson hung back all the way to the shop, making audible chuffing noises and staying close to Saxon as if he were afraid Buell might whirl and attack him.

Inside, a single bulb burned palely overhead and more light came through an open door behind the counter; but none of it did much to dispel the heavy gloom. Shadows crowded in close to them, clinging to the random scatter of goods. Saxon shut the door and stood between and apart from the other two, so that the three of them formed a triangle.

"All right," he said, "what the hell is this all about?"

"That's what I'd like to know," Buell said thickly. His body had a slight weave to it and his eyes were glassy; he looked and sounded more than a little drunk. "This son of a bitch broke in here."

"Broke in?"

"Damn right. I found him down in my workshop. Come down the stairs and put the light on and there he was on all fours like a goddamn dog. Scared the living shit out of me."

Iverson shook his head in frantic broken movements that sprayed snow from his cap and his glasses. He was still making those chuffing noises, as if he were hyperventilating. On the palm of one bare hand, lifted in front of his face, Saxon could see a black stain that might have been blood.

He said to Buell, "Did you hurt him?"

"Hurt him? Christ almighty, he come up off that floor screaming like a woman and run straight at me, knocked me over before I could get out the way. Anyone got hurt down there, it's *me*."

"What are you doing with that rope?"

"Rope?" Buell looked down at the coil in his hand as though

he had forgotten he was carrying it. "*He* had it, by God. Had it looped around his arm. Dropped it when he run into me, and I—"

"Murderer—he's the murderer!"

That came from Iverson in a liquid croak. Saxon stared at him; he could feel his nerves contracting.

Buell said incredulously, "Murderer?"

"You did it, you killed Gloria and the others—"

"You're crazy!"

Iverson fumbled in his coat pocket and came out with a handful of something that looked like strips of leather. He held them out to Saxon. "Buell used one of these to strangle them," he said, "and he used rope like that to hang them afterward."

"Jesus Christ," Buell said. He let go of the rope as if it had come alive and squirming in his fingers.

Saxon said, "That's a strong accusation, Iverson."

"It's the *truth*, that's what it is." Iverson's voice was stronger now; he had gotten his breathing under control. "I told you I was going to solve the case, didn't I? I told you about my intimations. This afternoon they all finally came into focus while I was urinating—"

"Urinating?"

"—and I had a precognition. I saw myself in Buell's workshop and I saw the rope and the leather strips and I knew he was the one. I *knew* it. That's why I used one of my credit cards to get in here; I had to fulfill the vision and get the evidence."

"Crazy," Buell said. "Damned if he ain't."

"Crazy? I'm not the crazy one, you are. You're a psychotic with an obsessive hatred for clairvoyants and you murdered three of us already and you would've killed me, too, if I hadn't gotten away—"

"I never killed nobody!" Buell shouted. Then a thought seemed to strike him, and he blinked and pointed a shaking finger at Iverson. "Maybe *you're* the one. Damn, maybe you killed them three friends of yours and you was waiting in my workshop to do me the same way. You had the rope and you had them pieces of leather—"

"That's enough," Saxon said sharply. "Now, I want to hear answers to questions and that's all I want to hear."

Buell jammed his hands into his pockets. He seemed to be sobering a little; his expression was less glassy and more nervous. Iverson stared at the gun in Saxon's hand as if seeing it for the first time. His Adam's apple bobbed up and down like a cork on an elastic band. Neither of them said anything.

"You first, Iverson. This vision you claim to have had—"

"I don't *claim* to have had it, I *did* have it. I'm having more intimations right this minute, more psychic birds fluttering in my consciousness. I might even have another vision pretty soon."

"Bullshit," Buell muttered. But he didn't say anything else.

"All right, you saw yourself in Buell's workshop and you saw the rope and the leather. What else did you see?"

"Nothing else."

"Then on what basis did you decide Buell was the murderer?"

"I *knew* he was. Is. The birds came together in my psychic eye just like I knew they would and gave me the answer."

Buell made a disgusted noise in his throat and then belched. Whiskey fumes soured the air around him.

Saxon had begun to feel disgusted himself. He said to Iverson, "Why didn't you come to me about this vision? Why did you break in here on your own?"

"Because I was here alone in the vision and you can't change a precognition. If you do, you're just fighting determinism, and that can be very dangerous because it can't be fought, it has to happen, so I had to come here alone. Besides, I solved the case with my gift and it was up to me to get the evidence."

Christ, Saxon thought. "Did you search the workshop?"

"I didn't have time to search it. Maybe there's something else incriminating down there—"

"Nothing incriminating in my workshop," Buell said.

"—but even if there isn't, it doesn't matter. My vision and the rope and the leather strips are enough, aren't they?"

"No, they're not enough," Saxon said. "None of the victims was strangled with strips of leather."

Iverson gaped at him. "They weren't? How do you know that?"

"Never mind how I know it." He wasn't about to tell this idiot about Leslie's vision at the Harris farmhouse; about the blue velvet cord she had seen. "And another thing: Each of the victims was hung with a different kind of rope—Sandra Harris with a clothesline that probably belonged to her. What you saw and what you found here aren't evidence of anything, Iverson."

Iverson scowled and folded his arms across his chest. He had the stubborn, sulky look of a kid who thinks he knows something important and can't get anybody to listen to him. "I don't care what you say," he said. "You're wrong and I'm right. I *know* I'm right."

Saxon looked at Buell. "You make a habit of working on Sunday?"

"What? No, I don't make a habit of it."

"Then why did you come here today?"

Buell's eyes flicked. "Felt like it, that's all."

"Not good enough. Answer my question."

Hesitation. And then a resigned, hell-with-it gesture. "I think I got a pint of rye stashed down in the workshop. Remembered it might be there after Colebrook chased me out the inn."

"Why did Colebrook chase you out of the inn?"

"Hell, I don't know. Said he was closing the bar until later, had something to take care of."

"Okay. So you came here and went down into the workshop and found Iverson. And he knocked you over and then ran."

"That's what he done."

"He also dropped the rope. You picked it up."

"I guess I did."

"Why?"

"It was there and I picked it up, that's why."

"What would you have done if you'd caught him?"

"Done? I never thought ahead that far. Had him arrested, I suppose. I still want him arrested. Bastard broke in here, scared hell out of me. Might have been waiting to *kill* me, by God, he's crazy enough—"

"You were going to kill *me*," Iverson said passionately. "If I was a psychotic murderer, do you think I'd have run for my life the way I did?"

"Ain't no telling what a crazy psychic's liable to do."

"There's no telling what a *psychotic* is liable to do."

"Don't you call me no psychotic—"

"Psychotic! Murderer!"

"Crazy psychic fuck!"

"*Both of you shut up!*"

Saxon bellowed the words, and the authority in them seemed to make Iverson and Buell shrink away from each other. The frustration was sharp inside him again. He didn't like either of these two and he didn't trust the word of either; but there was nothing in their stories to indicate they were guilty of anything except abnormal behavior: a buffoon and a dull-witted village drunk. It was possible one of them *was* the murderer—he wasn't about to rule out anybody yet. But even if that were the case, it didn't seem reasonable that one had come here to kill the other.

False alarm. Just another segment in a lunatic time of irrational happenings, irrational people, fear and hostility, death visions and meaningless visions. Too many questions and no answers, and not one single lead from anyone he had spoken to in Whitehall today or the past two days.

And Leslie's still alone in her house, he thought.

Iverson and Buell were staring at him. He got a grip on himself. Saw that he was still holding the revolver on them and tucked it away inside its holster. "I've heard enough for now," he said. "Iverson, I want you to go back to the inn and stay there. And I mean *stay* there."

"Now? You mean now?"

"That's just what I mean."

"What about Buell? I tell you, he's the murderer—"

"If he is, then I'll arrest him. If and when I have proof."

Iverson looked as if he wanted to cry. "Why won't you believe me? I've solved the case for you, and now you're going to let the killer run around loose."

"Letting *you* run around loose," Buell muttered.

"Back to the inn, Iverson. And don't come back here, don't bother Buell again." He looked at the wizened little man. "That goes for you, too. Stay away from Iverson."

"I don't want no truck with him. But I'm gonna press charges against him with the county police, you can count on that."

"That's your privilege."

"You're making a big mistake, Mr. Saxon," Iverson said. "You mark my words." He pulled his checkered cap down over his ears, glared once more at Buell, and stalked over to the door. "You mark my words," he said again. The door clattered behind him in the wind.

"You ought to of put him in custody," Buell said sullenly. "What if he does come after me a second time?"

"He won't come after you. But *I* will if you cause trouble. Just remember that."

Saxon left him. Outside again, he hurried through the snow to the street. The sky was dark now, massed with heavy bloated clouds; snow fell in spinning whorls. Fifty yards away, slogging toward the inn, Iverson was a misty silhouette.

The Toyota's windshield was caked with half-frozen flakes; Saxon scraped it clear, slid in under the wheel, and put on the wipers. It was another minute before he could see well enough to drive. And another five minutes after that before he crawled up Maplewood Road and plowed the car into Leslie's driveway.

There was a light burning in one of the front windows, but otherwise the house appeared dark. He got out, pushed toward the door. And came to an abrupt halt, staring at the snow on what would be the path to the front gate.

It was marred by blurred tracks, recently made because the storm had only partly filled them in. Someone had come to the house, or gone away from it, within the past few minutes.

Apprehension clawed at him. He ran in awkward strides to the door and twisted the knob. It was unlocked; the wind hurled it inward out of his grasp, dislodging a piece of cardboard that Leslie had tacked over the broken pane of glass. He drew his service revolver again, lunged inside.

"Leslie!"

Silence.

The living room was deserted. Banked fire on the hearth, one of the floor lamps burning; nothing disturbed. He ran into the kitchen, the bedroom, the study. Raced upstairs to the studio.

Empty, all of them. Empty.

Leslie was gone.

4:55 P.M.

Broadelm Road, where it passed through the birch woods east of the inn, was like a white-floored tunnel: the dark pressing sky its roof, the thick pillar shapes of tree trunks its walls. The cold made Jo shiver violently inside her coat. Snow cascaded down in shifting patterns, obscuring what lay more than a hundred yards ahead of her. The snowfall and the wind-whipped branches were all that moved within that hundred-yard expanse; there was still no sign of Oscar except for the faint tracks of his passage in the surface snow.

You're a damn fool, she told herself again, running around out here in the middle of a bloody blizzard. Turn around and go back, for God's sake. Let the FBI find Oscar.

But her legs kept scissoring forward as if independent of the more rational commands of her mind. There was an undercurrent of compulsion in her that had been born when she encountered Oscar in the hallway outside her room. That half-blind look of terror and anguish on his face—it had touched something deep within her, caused a kind of mental jarring and then the need to go after him, find out where he was going. It was as though a psychic force had emanated from him and connected with her own gift; as though in that instant they were joined. She had run back into her room, gotten her coat, and rushed down the back stairs and then onto Broadelm Road in the wake of his tracks.

Thin shadows of fear and menace brushed at her as she ran. Had Oscar had another death vision? Was that the reason for the stricken look on his face, for his running past her as though she weren't even there?

Had someone *else* been murdered?

Jo didn't want to believe that. She didn't want to believe Saxon was right and the madman who'd killed Gloria and the others was right here in this disgustingly quaint little village. She was afraid, yes, but it wasn't a crippling fear; if she wasn't a brave woman, neither was she a coward or one of those silly shrinking-violet types she had always detested. Twenty years as a woman alone, a theatrical agent in the New York jungle, had given her a protective veneer of toughness and cynicism thick enough to shut her feelings away from even herself. It hadn't cracked in all that time and it wouldn't crack now.

Doubt, resilience, the compulsion to find Oscar: She kept on going.

Ahead she saw the edge of the woods and the sharp southward bend of the road. She struggled to quicken her pace—the surface snow was already calf-deep—and came out finally to where she could look along the curve to the covered bridge. Still empty, still no sign of Oscar.

Where was he, damn it? Where was he going?

Leslie's house wasn't far from here, Jo remembered suddenly. And Leslie hadn't been at that awful meeting at the inn two hours ago; no one had seen her, in fact, except young Saxon, since Friday night. Which meant she had been alone in her house this afternoon. Alone and vulnerable.

Good God, suppose she was victim number four. . . .

Stop it, Jo ordered herself. Nothing has happened to Leslie. Her house may be Oscar's destination, but even if it is, she's all right. Of course she is. She's all right, and so is Oscar.

His tracks followed the curve of the road: an erratic course down its approximate center. Jo kept them in front of her, making the same wide loop. The covered bridge loomed ahead, outlined gray-black against the sky; its yawning entrance looked like the opening into a cavern. She recalled her trek through the bridge yesterday with Oscar—the scurrying noises, the damp and musty smell—and a feeling of repugnance came to her. She didn't want to go in there again, not in the dark, not with bats and God knew what else probably nesting in the shadows.

Except that Oscar's tracks went straight to the entrance and vanished into the blackness within.

When she reached the bridge, she stopped and tried to penetrate the gloom. She could just make out the grayish rectangle of its opposite end; everything else was obscured. The compulsion tugged at her again, drawing her forward as if on wires of energy. She took a breath, felt the air burn like ice in her lungs. And moved ahead into the bridge.

After ten paces, the sound of the storm became concentrated: The wind in there was an eerie, whistling moan. The musty smell dilated her nostrils, brought a sour phlegmlike taste into her mouth. Except for the faint light ahead, the darkness was thick and enfolding. She could barely make out the thin carpeting of snow across the wooden floor.

She resisted an impulse to run on the uneven surface; forced herself to take long, rapid walking strides instead. Halfway through. The old wooden walls groaned under the thrust of the wind; the whistling sound was like a siren. Two-thirds of the way through. Ahead the grayish rectangle grew more distinct. She could see flurries of snow outside, the skeletal and wind-tossed shapes of trees. She could see—

—a blob of something lying in the snow just inside the entrance.

Jo's stride faltered, broke. She stood staring ahead with her body poised and tilted forward. Just a shadow, she thought. Or maybe a rock or a snowdrift.

Or maybe Oscar?

Her fear sharpened; menace swirled around her as though carried on gusts of wind. She felt dizzy, weak-kneed. Dim things like evil winged creatures began to move inside her mind: psychic flutterings, formless symbols—

Something rustled in the shadows behind her.

Muscular arms grabbed her, wrapped around her, and pinned her elbows at her sides. A knee jabbed against the base of her spine; her body was wrenched backward.

A voice whispered in the darkness, "I'm sorry, Jo Turner. I'm sorry."

And in that instant, in one bright flash, she understood the dark forces that had used her gift to bring her here: She hadn't been compelled to find Oscar at all, she had been compelled to attend her own death.

A whining cry burst out of her.

The strong arms slid upward and a velvety band caressed her throat. Bit into the flesh. Tightened.

The last sound she heard, the last sound in the world, was the wind like a mad echo of her scream.

5:15 P.M.

With the white wind like a hand shoving at her back, Leslie trudged steadily through the layers of snow on Broadelm Road. But her awareness of the temperature and the elements was peripheral; her mind was turned inward, walled off from externals, attuned to psychic impulses that were almost hypnotic.

She had been sitting before the fire in her living room, waiting for Brad, when the vibrations began to grow stronger, to bombard her mind with symbols of evil and menace and terror. Loathsome. Irresistible. Pulling at her magnetically, forcing her to put on her parka and mittens, to go out into the storm and make her way east along Maplewood Road, north on Broadelm.

She had no idea where the impulses, the controlling forces, were taking her. But she was compelled to follow.

The road sloped upward to a short rise. Hunched forward, her boot soles slipping on the frozen crust beneath the surface snow, she made her way up the incline. But more slowly now, with a vague sense of hesitation as she neared the crest. She knew what lay beyond, but when she reached the point where she could see it, she stopped so sharply she might have walked into an invisible wall.

The covered bridge stood seventy yards away, indistinct and ghostly through the flurries.

She stood staring at it—and it seemed to tilt off-center, to lose dimension and definition. The tossing shapes of trees took on the same surreal look in the darkness; everything within the range of her sight shifted, blurred, flowed together.

There was a sudden twisting in her mind that made her gasp. The bridge and the trees and all of the night dissolved into a swirl of blue and black, red and white.

Then the screaming began.

5:15 P.M.

He had brought the rope with him this time: the vision—always the vision. As soon as the woman lay crumpled and still at his feet, he tied one end of it in a slipknot around her neck. Threw the other end over a crossbeam above, laid his flashlight down, and desperately began to haul the dead thing up off the snowy floor of the bridge.

Hurry, he kept thinking, hurry hurry. He had to get back before he and the host were missed, before someone could come unexpectedly and catch him as he had almost been caught last night in Storm Junction.

Last night in Storm Junction. And now again today. Two

visions in twenty-four hours, two deaths and two salvations. But the vision this time had been different from any of the others—more urgent, less clear and detailed—and the panic it had carried was with him still. They were coming too fast now, much too fast. He felt as if he were out of control, as if the forces themselves behind the visions were out of control. Everything seemed to be gathering a kind of wild momentum, like a snowball rolling downhill with him trapped inside it, and there was nothing he could do to stop it. He was helpless.

Obey or die.

Life was the secret. An end to the secret was the end of him.

Protect the secret or die again.

His breath came in gasps as he pulled on the rope; his face was stiff with frozen sweat. Jo Turner's scream was in his mind, and that, too, seemed frozen, a constant wailing note that drowned out the storm raging around him. But at least there was no death smell here; at least that. The chill air and the musty odor inside the bridge had taken it away.

He thought he heard the dead thing's heels scrape on the floor, tugged harder on the rope, and then saw the body sway in front of him, suspended. He had put the flashlight on a horizontal two-by-four serving as a crossbrace for the near wall; now he canted it so that the beam was centered on a wide chink between two of the vertical boards. He managed to loop the rope through the chink and around the crossbrace, to tie it off without letting the body slip. Then he caught up the flash and swung it around and up. His hand trembled so badly from strain and fear that the light flickered and danced across the blue-purple face, the blackened tongue, the distended eyes.

The vision.

And it was done.

He shut off the flash, backed away through the darkness toward the south entrance. The scream remained frozen in his mind. No relief this time, he sensed that. No peace, no return to the warm place deep inside the host where there was little pain and little fear.

Because it was all going to happen again too soon: another vision, another death, another salvation.

Soon. Too soon.

"No," he said aloud. "Please, no."

But there was no one to hear him, now or ever. There were only the visions; there was only the secret to protect. It didn't matter that everything might be out of control. It didn't matter how much risk there would be. If it happened again, he would obey.

He would obey.

5:25 P.M.

The tracks leading away from Leslie's house were all but obliterated now by the wind and the new snow, but the Toyota's headlights picked up just enough traces of them to lead Saxon east along Maplewood Road, then north along another lane signposted Broadelm. He kept telling himself there had only been a single set of them, because that meant she was alone. But why had she gone out in this goddamn storm?

Saxon could feel and hear his pulse hammering like the accelerated ticking of a clock; it seemed to fill his ears above the whirring of the car engine. If she had stayed on the road, he should be getting close to her. But if she had left it somewhere, and if the storm worsened enough to wipe out her tracks entirely . . .

He drove as fast as he dared, his hands clamped so hard around the wheel that the muscles in his arms ached. Beyond the thudding windshield wipers, the headlight beams reflected off the falling snow as much as they penetrated it; he couldn't see much more than a hundred feet. The road in front of him stayed empty. Nothing but whiteness and blackness—

A shape materialized at the far reach of the headlights: somebody standing on a rise a hundred yards ahead, motionless, facing away to the north.

When he plowed closer and recognized Leslie's parka and the familiar contours of her body, anxiety made him over-accelerate. There was a tearing sound and for a sickening moment he lost traction; the Toyota's rear end started to fishtail. He jammed the transmission into low gear, battled the wheel. Got the car under control again.

He forced himself to ease forward until he was within twenty feet of her. She didn't turn around to look at the lights; she just kept standing there, looking away, as if she had been frozen into position. He threw the car into neutral, pulled on the emergency brake, and bolted out of the door. Ran to her in slipping strides and caught hold of her arms and spun her toward him.

The sight of her face frightened him, filled him with anguish. There was a trancelike fixity to her expression and her eyes were open, staring blankly, the lashes flecked with ice. But then, when he shook her, she began to blink and he saw her eyes focus. A spasm went through her. Her mouth opened, formed words that were lost in the shriek of the wind.

He wrapped an arm around her shoulders and pulled her back to the car. The passenger door was stuck, iced shut; he took her around to the driver's side, got both of them into the front seat. In the glow of the dash lights he could see that the trancelike expression was gone, that it had been replaced by one of dull terror.

"Leslie," he said, "what are you doing out here? What's happened?"

She began to shiver. "The bridge. Oh, God, the bridge."

"Bridge?"

"It's Jo this time. Dead, hanging in there, I saw her eyes like jelly and her mouth a bowl of black."

The sound of her voice, the words she was saying, scraped through him like sandpaper on an exposed nerve. Jesus! "Where?" he said. "Leslie, where?"

"The bridge. Down there, the covered bridge."

He peered through the windshield, past the top of the rise. Through the swirls of snow, he could make out the silhouette of a barnlike structure spanning the roadway.

He released the brake, took the car over the crest and down toward the bridge. Beside him, Leslie was still shivering, so spasmodically that he could hear the clicking of her teeth. He reached out to turn the heater up as high as it would go.

"I don't want to see her," she said, stuttering the words. "I won't look at her." She turned sideways on the seat and shut her eyes.

Grimly Saxon slid his service revolver out of its holster and held it in his lap. If Jo Turner was dead inside the bridge, then her killer might still be in there, too. Or somewhere in the vicinity. He had no way of knowing how long ago any of this had happened.

The entrance to the bridge loomed ahead. Like a black mouth, he thought, and remembered Leslie saying "her mouth a bowl of black." The muscles in his groin were knotted as the headlights probed ahead through the snowfall, probed inside the darkness of the bridge.

The car was thirty feet from the entrance before the lights picked up what was in there. And twenty feet away before he saw it clearly. The hackles on his neck erected into bristles that were as cold as ice. He brought the Toyota to a stop with its nose just inside the bridge, set the brake, got out, and started forward with his gun extended in front of him.

Toward Jo Turner's body hanging from one of the cross-beams overhead.

And toward Oscar Koskovich standing in front of it, crooning to it in a querulous voice, saying over and over, "Jo? Jo? Jo?" while he pushed it gently with his fingertips and made it swing back and forth, back and forth, like a pendulum in a giant clock. . . .

CHAPTER 5

Sunday Night, January 21

6:30 P.M.

Walker knew something had happened as soon as the three of them—Saxon flanked by Leslie Abbott and Oscar Koskovich—came into the inn. One look at their faces was enough to tell him that, even from a distance. Saxon's was drawn and tense and his eyes were molten with supressed fury; the Abbott woman's was pale and frightened. But Koskovich's was the worst of all. It was the color of old snow, and it seemed void of intelligence; the eyes were wide open, blank and unfocused, as if he were staring at something a long way from here. Or at nothing at all. There were gray blotches of frostbite on his cheeks, a dark stain of something that might have been frozen blood over one ear. Saxon and the woman were glazed with snow, but Koskovich looked as though he'd been buried in it.

Walker threw aside the magazine he'd been reading, stood from his chair, and went toward them. Saxon waved him aside. Led Leslie Abbott past him to the fire and dragged a chair onto the hearth, eased her into it.

Koskovich hadn't moved; he was still standing near the

foyer, still staring in that empty way. Saxon went to him, took his arm, and brought him over to the fire and sat him down in another chair near the woman. Walker had seen a man suffering from catatonia once, on a case while assigned to the Washington office. It struck him that Koskovich had most of the same symptoms.

Saxon turned to him. "Where are the Colebrooks?"

"I don't know," Walker said. "I haven't seen either of them."

"You haven't seen a goddamn thing, I guess."

"Easy, Brad. What the hell's happened?"

"Another murder, that's what happened."

"Christ! Who?"

"Jo Turner."

"When was she killed? Where?"

But Saxon was already moving, heading toward the entrance to the bar. Walker followed him, and in his mind he could see the Turner woman: brassy, sharp-tongued, attractive for her age; worried, nervously chain-smoking cigarettes. Dead. Murdered. A sensation of something black and ugly slithered through him. Then vanished in anger and urgency.

There was only one person inside the bar—the gangly kid with acne, Buddy Quint. He was behind the bar, filling the cooler with bottles of beer from a cardboard case. He looked up as they entered, with wary eyes at first and then with alarm as he saw the expression on Saxon's face.

"Colebrook," Saxon said to him. "Where is he?"

"Over to his house, I think—"

"Mrs. Colebrook?"

"She's in the kitchen."

"Get her. Tell her I want two heavy blankets, a pot of strong coffee, and something for frostbite. You understand?"

"Yes, sir."

"I don't suppose there's a doctor in Whitehall."

"Doctor? No, nearest one's over in Pycott—"

"Anyone with nurse's training?"

"Not that I know of."

"All right. Move out. And then go find Colebrook and bring him back here with you. On the double."

"Yes, sir."

Quint came out from behind the bar and hurried toward the dining room, casting worried looks over his shoulder as he went.

Saxon ducked under the hinged section at the end of the bar, found a bottle of brandy among the other bottles under the back bar mirror. He caught up two snifters, and as he poured one of them half-full, he said to Walker, "Where's Iverson?"

"Upstairs in his room, I guess."

"You guess. Koskovich slipped out, Jo Turner slipped out, and you didn't see either of them leave. And you don't know where the hell anybody is. For Christ's sake, what have you been doing for the last couple of hours?"

"Brad, don't lay the blame for this on me. I was in my room part of the time, down here part of the time. I assumed Koskovich and the Turner woman were in their rooms; I had no reason not to. No reason to suspect another murder after your warning this afternoon."

"Yeah, my warning." Saxon finished pouring brandy into the second snifter and then passed a hand over his face. "Okay. You're right, it's not your fault."

"Give me some idea of what happened, will you? How was she killed? When? Where?"

"Same way as the others. Sometime after five o'clock, apparently." He came out beside Walker with the two snifters. "There's an old covered bridge on a back road about a quarter of a mile from here. I found her inside."

"No sign of who killed her?"

"I don't think so."

"You don't *think* so?"

"Koskovich was with the body when I got there."

"Doing what?"

"Talking to it," Saxon said, and moved away again, back into the lobby.

Walker went after him, but before he could say anything else, the antique clock chimed the quarter-hour. The sound of it was hollow and mournful in the quiet room. When the echoes faded, he was aware of the storm howling outside, chattering around the windows, throwing snow against the glass in sandlike ticks. A draft of wind in the chimney made the birch fire dance crazily. It all reminded him of how cold he was—bone-marrow cold. It would be a long time before he knew warmth again.

Saxon crossed to Leslie Abbott, gave her one of the snifters, and leaned down to say something to her. She nodded, held the glass between her palms, and drank from it in small sips. Koskovich was still motionless in his chair; he didn't move when Saxon pushed his head back and held the second snifter up to his mouth, not until some of the brandy passed between his bluish lips. Then his throat worked and he coughed, blinked for the first time. A dull flicker of intelligence came back into his eyes. He turned his head and looked up at Saxon like a child.

Myrna Colebrook came into the lobby from the dining room, carrying two large folded blankets over one arm and balancing a tray laden with cups and a pot of coffee. Her face was closed up tight, but a shadow of fear slid over it when she saw Koskovich and Leslie Abbott; her gaze flicked nervously to Saxon, to Walker.

When Saxon went to her, she said in a wooden voice, "Something's happened, hasn't it? There's more trouble."

He ignored that, took the blankets from her, shook one out, and draped it around Leslie. Did the same with the second blanket for Koskovich. Then he asked Mrs. Colebrook, "Did you bring medicine for frostbite?"

"Yes."

"Stan," he said to Walker, "you and Mrs. Colebrook take Koskovich up to his room, get him out of those clothes and into bed. Then find Iverson."

Walker nodded, went to Koskovich, and eased him up out of the chair. There was no resistance; it was like handling a life-size windup doll. With Myrna Colebrook trailing reluctantly behind, he guided the man into the foyer and up the stairs and into his room.

He had to tell Mrs. Colebrook to help him peel off Koskovich's sodden clothing; she just stood stiff-backed by the door, watching, until he did. Between them, they got Koskovich stripped and into pajamas that were lying across an open suitcase, into bed and covered with three heavy blankets. She didn't say a word the entire time.

"Tend to his frostbite," Walker told her then, "and to that wound on his head." It was frozen blood above his right ear, all right; the area there had a pulpy look, as though he'd been struck with some sort of blunt instrument. "When you're done, come back downstairs."

More silence. But she sat on the bed, took a tube of something from her shirt pocket, and began to squeeze ointment onto her fingertips.

He left her, hurried to Iverson's room, and knocked sharply on the door. No response. He knocked again and rattled the knob, but it was locked. He was just starting to turn away, tight-mouthed, when Iverson's voice came from within.

"Who's there?"

"Agent Walker. Open up, Iverson."

"I can't right now. I'm naked."

"Naked?"

"I was taking a shower. I always do before dinner."

"Open the door."

"But I told you, I'm *naked*—"

"Open the damned door!"

The lock scraped, clicked, and the door opened. Iverson stood there, holding a towel in front of his bare white body. His posture was that of a prudish woman, bent and half-twisted, and there was a faint embarrassed blush on his cheeks. He wasn't wearing his glasses: He squinted at Walker myopically.

"There," he said in a petulant voice. "You see?"

"Yeah, I see. Get dressed and come down to the lobby."

"Why? What's the matter?"

"Just do what you're told. And make it quick."

Walker turned away before Iverson could say anything else and went back downstairs. When he reentered the lobby, he saw Saxon standing next to Leslie Abbott, watching her drink from a cup of steaming coffee. Wrapped in her blanket, she looked like a giant gray larva, but there was color in her face now and she appeared to be less frightened.

Saxon touched her shoulder gently and then came away from her to join Walker. "What about Iverson?"

"In his room. He'd just finished taking a shower. He'll be down as soon as he's dressed."

Saxon nodded.

"How's Miss Abbott?"

"She'll be okay."

"I don't like the way Koskovich looks."

"Neither do I. He's in deep shock."

"You try questioning him before?"

"I tried. He didn't respond."

"You said you found him *talking* to the body?"

"That's right. Delirium."

"Could he have killed her?"

"Maybe," Saxon said. "But it's more likely he had another vision. Of *her* murder, this time. You saw that wound on his head; I think he went to the bridge in the same kind of state he drove to Storm Junction in last night, and the killer was waiting there and slugged him. Either before or after the murder, there's no way of telling."

"Did you leave the body at the bridge?"

"No. Somebody might have stumbled on it, and it would have frozen solid by morning. I cut it down and wrapped it in a tarp that Leslie had in her car. It's in the trunk, out front."

"How did you find it? How did you know to go to the bridge?"

"Leslie had a vision, too—" Saxon broke off and made a gesture of frustration. "Look, what's the use of going into it?

You don't believe in clairvoyance or psychic emanations; you won't accept the only explanation I've got to give you."

"I don't know what I believe anymore," Walker said, and that was the truth. With all that had happened in the past few days, was still happening, it seemed that any number of things were possible. Maybe clairvoyance *was* nonsense, as he had always believed. But for the first time his mind wasn't closed to the possibility that it wasn't. "Try me."

Saxon hesitated, studying him. Then he let out a breath and said, "All right then, here it is," and gave a terse account of the past couple of hours. He finished by saying, "It was psychic impulses that drew Leslie out into the storm. Those same forces must have affected Koskovich, maybe even brought Jo Turner to the bridge. Christ, Stan, I can almost feel them myself, like something palpable in the air."

It all sounded incredible, and yet the facts as Saxon outlined them seemed to have a rational basis with a parapsychological interpretation. And there did seem to be something around them: an aura, a kind of energy that went beyond tension and the atmospheric effects of a storm. Power of suggestion, maybe. And maybe not.

He said, "What would cause these impulses? Where would they come from?"

"A concentration of violent emotions," Saxon said. "All the clairvoyants here in Whitehall. The presence of a psychotic who's already killed four people. All of those things together would be enough."

"A psycho," Walker said, and he was thinking then that it didn't really make any difference if parapsychology was fact or fiction. The murders were real; the psycho was real. And a homicidal lunatic in closed, isolated surroundings such as these was the worst possible kind of adversary. "He went out and killed Jo Turner two hours after your warning. He's either taunting us, or he's too crazy to care that we're around. Either way . . ."

Walker left the sentence unfinished, but Saxon understood well enough what he had been about to say and nodded grimly. The unspoken words seemed to hang between them, suspended like small invisible bodies from the lobby's beamed ceiling.

Either way, he was liable at any time to kill again.

7:05 P.M.

From where she was sitting before the fire, Leslie watched Brad and Walker talking in urgent whispers across the room. The heat of the flames at her back, the brandy and the coffee she had drunk, made her feel almost warm now. There was warmth in her mind, too, but it was an ugly warmth: pulses of heat, the same psychic vibrations beating rhythmically, even stronger than they had been at her house earlier. As if they were concentrated here inside the inn, because this was where she was and where Oscar and Neal were.

Because this was where the murderer was?

I don't want to stay here tonight, she thought. Brad would want her to do that, but maybe she could talk him out of it. Neal, Oscar upstairs all shattered by what the vibrations had done to him; the Colebrooks and Buddy Quint and Ephraim Buell nearby. No, not here tonight. Home was where she wanted to be. Alone with Brad in her dead house.

Where the painting was.

Here with the others; home with the painting. But home was still better—or was it? Where was she *supposed* to be tonight? Tomorrow night? All the nights until this was finished and she was either dead or she had some control of her life again?

Leslie took a sip of her coffee. The surprising thing was that she felt calm enough at this moment, even with the impulses. Even with the visions and the murders, the afterimage of Jo hanging inside the covered bridge, eyes like jelly and mouth a bowl of black. She couldn't seem to feel much of anything; even the fear had dulled and receded. She wondered if she was losing the capacity to feel, turning into an insensitive creature who was only able to respond to acute stimuli: pain and terror and animal passion.

The sound of heavy footfalls came to her from inside the dining room. She looked up to see Harmon Colebrook and Buddy Quint, wearing snow-dusted mackinaws and worried, churlish expressions, emerge into the lobby. At almost that same moment, Myrna Colebrook came downstairs again and entered through the foyer. The three of them moved together with Brad and Walker and formed a loose pentagon. Leslie drank more coffee and listened.

"What's happened now?" Colebrook said. "What's going on?"

"There's been another murder," Brad told him flatly.

"Here? You mean here in *Whitehall*?"

"That's right."

"Jesus Christ!"

Buddy Quint said in an awed voice, "Who was it got murdered?"

Brad told them. About Jo and about the covered bridge. They exchanged glances; their faces were pale and stark.

"You have any idea who did it?" Myrna Colebrook asked nervously. "We have a right to know if you do."

"We don't have an idea, not yet. But we will before much longer."

"It's one of them, by God," Colebrook said. "One of them psychics doing it to their own. It's not any of us."

"We'll see about that."

Colebrook and Quint cast looks in Leslie's direction. There was hatred in their eyes: *You brought the whole bunch here, you're one of them. Damned witch, it could even be you.* Or was one pair of those eyes really saying something else, saying, *You're next, Leslie Abbott, I'm going to kill you next?*

The dark figure in the painting. Colebrook's face? Quint's? Whose face?

Brad said, "Where were you at five o'clock, Colebrook?"

"Me? Listen here, I tell you it's not any of us—"

"Answer the question. Where were you?"

"Over to my house. I was there from four-thirty on."

"Doing what?"

"Working on the furnace. Been acting up all winter."

"The whole time?"

"Most of the time."

"What else did you do?"

Colebrook hesitated.

"Talk to me, Colebrook. Ephraim Buell told me you closed the bar because you had something important to do. I won't buy fixing your furnace."

"All right," Colebrook said defiantly. "I made a couple of phone calls to Rutland. To the state police and a lawyer."

"About Agent Walker and me, is that it? About the way we've been handling things here?"

"Man's got a right to find out where he stands, doesn't he?"

"That depends on the man. Did you leave your house between four-thirty and six?"

"No."

"Were you alone during that time?"

"I was. I didn't see anybody until Buddy come for me."

"Mrs. Colebrook, where were you at five o'clock?"

"At my mother's house," she said. "I drove over there after the meeting and stayed to cook for her. She's old and sickly; she can't do for herself like she used to."

"What time did you leave her?"

"Some past six."

"You come straight back here?"

"Yes. Put the car in the garage and walked over."

"Did you see anyone on Broadelm Road?"

"No."

"Anyone on Main Street?"

"No. Nobody."

"Did you go inside your house? See your husband?"

"No. The lights were on; I supposed he was there. But it was time to start getting ready for dinner."

Brad turned to Buddy Quint. "What about you? What were you doing between four-thirty and six?"

"Cleaning up the storeroom." Quint ran nervous fingers over the bouquet of pimples on his chin. "Mr. Colebrook asked me to do that this morning."

"I suppose you were alone."

"Yes, sir."

"And I suppose you didn't see anybody."

"No, sir, I didn't. I swear it."

Brad made a fist of his right hand and smacked it into the palm of his left: a sudden angry gesture. The sound caused Myrna Colebrook and Buddy Quint to jerk as if it were them he had struck. "Nobody saw anything, nobody did anything, nobody knows where anybody else was. Christ!"

"It's not our fault we don't know anything," Colebrook said in a whining tone. "We're trying to cooperate here. We want this crazy caught as bad as you."

"Sure you do," Walker said. "Just take it easy."

Watching, Leslie understood that he was talking to Brad as well as to the others. Walker was so quiet and unobstrusive, such an obvious skeptic, that she had almost forgotten his authority.

Brad had himself under control again. He said to Colebrook, "Just keep on cooperating, that's all. From now on, we want to know where you people are and what you're doing at all times. If you have to leave the inn for any reason, report to Agent Walker or me first. Is that understood?"

Slow tight-lipped nods.

"All right. Leslie Abbott's Toyota is parked in the lot out front; Jo Turner's body is in the trunk, wrapped in a tarp. Colebrook, you and Quint get it out of there."

Quint's mouth quirked squeamishly. Colebrook said, "What do you want us to do with it, for Christ's sake? I won't have it in here—"

"I don't want it brought in here. I want you to find a cool place to put it until we can get the state police in here."

"The old icehouse out back, Harmon," Myrna Colebrook said. "Nothing in there except tools."

"Good," Brad said. "Go ahead, get it over with."

Colebrook and Quint moved away. A moment later, Leslie heard the keening of the storm magnify as the front door opened; particles of windblown snow sifted through the foyer, settled to the floor like white dust. Then the door banged shut —and the grandfather clock tolled the half-hour in a hollow voice. She pulled the blanket more tightly around her and pushed her chair backward a few inches, closer to the fire.

There were clumping sounds on the stairs. Neal appeared in the foyer, wearing his idiotic vision cap. He looked the way he always did: excited, boyish, full of himself. But there was a tenseness in his face and bearing that Leslie had never seen before. She wondered if the psychic vibrations had affected him, too, unsettled him; she wondered if he was capable of being unsettled by the visceral pain and terror of others.

Whose face? Could it even be Neal's?

Walker said, "You took your time getting down here, Iverson."

Neal came into the lobby. "I would have been down sooner, but I had another vision while I was putting on my undershorts."

"Vision?" Brad said. "What sort of vision?"

"It was Buell's workshop again. I wasn't there this time, but I saw it just as clear as before. Only it was in full color this time, not in black and white."

"What did you see?"

"Nothing specific, just the workshop. But there's something there, Mr. Saxon, I could feel it like those same psychic birds that keep fluttering around in my consciousness. Buell's guilty, all right, and if you search that workshop I'll bet you'll find evidence I'm right. I'll just *bet* you will."

"I intend to search it," Brad said.

"You do? Good! I knew you'd have to believe me sooner or later—"

"Jo Turner's dead, Iverson," Walker said. "She was murdered tonight."

Neal's mouth fell open in a way that was almost hideously

comic, like the mouth on a ventriloquist's dummy. His eyelids flapped. "What?" he said. "What?"

"You heard him," Brad said. "Found her hanging, same as the others. In a covered bridge not far from here."

Neal took off his cap and squeezed it between both hands; his shock seemed to be genuine. "Buell," he said. "Buell did it. He went after Jo when he couldn't get me."

"Maybe it's Buell and maybe it isn't. Where were you at five o'clock?"

"Five o'clock? I was here in my room; I came straight back here from the antique shop like you told me to." He grimaced. "Why do you want to know where I was? You don't think—"

"Did you talk to anyone? See anyone?"

"No. I went right up to my room and called my wife on Long Island and then worked with my tarot cards. Listen, you've got to arrest Buell before he comes after *me* again. You should have arrested him before—"

"Shut up, Iverson," Walker said. "Just shut up."

Brad and Walker moved away from Neal, left him staring at them and holding his vision cap like an offering. They held a brief conference in an undertone that Leslie couldn't hear. Then Brad pivoted and crossed to where she was sitting.

"I've got to go out for a little while," he said.

Leslie nodded. "Where are you going?"

"To talk to Ephraim Buell. I'll be back as soon as I can."

"Yes, but then what? Brad, I don't want to stay here tonight. I don't want to sleep alone in this place."

He was silent for a moment. Then he said, "I don't think going back to your house is a good idea. The closer together we are, the safer it'll be."

"Walker can watch over Oscar and Neal, can't he? Just for tonight? Just until morning?"

"Is it that bad for you, being here with them?"

"Yes."

"All right then. We'll talk about it when I get back."

He touched her cheek gently with the back of one hand and then turned and went out. Leslie saw that Neal was staring at her with his protuberant eyes; his gaze seemed almost childishly triumphant, as if she were an adversary whom he had somehow managed to outwit. When she heard the inn's front door close, she put her coffee cup down and unwrapped the blanket from around her. Stood beside the chair, staring into the fireplace.

The flames danced and flickered in the chimney drafts—just as the flames of psychic energy danced and flickered inside her mind.

Whose face?

8:00 P.M.

There were lights on in the cottage behind Buell's Antiques; Saxon could make out two misty, diffused rectangles glowing there as he plowed the Toyota to a stop on Main Street. The antique shop was dark. He shut off the engine and headlights and stepped out into surface snow that was already knee-deep, bracing himself against the force of the wind. Another couple of hours and the village streets would be impassable by car.

The bile-taste of frustration was sharp in his mouth as he waded around the car and started through the drifts alongside the shop. No answers from anyone at the inn; not even one goddamn alibi that would eliminate at least one of them as a suspect. Chasing shadows, that was all he'd been doing the past twenty-four hours. No apparent leads. A list of suspects that had been narrowed to twenty or so but couldn't seem to be narrowed any further. He'd thought he was frustrated in Syracuse in 1969; he'd thought he was close to self-hatred then. But nothing in his career or his life had made him feel as he did now. He couldn't stand to be ineffectual, and that was exactly what this lunatic time had made him. Ineffectual on a case that was a hell of a lot more than just a case because of Leslie.

Unless Iverson is right, he thought, and Buell's the killer. But, Christ, there was nothing to point to Buell except the accusations of a clairvoyant buffoon. The victims hadn't been strangled with strips of heavy leather; they had been strangled with a blue velvet cord.

Well, maybe it *could* be Buell. Sure it could. And it could be Iverson. And it could be Colebrook or Buddy Quint or Quint's father or even Oscar Koskovich. It could be just about anybody in this fucking village.

He wants all of us dead, Brad. He wants me *dead . . .*

Ahead, the cottage looked spectral and indistinct through the flurries; only the rectangles of light lent any reality to it. The temperature seemed to have dropped another few degrees. The firn beneath the surface snow was frozen and his booted feet cracked it like glass as he moved. He slogged ahead to the cottage porch.

The stairs were slick with crusty snow; he climbed them cautiously. There was no bell button beside the door, so he hammered several times on the wood panel. Waited. Heard nothing except the wail of the storm and hammered again. The door remained closed.

He moved away from it to the nearest window. Hoarfrost made the glass opaque; he could make out blurred shapes inside but nothing more, nothing moving. He came back to the door and rotated the knob. It opened under his hand. A wave of thick, oil-stinking heat slapped at his face; Buell must have had the temperature near eighty in there.

Saxon stepped inside quickly and shut the door behind him. With the sound of the storm muffled, he could hear the faint mechanical thrum of the oil furnace and the staticked sound of a radio. On instinct, he unbuttoned his coat, dropped his hand to the butt of his service revolver. Then he went to his left, toward the noise of the radio, and emerged into a parlor full of mismatched antique furniture and a careless clutter of magazines, newspapers, unwashed dishes, and empty bottles.

Another sound came to him: the wheezing nasal rasp of

someone snoring. He found the source of it a second later. It was coming from an old-fashioned wing chair faced away from the doorway, toward a table on which a 1930s-style radio sat. He went over to the chair for a close inspection, then let himself relax and took his hand away from the revolver.

Buell was slumped down in the chair, his feet splayed out at loose angles, his head tilted to one side against a wing. His mouth was open and his lips vibrated with each snoring exhalation; the sour odor of whiskey was strong on his breath. Beside the chair, Saxon saw an empty pint of rye and an empty glass.

A feeling of disgust came into him. He leaned over and caught the man by both shoulders, shook him hard. It was like shaking a bundle of rags: Buell's head wobbled from side to side and his body had a boneless laxity. He made a protesting noise in his throat, but his eyes stayed shut.

Saxon let go of him and slapped him forehand and backhand across the face. "Wake up, Buell. Wake up!" Buell's eyelids raised, but the pupils were half rolled up so that only the bottom edges of them showed; the whites were like milk swirled with blood. He said something incoherent, gagged as if he were going to vomit on himself, then sagged lower on the chair. His eyelids came down and he began to snore again.

Waking him to the point where he was rational would probably take time, Saxon decided. He'd drunk himself into a stupor. But why? Guilt, maybe? Except that that didn't seem consistent with the kind of lunatic on the loose here. Buell was an obvious alcoholic; drunks didn't need much of an excuse to drink themselves into a stupor.

The heat and the combined smells of fuel oil and whiskey were making him nauseous. He hadn't eaten anything since breakfast, and his stomach was sensitive and too-long knotted up with tension. He backed away from Buell, stood sweeping the room with his eyes. On the inner wall he located a thermostat and he went to it and turned it down from eighty to sixty-five.

He searched the parlor first, methodically, looking for anything that might tie Buell to the murders. What he found was nothing. Adjacent to the parlor was the bedroom, and he sifted through that next. Nothing. And nothing in the kitchen, or in a second bedroom that had been converted into a storage room for junk, or on the enclosed rear porch. The only things he knew about Buell when he was done were that the man apparently kept no personal correspondence or business records of any kind, that he was a sloppy housekeeper and not very interested in personal hygiene, and that he either didn't trust banks or preferred to keep a large amount of cash on hand: There was a strongbox on a shelf in his closet that contained at least $2000 in tens, twenties, and fifties.

Saxon went back into the parlor. Buell was still sprawled in the same position, snoring more noisily, and he didn't move when Saxon patted down his pockets and removed a wallet and a ring of four keys. The wallet yielded nothing of interest; he replaced it, but kept the keys. Then he went into the hallway and let himself out.

The night seemed even colder after the overheated cottage; the wind burned like dry ice against his exposed face. He was shivering by the time he reached the front door of the antique shop.

The second key he tried unlocked the door. He let himself in, found a switch for the lights, then crossed behind the counter to what looked to be the cellar door. That was locked, too; another of the keys opened it. He made his way carefully down the stairs, located an overhead bulb with a long cord suspended from it, and used it to chase away the darkness.

The workbench drew him first. He went over it with the same methodical care with which he had searched the cottage. Opened drawers, examined containers and shelves full of chemicals, paints, varnishes, brass ornaments, clockworks, hinges, wood screws, squarehead nails, and wooden pegs. There were a hundred different kinds of tools, plus a lathe and an electric bench saw. But there wasn't anything at all incriminating or even interesting.

He prowled through clock casings, stacks of lumber, bits and pieces of what appeared to be half-restored furniture, sheets of metal and glass, disassembled lamps and other lighting fixtures, crates of china and glassware. He found rope, leather, twine. He found a packrat's nest behind a dust-coated washbasin.

He found nothing.

At the end of twenty minutes, he gave it up. Shut off the light and climbed the stairs and relocked the cellar door. Then he went back into the freezing night and retraced his path to the cottage.

When he stepped inside the still-overheated parlor, he found Buell in the same position he had left him: slumped in the wing chair, snoring gustily. A thin line of saliva glistened like a snail's track from one corner of his mouth down over his chin. Saxon crossed to him, shoved the ring of keys into the trouser pocket from which he'd gotten them, and gave the man another shaking and half a dozen sharp slaps. What they got him this time were moans, an unfocused bleary stare, a hand raised as if to ward off alcoholic demons.

He dragged Buell from the chair and half-carried him across to the nearest window. Buell made muttering protests, but he didn't struggle and he didn't come out of his stupor. Or he didn't until Saxon managed to unlatch the window, haul it up several inches, and shove the man's head down into the icy blast of wind and snow that swept in from outside. Then he shuddered and thrashed like an animal in Saxon's grip, saying something that sounded like "Jesus Christ the fuck you doing to me?" in a ragged slur.

Saxon held him in front of the open window for another ten seconds before letting go of him and slamming the window shut again. Buell lurched upright, reeled into the wall, and pawed at his face with both hands. His eyes seemed to crouch behind slitted lids; he looked sick and confused. But as his vision cleared and his brain registered what he was seeing, fear crawled into his expression and dominated it. He stumbled away from the wall, groped his way to the chair, and flopped down on its arms.

"You doing in my house?" he said thickly. "You want with me?"

"Answers, Buell. How long have you been here? What did you do after I left you at the shop earlier?"

Buell shook his head and peered at the empty bottle beside the chair. Made a victimized sound, sobbed, and kicked the bottle away, kicked the empty glass after it.

Saxon said, "Did you understand what I just asked you?"

"Yeah." Buell ran his tongue around the inside of his mouth as if it were something painful and burned-out. "Jesus, I need a drink."

"No drinks. Just answers."

"I didn't do nothing after you left. Just got the pint out the cellar and come here. Must of passed out. . . ."

"You see anybody, talk to anybody?"

"No. Just come here with the bottle. Listen, what you doing in my house? Got no right to come into my house!"

"I've got every right. Jo Turner was murdered this afternoon. Strangled inside the covered bridge on Broadelm Road."

It didn't seem to register at first. Buell kept on staring at him out of his slitted, blood-flecked eyes. When it did register, a moment later, he stiffened and then came up off the chair and stood swaying. Pinheads of sweat formed into a scattered pattern across his forehead.

"Someone in Whitehall killed her," Saxon said. "Someone here killed the other three PSYCHICs, too. I'm going to find out who it is, Buell, one way or another. And I'm going to take care of him when I do. One way or another."

A sick belch came out of Buell, turned into a gagging rattle. One hand wobbled up and covered his mouth. He spun away, bent forward at the middle, and staggered out into the hallway. Saxon could hear him banging into walls, then a door slapping open, then the hollow thump of a toilet lid being thrown upward against the tank.

Saxon stood for a couple of seconds, debating. But he hadn't found a damned thing in his searches; and Buell hadn't told him anything in those first confused minutes—if he had anything to tell or admit—which meant prying anything out of him as he sobered was unlikely. And Saxon had said all there was to say already.

He crossed into the hallway, over to the front door. The last thing he heard before he took himself back into the storm was the sound of Buell vomiting noisily into his toilet.

8:00 P.M.

At the inn, Neal sat fidgeting across from Walker. Across the chess table again, with the black wooden pieces on his side again—more of Walker's transparent psychological maneuvering, for all the good it was going to do him. Leslie was still standing in front of the fireplace, staring into it; but Walker wasn't bothering *her* with more pointless questions about what *she'd* been up to when Jo was killed.

Neal resisted an impulse to turn the table around so that the white chessmen would be on his side. The news of Jo's death had upset him pretty badly; the Prince had real feelings, even if nobody believed that but him.

He said, "I know you don't want to believe it, Mr. Walker, but what happened to Jo is Agent Saxon's fault. If he'd arrested Buell this afternoon, when he had the chance, she'd still be alive."

"Crap," Walker said flatly.

"Well, it's true. I told him what I saw in my vision, I told him Buell was the murderer, but he just wouldn't listen. Nobody wants to listen, nobody wants to believe *anything* here."

Walker gave him a silent stare. He seemed to be making an effort to maintain his professional control, Neal thought. Which was another myth about FBI agents: that they were always in complete control of every situation. Walker wasn't in complete control, and Saxon wasn't either. The Prince was the only one here who knew how to be decisive, it seemed. Oh, he had to admit that his own control had slipped a little this afternoon, when Buell surprised him in the cellar workshop—but whose control wouldn't slip in a crisis like that, alone with a psychotic killer who wanted to strangle you and hang you from a rafter?

Walker said at length, "This evidence you imagine to be in Buell's workshop . . . what do you think it is?"

"I don't know. Maybe a diary or something."

"Diary?"

"Lots of psychotic murderers keep diaries."

"Is that right? Why do they do that?"

"So they can have a permanent record of their terrible crimes. Some of them keep scrapbooks, too. They read their diaries and look at their scrapbooks and brood about them all the time until they're caught and put away in mental institutions."

"You seem to know a lot about it, Iverson."

"That's because I read newspapers and watch television."

"Uh-huh. You keep a diary or a scrapbook yourself, do you?"

"What? What kind of question is that? No, I don't keep a diary or a scrapbook, and, no, I'm not the killer. Buell is, I tell you. *Buell.*"

Walker unwrapped a stick of Juicy Fruit gum and slid it into his mouth; his jaws began to grind it steadily, distractingly. Another psychological ploy? Neal wondered. These FBI agents could be pretty sneaky and devious when they wanted to be. You had to be on the alert with them every minute so you didn't fall into one of their clever little traps.

"When you were alone in your room around five o'clock," Walker said, "did you have any sort of psychic experience?"

"Of course I did. I had a series of shadowy symbols pecking around the edges of my third eye. It was Buell murdering Jo; I was responding psychically to the violent emanations of her death." A thought struck him and made him frown. He glanced over at where Leslie was sitting. "Did she have a vision, too? Is that how you found out about Jo?"

"It's how my partner found out."

"What about Oscar? Did *he* have a vision?"

"It seems that way."

"Seems that way? Where is he, anyhow? Why aren't you questioning him?"

"He's upstairs in his room," Walker said, "and he's in a state of shock. I don't want you bothering him, Iverson. I want you to stay away from him."

"State of shock?" Neal said. "Why is he in a state of shock?"

"Because it appears he was the first to discover Jo Turner's body. Because violent death affects some people a hell of a lot more deeply than it affects others." Walker looked angry again. "*You* don't seem particularly upset about Miss Turner. Doesn't it bother you that four of your friends have been murdered?"

"Well, of course it bothers me. Why does everybody think it doesn't bother me? I have feelings, too, damn it. It's just that I'm able to keep them under tight control."

"Yeah," Walker said. He stood and loomed over the chess table. His face was congested, full of little veins that looked like worms wriggling under the surface. "I'm going upstairs to check on Koskovich," he said. "You stay right here, Iverson. Don't make me come looking for you when I get back."

No control at all, Neal thought as Walker went into the foyer. He shook his head. Just no control at all.

Across the lobby, the grandfather clock played its quarter-hour melody; the sounds seemed to echo in Neal's mind, stirring the faint psychic rhythms and focusing them for an instant in his third eye. He reached up to adjust his vision hat. But it was just another false alarm. The psychic eye remained closed and dark.

Crockery rattled in front of the fireplace. He glanced over there, saw Leslie pouring herself another cup of coffee from the tray beside her chair. On impulse, he got to his feet and went to her.

"Hello, Leslie," he said.

She glanced at him briefly, then looked down at the cup in her hands without answering.

"How come you were wrapped up in that blanket? Were you at the covered bridge, too?"

She seemed to flinch. "I don't want to talk about it."

"Well, Walker said you had a vision of Jo's murder. But I guess you didn't see who the killer is, right?"

Silence.

"*I* know who the killer is," Neal said. "It's Ephraim Buell. I had a vision this afternoon of myself in Buell's workshop and there was rope and leather strips there, the murder weapons even if Agent Saxon doesn't think so, and I knew he was the one. So I went there to get the evidence, and Buell came and almost murdered me, too. He would have if I hadn't knocked him over and gotten away."

A muscle jumped on her cheek. She said nothing.

"I tried to tell Saxon that it was Buell, but he wouldn't believe me. I hope he believes me now and puts Buell in handcuffs before he can come after you or me or Oscar. He'd *better* do it, or else."

"Leave me alone, Neal."

He squinted at her. "Why? I'm only trying to tell you the truth here. You've been having visions about the murders and so has Oscar, you're both sensitive like I am, but it's *my* gift that solved them. Don't you see that? I've solved the murders and maybe I've saved your life."

Her head lifted and her eyes raked his face like nails. He took an involuntary step backward. "Goddamn you," she said, "leave me alone!"

He swung around and returned to the chess table, making sure to take the white side this time. Sat there with arms folded across his chest. Damn everybody, he was thinking. They just wouldn't pay any attention to him. Solve the case, save their lives, and what did he get? A sympathetic ear? Gratitude? No. Scorn, that was what he got. Nothing but scorn.

Well, let them be scornful. *He* knew the truth, and they would, too, before much longer. *He* was the one who would reap the harvest of fame that was going to sprout for him.

It was the Prince who would have the last laugh.

8:05 P.M.

When they finished transferring the Turner woman's body to the old icehouse, Colebrook and Buddy Quint struggled back to the inn and entered through the storeroom. They were both wrapped in a glaze of snow and ice and they stood slapping it off their clothing. Colebrook's ears and nose felt numb. Colder than a witch's tit out there. His mouth crooked bitterly. Colder than Jo Turner's tit, more like it.

Buddy said, "I'd best call my dad. He's got to know what's happened tonight."

"Yeah. If the FBI ain't already spread the word."

"It's spooky, that's what it is," Buddy said. "Downright shit-scaring spooky. A murder here in the village; murder and psychics and the FBI." He licked snow off his lips and looked at Colebrook like a flushed rabbit. "You don't think it could be one of our people, do you, Harmon?"

"Hell, no, I don't. It's one of them, all right. Iverson most likely; he's got my vote."

"Mine, too. But the FBI sure don't seem to be looking at any of them. Seems like they reckon it *is* one of ours."

"Bastards."

"What're we going to do, Harmon, snowed in here with a murderer loose?"

"I know what I'm going to do," Colebrook said grimly. "I'm going to make sure he don't come after *me* with a goddamned rope. You go on and ring up Tom. I've got something to do."

As soon as Buddy had disappeared into the kitchen, Colebrook went to the alcove where he kept his hunting and fishing equipment stored for the winter. He took down his Stevens side-by-side shotgun from one of the shelves, unwrapped its cloth covering, and broke it open. Took two shells out of his ammunition box and slid them into the breech and snapped the weapon shut again. The shotgun had a sturdy, comforting feel in his hands. Blow a man's head clean off at close range, this baby. Wasn't anybody in the world crazy enough to buck a double-barrel pointed square at his eyes.

He came out of the alcove with it, holding it cradled across his chest. Myrna was standing in the kitchen doorway. Just standing there looking at him with her face squeezed up and her fat hands on her fat hips.

"What's the idea of that, Harmon?"

"What the hell you think the idea is?"

"The FBI won't stand for you parading around with a shotgun."

"Screw the FBI. We got to protect ourselves. They're sure as Christ not doing the job for us."

"They're in charge as long as we're snowed in here," she said. "We've got to trust them now."

Trust them? Colebrook thought. That was just about what the state police and the lawyer in Rutland had told him when he'd made his calls earlier. Cooperate with them, trust them. Shit. What you could trust the FBI to do was put you under suspicion and harass you and run around doing nothing like castrated bulls in a cow pasture. Man had to look out for his own ass in a situation like this. Otherwise, you were helpless.

"I mean it, Harmon," Myrna said. "You're only going to cause trouble for us if you start acting like a damned fool."

"Damned fool, am I?" Colebrook felt heat rise in his cheeks. He'd had about all he could take from her, too. "Now you listen to me, woman. I know what I have to do and I intend to do it. Not you or anybody else is going to tell me different. And if you don't like the way I handle things, then you can just pack your bags once this is done and find yourself another man to put up with you."

Her eyes glittered. "You asking me to leave you, Mr. Colebrook?"

"Take what I said any way you care to, Mrs. Colebrook."

"You'd like it just fine if I was gone, wouldn't you? Then you could traipse off to Rutland two or three days a week and bed down free with those sluts of yours. Don't think I don't know about your whoring ways; I've known for a long time. But I own half of this place and I put just as much into it as you since we got married. I'm not about to throw it all away because you're a fornicator and a fool and you invite me to leave."

She swung back into the kitchen and slammed the door behind her.

Colebrook stood with his hands tight around the shotgun. Rage and tension made the blood pound in his head. So she knew about the tramps in Rutland, did she? Well, the hell with it. And the hell with *her*, too. He just didn't give a hoot or a piss anymore, not where she was concerned, and he wasn't about to keep on sharing his bed and board with her, no matter what she said. She wouldn't give him a divorce, he'd find another away to get shut of her. There were ways, all right.

He tilted the shotgun's muzzle toward the floor, held it crooked under his right arm, and pushed into the kitchen. Myrna was over by the stove with her back to him, stirring something in a kettle. She didn't turn around. The smell of baked ham and simmering beans made his stomach churn. He stomped across to the dining-room door and cracked it and peered through.

Beyond the dining room, inside the lobby, Leslie Abbott was standing in front of the fireplace, and Iverson was sprawled in another chair, fiddling with that goddamn cap of his. There wasn't any sign of Walker or Saxon. Colebrook stepped out, veered over to the bar entrance. Took the shotgun behind the bar and propped it up underneath, out of sight against the stainless-steel sink. Then he poured himself a small hooker of gin, tossed it off neat.

He was ready for anything now, by God. Any damned thing at all.

8:45 P.M.

Oscar was cold. Cold and old, frightened not bold. He had the bedcovers tight around his chin, but they didn't seem to help much; little shivers and slivers of chill worked through him. His eyes felt wet. Wet like a pet, it's not over yet.

Animals gamboled in the bottom half of his mind. Rabbits and puppies and kittens. Canaries sang and shit and broke down. Susan was there, sitting in her rocking chair with the cancer eating away at her like acid. Gloria held out her hands to him and said, "Oscar, why did you do this to me? Why, Oscar?" Tony and Sandra showed him pieces of rope, no hope, no hope, and stuck out their black tongues at him.

The upper half of his mind belonged to Jo. Hanging there in the black and white, hair fluttering, swinging to and fro, fast and slow, poor dead Jo. Pendulum of a clock. Tick-tock, tick-tock. Time running out. Tick-tock. Black and white and dead. Tick-tock. Jo? *Jo?*

"Snap out of it, darling," she said. "Get a grip on yourself. Why are you lying here like this? Maybe dying here like this?"

No hope, I can't cope. I'm sorry, Jo.

"Sorry, sorry, sorry, sorry."

Stop swinging. Won't you stop swinging?

"No, dear. To and fro, here we go."

Tick-tock, tick-tock.

Other sounds in the room: snow scraping at the window like fingers, wind beating at the window like fists. Cold, cold. Oscar grasped the covers tightly in both hands and drew them over his head, used them to scratch itching, burning places on his cheeks. But the itching would not go away. The cold would not go away. Like Jo. Like the pendulum. To and fro, here we go.

Scraping and beating, tocking and ticking. Cold and old and cold. Can't get warm.

Except that he *was* getting warm. The cold seemed to go

away all of a sudden and dull pulses of warmth spread out in its place; the covers, now, were smothering him. Heat at the center, growing, flowing. Sweat on his face. The image of Jo melting like hot wax in the upper half of his mind; pets and Susan and Gloria and Sandra and Tony melting in the bottom half. Tick-tock, melting clock. Tick-tock, mental block. Tick-tock, psychic shock.

New shapes began to form beneath the wax. Ugly, demanding, but hidden. Hidden. Gift, rift. Lift, sift. Get out of bed or you'll be dead.

He threw the covers down and away, wrenched himself from the tangle and stood unsteadily. The wax froze; Jo was swinging again, black and white and dead. *Sorry, Jo! Sorry!* To and fro, here we go. Tick-tock, tick-tock, tick-tock.

Oscar moved over against the wall and crouched there.

Listening.

9:10 P.M.

Leslie prowled the lobby, the foyer, the dining room, in a restless circuit. She felt caged, like an animal put on display for hostile eyes. Neal still sitting over by the chess table, pouting and moving his lips as if he were holding a conversation with himself, now and then giving her sullen and reproachful looks. Buddy Quint and Myrna Colebrook impaling her with eyes like wooden stakes whenever they passed in and out. Harmon Colebrook crossing the dining room a little while ago with a shotgun in his hands, glancing at her as if he thought she'd make a good target. Walker's eyes were the only ones that showed any sympathy, but they were impersonal and they offered little reassurance and no comfort at all.

And then there was Oscar upstairs with his mind torn and battered by the same forces, the same curse, that kept working inside her own head.

Why doesn't Brad get back? she thought. What's taking him so long?

Ephraim Buell. Maybe Neal was right after all—even fools were right sometimes—and Buell *was* the murderer. Maybe Brad had found proof and arrested Buell and it was all over or about to be over at any minute. But she couldn't make herself believe it. The vibrations were too strong and still getting stronger; too full of obscene promise for an ending that quick and that simple.

More to come, she thought. Much more to come.

The Simon Willard clock chimed again and the hollow sound of it made her stop halfway across to the foyer. Neal glanced up, not at her but at the clock, and she saw him frown and then take off his glasses with one hand and his vision cap with the other. He sat stiffly, his head cocked to one side. He does feel the impulses, Leslie thought. He's a clairvoyant, whatever else he is. Maybe he doesn't understand the sense of them, but he feels them, too.

The inn's front door rattled open, letting in a sworl of snow and the cry of the wind. Letting in Brad. She moved into the foyer, saw him shove the door closed. When he pulled off his hat and turned toward her, his expression, still tense and worried, told her all she needed to know about his session with Ephraim Buell.

Before she could say anything to him, or he to her, Neal came rushing in from the lobby. He had put his glasses back on, but he was still holding his silly cap in one hand. "Where's Buell?" he said to Brad.

"Where I left him. At his cottage."

"You didn't arrest him?" Neal shook the cap accusingly. "Why didn't you arrest him, for God's sake?"

Brad stared at him. "Don't start in with me, Iverson."

"But he's the murderer! If you'd searched his workshop—"

"I did search his damned workshop. And I searched his cottage, too. There's no evidence to implicate him. You understand that? No evidence at all."

"Yes, there *is*. You must have overlooked it—"

"That's enough," Brad said. His voice was low, but there was an undercurrent of danger in it. The other side of Brad

Saxon: the implacable government agent, the symbol of authority. "Now back off. I mean it."

Neal's lower lip quivered. "If Buell comes after me next, it'll be your fault. You'll have my murder on your conscience, too." Snuffling, he went back into the lobby.

"Christ," Brad said. Then he looked at Leslie and his eyes softened and his voice was gentle when he said, "How do you feel?"

"Restless. Knotted-up inside."

"Psychic impulses?"

"Yes. Worse now. Much worse."

"You haven't had any more visual impressions?"

"No. Thank God for that, at least."

"Did anything happen while I was gone?"

"No. Nothing."

"Where's Walker?"

"I think he went into the kitchen," Leslie said. She stayed his hand as he started to unbutton his overcoat. "Brad, I meant what I said earlier. I can't stay here tonight. I just—can't."

He hesitated.

"Please," she said. "There's nothing more you can do tonight anyway, is there? At this hour?"

"No. Probably not."

"Then take me home, stay with me."

He let out a breath. "All right."

"Now? Can we go now?"

"Pretty soon. But I've got to talk to Walker first. Get your coat on; I won't be long."

She followed him into the lobby, went across to where she had draped her coat over the chair on the hearth. Neal was standing near the Simon Willard clock; he avoided eye contact as Brad passed him and went into the dining room, but then his myopic gaze lifted and settled on her. When she swung her coat around her shoulders, he started toward her tentatively. But she made a deliberate point of ignoring him and hurried back into the foyer, and he didn't come after her.

She leaned against the reception desk, waiting. Home, she thought. I don't want to go there either; I don't want to be alone there even with Brad.

The painting.

Whose face?

The psychic pulses assailed her mind. Like mute voices screaming in the night.

9:25 P.M.

Walker was alone in the kitchen, leaning against a butcher-block table and wolfing a thick sandwich, when Saxon entered. He looked up in a mildly startled way, as if he had been caught bending a Bureau commandment, and then put the sandwich down on a plate beside him and wiped his mouth with a paper napkin.

He said, "I got hungry. I've always been a compulsive eater."

"You don't have to apologize to me for eating."

"I just want you to know. Anything with Buell?"

"No," Saxon said. He gave a brief account of his time at Buell's house and antique shop. "If he's our man, there's not a damned thing I could find to prove it."

"Nothing here to point to anybody either," Walker said. "I searched Koskovich's room a little while ago, and Iverson's, too, on the sly."

"You didn't come across a blue velvet cord, did you?"

"Blue velvet cord? No, I didn't. Why?"

"That's what the victims were strangled with, apparently. Leslie saw it in her vision at the Harris farmhouse."

"Why would the killer use something like that?"

"Yeah, why?" Saxon said. "Koskovich still in the same shape?"

"He was the last time I looked in on him. I locked him in —I got both sets of passkeys from the Colebrooks."

Saxon nodded.

"I also called Hartford, and notified the state police. They'll get men in here as soon as the roads are passable."

"Okay. Good."

"Doesn't seem to be much else we can do tonight," Walker said. "I thought about talking to some of the other locals on the phone, but there wouldn't be any point in it. And it's too late and too stormy to go around making any more house calls."

"You're right. All we can do is make sure nobody else is attacked before morning."

"Yeah."

Saxon met his eyes squarely. "I'm going to take Leslie back to her house," he said. "Now. And I'm going to stay there with her."

Beyond a slight lifting of his eyebrows, Walker showed no reaction. "You sure that's a good idea?"

"No, I'm not sure. But it's what she wants and I'm going to go along with it, for her sake. Those psychic impulses I told you about are playing hell with her nerves; I don't want her to wind up like Koskovich."

"All right," Walker said.

"No moral objections?"

"Come on, Brad, don't start judging me again. I may have thirty years in the Bureau, but that doesn't make me a prude. Besides, it's been obvious for a while that the two of you are involved." He paused. And then asked surprisingly, "You in love with her?"

Saxon didn't know what to say. It was a question he hadn't even asked himself yet. But maybe it was a question that didn't need to be asked because he already knew the answer. Had known the answer since last night.

"I guess that was out of line," Walker said. "It's none of my business."

"You weren't out of line. How I feel about her is obvious, too, isn't it?"

Walker nodded, and they looked at each other for a time. Saxon felt a sudden warmth for the man. They had a great deal more in common than he could possibly have imagined before this weekend; and there was not only a rapport developing between them, not only a mutual respect, but a sense of friendship.

"I can handle things here," Walker said finally. "I'll get Colebrook to put a couple of cots in Koskovich's room for Iverson and me. Nobody's going to get at either of them with me there."

"Good. I'll check in with you later by phone."

Saxon went back through the dining room, into the lobby. Colebrook was standing just inside the bar, tight-faced and gimlet-eyed, but when Saxon approached he turned away wordlessly. Iverson sat now in a chair near the fireplace, brooding; he didn't move or look up.

Leslie stood waiting in the foyer, bundled inside her coat. Neither of them said anything as he took her arm and they went to the door. Outside, the snowfall seemed to have lightened a little and the gusts of icy wind were less severe; there were rifts here and there in the thick cloudbank overhead. But there wasn't any way of telling yet if that meant the storm was starting to break, if the eye of it had already passed.

In the car, Leslie sat close to him; her body felt rigid, coiled with tension. He looked at her pale face in the glow of the dash lights. And he was aware, then, of a kind of ache deep inside him.

Yes, he thought. Yes, I love her.

9:55 P.M.

There was a sour burbling in Walker's stomach as he climbed the stairs for another check on Koskovich. The two sandwiches he had eaten lay in there like a solid mass; he could swear he felt their edges. He chewed two more Rolaids tablets, belched when he reached the upper landing, belched again as he started down the hall. The sounds seemed to echo coarsely in the deserted stillness.

He felt bleak and wired-up inside. Nerves had never been a problem for him on an assignment, but this wasn't an ordinary case. Christ, no, it wasn't. The parapsychological angle was part of it; his beliefs on the subject had been profoundly shaken, and there was something damned unsettling in the idea of psychic vibrations and visions of murder so powerful they could unhinge the mind. The other part of it was being isolated in a place like this with a lunatic on the loose.

He didn't much care for the responsibility of having to watch out for Koskovich and Iverson on his own tonight. Koskovich was in an unbalanced state, and Iverson was a goddamned nut case who was liable to do or say anything. Suppose one of them had another vision? Or both of them did? Suppose things happened that he didn't have the experience to understand or handle? The thought nagged at him. Saxon, at least, had a background in this kind of thing. But it was out of Walker's element, and when you were out of your element, you were prone to mistakes.

Still, he couldn't fault Saxon for taking Leslie Abbott away from here. It wasn't really a professional decision, but the circumstances made it acceptable enough. At least to Walker. Hell, if he'd just fallen in love—if it had been Beth in Leslie's position and *she* was in the midst of an emotional crisis—he'd have done the same thing. He knew damned well he would.

We're not so different after all, Saxon and me, he thought. He'd learned a few things about the man this weekend, and Saxon seemed to have learned a few things about him, too. Maybe they'd even learned a few things about themselves.

When he came to Koskovich's door, Walker reached out to test the knob and satisfy himself that it was still locked. Then he got one of the sets of passkeys out of his pocket, suppressed another belch, and let himself inside.

The bed was empty. He saw that immediately in the light from the nightstand lamp. And saw, too, that the room seemed to be empty as well. He let go of the doorknob and took two quick steps deeper into the room, swinging his gaze to the right where the bathroom was. Then he came to a standstill, his stomach kicking up the bitter taste of gall.

Koskovich was crouched against the wall three feet away, behind the door. Just crouched there with one hand splayed against the pine boards and his head tilted to one side as if he were listening to something. His eyes were vacuous and his frostbitten cheeks shone greasily with the ointment Mrs. Colebrook had rubbed on them. Inside his loose-fitting pajamas, his body trembled and quivered.

Walker took hold of one dangling arm. "Mr. Koskovich? What are you doing out of bed?"

The white-maned head turned toward him, but the eyes remained blank. The trembling lips moved and made words that Walker could barely hear.

"Tick-tock," he said. "Tick-tock, tick-tock."

The coldness lodged inside Walker seemed to spread outward again, making his hands and feet feel icy. "Come on, now. Back to bed."

"To and fro, here we go," Koskovich said.

Jesus. Walker guided him to the bed and he came along docilely. Offered no resistance when Walker pushed him down onto the mattress, swung his stockinged feet up off the floor, and covered him with the blankets. He lay there staring at the ceiling, looking old and broken and pathetic in repose—a shell in which the human essence had retreated like something hiding in a dark corner. Quickly Walker shut off the bedside lamp and moved over to the open door.

"Tick-tock," Koskovich said in the darkness. "Tick-tock."

Walker went out into the hall, shut the door, and relocked it with the passkey. Ate two more Rolaids to settle his jumping stomach. God, he thought, what a night this is going to be.

He went back to the stairs, started down. He was nearing the bottom when he heard the voices: an angry, raised babble that seemed to be coming from either the lobby or the bar. One of them belonged to Colebrook and one to Iverson. There was a third voice, too—not Quint's and not Mrs. Colebrook's because he'd already sent both of them home for the night. He thought he recognized it as Ephraim Buell's.

Now what the hell? he thought. He took the last few steps two at a time, swung around the newel-post toward the lobby entrance. The voices grew louder, became distinguishable.

Buell: Get away from me, you crazy fuck!

Iverson: Murderer! Murderer!

Colebrook: That's *enough*, I won't stand for it!

They weren't in the lobby. Running now, his hand clamped on the butt of his revolver, Walker veered toward the entrance to the bar.

Buell: Put that thing up, Harmon, you gone crazy, too?

Colebrook: Hell I will! You—

What Walker saw when he pounded inside the bar started his stomach heaving again. Buell, hatless but wearing an old turned-down parka, was leaning against the edge of the bar as if for support; his free hand, upraised beside his head, was trembling. Iverson was backed up against the opposite wall, between two of the tables. And behind the bar, Colebrook stood with his feet planted and his eyes flashing dangerously. In his hands, pointed at a loose angle toward Iverson, was a double-barreled shotgun.

Walker went into a half-crouch and drew his weapon. He snapped, "Put it down, Colebrook. Right now!"

But the innkeeper had already begun to lower the shotgun. The sight of Walker and of the drawn .38 had taken the edge off his aggression. He laid the weapon on the bartop and wiped his hands down the front of his trousers.

Some of the tension went out of Walker. He straightened up, but didn't reholster the .38. "What the hell's going on here?"

"It ain't my fault," Buell said in a whining voice. His hair was wild, like tufts of dusty grass salted with snow, and his face was the color of spoiled meat. "I didn't start it, that son of a bitch over there did. I just come here for a drink, that's all."

Iverson's expression was half-outraged, half-frightened. "You started it, all right," he said. "You started it by murdering four people—"

"I never murdered nobody!"

"Shut up, both of you," Walker said. "Colebrook, you tell me what this is all about."

Colebrook came forward a couple of paces, away from the shotgun. He put his hands flat on the bar. "Buell showed up for some liquor, like he said. Wanted to buy a bottle. Then Iverson come running in and started accusing him of murder. Pointing his finger and hopping up and down like a fucking maniac."

"*He's* the maniac," Iverson said. "He's the one who—"

"I thought I told you to shut up." Walker turned to Colebrook. "What's the idea of the shotgun?"

"Protection. I'm entitled to protect myself, ain't I?"

"Not if it means shooting people."

"Wasn't going to shoot anybody. Just wanted to calm things down before they got out of hand."

"That's a hell of a way to do it, mister."

Buell said, "I don't want no more trouble. All I want is a bottle and I'll get on out of here."

"This is Sunday," Colebrook said. He sounded spiteful. "No off-sale on Sunday."

"You sold me a bottle this morning, Harmon—"

"Hell I did. Against the law to off-sale liquor on Sunday."

"Goddamn it, I need a drink! Can't you see that?"

"It's guilt," Iverson said. "He needs a drink because he's—"

Out in the lobby, the grandfather clock began to chime the quarter-hour. Walker wouldn't have noticed the sound except that Iverson went suddenly rigid, as if he were having some kind of seizure; his head tilted back, his mouth hung open, his face was alight with surprise and awe. Colebrook and Buell were staring at him, too. None of them moved until the chiming faded into silence.

Walker took a step forward. "Iverson, what's the matter with you?"

The kid just stood there like something molded out of clay.

But his mouth curved upward at the corners, as though he might be smiling.

God, Walker thought, his mind's snapped. I've got another Koskovich on my hands.

Buell jerked his gaze away and said sickly, "Pour me a shot, Harmon. Have some mercy, give me a *drink*."

Iverson moved. The sound of Buell's voice seemed to energize him; he whirled with such abruptness that Walker was caught flat-footed three long strides away, and ran headlong out of the bar.

Buell made a grunting noise. Colebrook said, "The hell?" and started to come out from behind the bar. Walker got his legs going then, ran for the lobby in Iverson's wake. When he got there, he saw the kid rush into the corner where the grandfather clock was, skid to a stop, and put both hands on the clock case. Walker slowed with a feeling of confusion and unease clipping away at him, watching Iverson run his palms up and down the clock, across the painted designs on its upper and lower glass. Caressing it, the way it looked.

"Come away from there," Walker said. He stopped with six feet between them. "You hear me, Iverson? Come away from—"

Iverson let go of the clock and spun around with the same suddenness as in the bar. There was wild excitement on his face now; his body gave the impression of twitching up and down even though he was standing still. He took off his checkered cap, crushed it between his hands, and held it against his chest in a way that made Walker think of a minister with a Bible.

"The clock!" he shouted. "The clock!"

Walker didn't know what to say or do. He remembered Koskovich upstairs a few minutes ago, saying "Tick-tock, tick-tock."

"I saw it all," Iverson said. "The clock was the catalyst, it triggered my gift. I know the truth! The Prince knows the truth!"

Understanding began to break in on Walker. A psychic

vision? Was that what this was all about? Maybe the kid's mind hadn't snapped after all; maybe he had just gone into some sort of clairvoyant trance.

He said, "What truth?"

"The *truth.*" Iverson jabbed his cap at where Buell and Colebrook were standing in front of the bar entrance. "About Buell. I know what he is, I know everything."

"Make sense, will you? What are you trying to say?"

"I know why he did it," Iverson said triumphantly. "I know why Buell has been murdering members of PSYCHICs!"

10:10 P.M.

She lay trembling in his arms, but not with cold. With desire. For him and for the sensations of coupling and orgasm that would purge her, if only for a little while, of the black pulses that even here, away from the inn, glowed inside her mind.

There was a wet tingling heat in her genitals; her breasts felt swollen, the nipples so rigid they ached. The feel of his body was exquisite: muscled, slightly hairy, as hot and urgent as her own. And his mouth was sweet, his tongue was fire. And his erection was diamond-hard and pulsing against her thigh. Pulsing, pulsing—

Pulsing in her mind black waves beating beating

No. The need, the sensations; nothing else. Nothing else. She kissed him desperately, clutched at his groin, caught hold of his hand and laid it on one of her swollen breasts. Rubbed his palm in quickening circles over the nipple. He started to lean across her, groping with his free hand for the lamp on the nightstand, but she held him still against her, broke the weld of their mouths, and whispered, "No, leave it on, I want the light. I want to see you."

His lips moved to her neck, to her ear; the throbbing warmth of his breath made her tremble harder. The black pulses shimmered and faded and were consumed by the high white flames of her need. She gave herself up completely to sensuality. Pushed his head to her breasts and gasped when he took the nipple into his mouth; held his erection in both hands and wanted to take it into her mouth even though she had never done that with a man before; summoned an image of herself doing it, summoned other images just as erotic until there was nothing in her mind except Brad and frenzy.

"Leslie," he said hoarsely, "Leslie," and kissed her again, entered her mouth with his tongue, and moved over her—yes!—and entered her body. Fusion, fusion. She rose against him, clutched him with her arms and legs, drew him in deeper. Motion, rhythm, flesh surging against flesh. Fast. Fast. Fast.

"This is what I want," she said into his mouth, "*this* is what I want."

Fast. Fast fast fast.

She kept her eyes open, watching his face, watching his hands on her breasts, his lips on her breasts. Fast fast fast fast. And she felt herself climbing, climbing—and climaxed in the next second with a cry that crested near a scream—oh, but a good scream, good scream, good scream. The shudder of her body, the good scream, the urging of her hands gave him his own orgasm: She could feel him coming, and it was as if he were disappearing into her, turning himself inside out. He made a soft cry of his own against her, and she came again at the sound and the sensations, and again, and it seemed that he did, too, that he never stopped disappearing inside her. . . .

They lay on their sides, still joined, and touched each other with eyes and fingertips. Not speaking, because there was no need for words: Eyes and fingertips said it all. This is the way sex is supposed to be, she thought. This is what it's all about. Not the way it was with Jim Parker or any of the others before Brad. Like this. Like this.

Jo died tonight, four of us are dead.

The thought crept out of the dreamy languor and burned it away like mist.

There's a maniac somewhere in this village who wants me dead, too.

And, oh, God, the vibrations assaulted her again, all at once. Stronger now, as strong as they had been at the inn. Dark ripples of heat, symbols, spots of color, images flickering in her psychic eye: Jo, Gloria, Sandra, rope, Jo, blue velvet cord, black tongue, Gloria, dark figure without a face—

She caught Brad's head and pressed it tight against her throat so that he wouldn't see the expression on her face. Held him in a desperate embrace. And because he was still half-erect within her, she began to move her hips, to stroke his back and his buttocks with urgent fingers—sex, more sex, drive it away with sex and love—and when he grew hard, she whispered against his ear, "Fast like before, darling, fast fast, make me come."

But this time the sensations and the erotic fantasies and the orgasms were not enough; the rhythms of love were not enough. The black pulses kept beating at her. Beating at her.

Beating beating beating beating beating—

10:20 P.M.

Neal stood in front of the grandfather clock and stared down at Walker, at Buell across the lobby. *Down* at them; he felt as if he were a towering figure in the room, ten feet tall at least. A looming giant. A giant Prince. His mind was awash with light and knowledge; it glittered and sparkled and he was sure the brilliance shone through his eyes and made them glow like searchlights. He was so excited that he had to urinate. But that could wait. You didn't take the time to go to the toilet when your mind was awash with light and knowledge and you were about to prove to the world that you were a hero.

He had never had a clairvoyant experience as stunning as this. Never. The first vision, triggered by the chiming of the clock, had come with magnificent clarity, in full color: Buell in his cellar workshop. What he had seen Buell doing had sent him running out here; and when he touched the clock, psychometric energy flowed upward through his fingers and created the second and third visions, each as vivid as the first. Then the pieces of knowledge had dropped into his consciousness like a line of falling birds, radiant and absolute. And he knew. He *knew*.

There was a breathless hush in the lobby now, a tense expectancy. This must be what it's like for a performer, Neal thought, what it's like when you take to the boards for the first time. Take to the boards, that was performer talk. The Prince was about to take his first bow.

He got his excitement under control, squared his shoulders, and moved forward with a princely stride to where Buell was standing next to a trestle table. He wasn't afraid of Buell now; he wasn't afraid of anything. The light of truth had freed him from fear.

The Prince fixed his shining eyes on Buell. "I know why you've been murdering PSYCHICs," he said again. He tapped his forehead. "It's all right here in my mind."

"That's for goddamn sure," Buell muttered. But there was sweat on his blotched cheeks—guilt oozing right out of his pores. He appealed to Colebrook, got a wooden stare in return, and said to Walker, "You can see how crazy this bastard is, can't you?"

"I don't know what I see yet."

The Prince said, "You're not only a psychotic murderer, Buell, you're a fraud. That's the key to everything—that you're an enormous fraud."

"Fraud?" Walker said.

"Fraud?" Colebrook said.

"You don't sell antiques, Buell. I mean, you sell some antiques, but mostly what you do is manufacture fakes that you *call* antiques."

"That's a lie!"

"You use chemicals and wood and hardware and all kinds of things," the Prince said relentlessly, "and you make fake antiques and sell them to tourists and the people that live around here. That grandfather clock over there, it's just one example. It didn't even exist before nineteen seventy-six. You made it down in your cellar workshop."

Colebrook said, "What? What the hell's he talking about, Buell?"

Buell was shaking. In the light from the lamp on the trestle table his eyes seemed to glow. "I don't know what the hell he's talkin' about!"

"I paid you a thousand dollars for that clock."

"It couldn't have cost him a tenth of that to make," the Prince said. "I *saw* him making it with my psychic eye and he used an old case and new brassworks that he dipped in a chemical solution to make them look old."

"Lies! Lies!"

Walker gave him a narrow look. "We'll see about that," he said. "It's easy enough to check out."

Buell shook his head and his stricken gaze went furtively from Walker to Colebrook. The Prince felt exultant. They're listening to me now, he thought. The audience is captive for the Prince's first bow.

"You lying, cheating son of a bitch," Colebrook said. His hands were drawn into fists; he took a step toward Buell.

"Hold it," Walker snapped, and made a motion with the revolver that was still in his hand. Colebrook held it. "All right, Iverson, maybe you're right. Maybe Buell is what you say he is. But what does that have to do with the murders?"

"It has everything to do with them. He makes fake antiques, and the stuff he uses is in his workshop. That's the evidence I've been telling you all along is there. And he's been murdering PSYCHICs because he was afraid one of us would have a vision about him being a fraud, just like I did have one, and he'd go to jail for twenty or thirty years."

"I ain't a murderer!" Buell shouted.

"The way I figure it," the Prince said, "he wasn't a psychotic killer in the beginning. I mean, he didn't want to have to kill people, he just wanted all of us clairvoyants to stay away from him. That's why he started making the threatening phone calls to Leslie."

Walker said, "Threatening calls?"

"Sure. Buell's the one. I saw him on the phone in his cottage, making one of the calls. In my second vision, just now. That's where I saw him. And I heard him, too. 'How many times you have to be told? You're not wanted in Whitehall, we don't want *any* of your kind here.' That was what he was saying."

There was a trapped expression on Buell's face; he looked like an animal caught in a snare.

"Then I had my *third* vision," the Prince said, "and what he was doing that time, he was inside Leslie's studio and he was breaking up her paintings and furniture and things and squeezing paint all over. It looked like he was drunk, because he was staggering around and mumbling to himself—"

Buell made a noise in his throat, grabbed the lamp off the trestle table, threw it at Walker, wheeled around, kicked Colebrook in the ankle as the innkeeper lunged at him, and ran wildly toward the foyer.

It all happened so fast that the Prince just stood there with his mouth open and the unfinished sentence hanging in his larynx. Walker was knocked backward, off-balance and half around so that he seemed to be running toward the fake grandfather clock; Colebrook hopped on one foot and then tried to run while he was leaning forward and clutching at his ankle, and fell down to one knee. When Walker got his balance back and his body and gun turned around, Buell was already disappearing into the foyer. Walker lumbered after him, almost collided with Colebrook, and the two of them got tangled up together like Laurel and Hardy in one of their movies. By the time they got untangled and Walker shoved ahead again, the Prince heard Buell go out and the storm come in through the front door.

Colebrook shouted something, Walker shouted something; they chased each other out of sight. It would have been kind of funny if they weren't after a psychotic murderer and the whole thing weren't so serious. There were banging sounds, the rattling of coat hangers, pounding footfalls. Then the front door slammed and the wind became a muted whine again. Except for that and the faint crackling of the fire, the lobby was as still as a dead man's heart. That was the phrase that came to the Prince as he stood rooted in position: *as still as a dead man's heart.*

But it came to him peripherally, the way everything else had in the past few seconds. He knew he ought to be moving himself, pursuing Buell himself, but the reason he was still standing here was that there were psychic birds wheeling around in his mind again. In his third eye. Shadow replaced the brightness there, brightness replaced the shadow; it held him transfixed.

Then the eye opened and the shadow and the brightness came together in another vision. He still had his cap clasped in both hands; he brought it up and pressed it against his forehead, rubbed it back and forth over the skin between his eyebrows. The vision settled into focus, took on sharpness and detail that weren't in color this time but in crisp black and white.

It only lasted for a few short seconds, but they were enough. Enough to drop more falling birds of knowledge into his consciousness. Enough to make the light of truth even more dazzling than before. Enough to fill him with a fresh rush of excitement. And enough to uproot him and send him charging out of the lobby.

Was his coat in the foyer cloakroom? Yes, right over there on one of the hangers. He pulled it free and struggled into it as he stumbled to the front door.

Except for a choppy line of tracks leading off toward Quint's Country Store, there was no sign of Buell or Colebrook or Walker in the darkness outside. But that didn't matter. He knew where Buell was heading, and now he was on his way to the same place. Without fear. No harm would come to him tonight; he knew that just as he knew everything else.

Toward the final confrontation, that was where he and Buell were heading. Toward the last deadly meeting of hero and psychotic killer. Because Walker and Colebrook weren't going to catch him; Buell was going to vanish into the night as far as they were concerned, and when he did, he would go after his fifth victim.

He would go after Leslie.

What the Prince had seen in his vision was himself standing in the snow near Leslie's house. Standing there and looking up at it and knowing, knowing, knowing she was about to die.

10:50 P.M.

Postcoital stillness. That was a phenomenon Saxon had noticed a long time ago with Evelyn—how still everything seemed after an intense period of lovemaking. Not just externally but inside him as well. *Tristesse*, the French called it, but it wasn't sadness exactly, more of a placidity that lay over events, emotions, thoughts.

With Evelyn, though, the postcoital stillness had never been anything like this. He had loved her a great deal, more than he had been willing to admit for a long time, but sex with her was always just a little unsatisfying. She had been passionate enough, especially in the beginning, and she had never denied him; but neither had she taken the initiative. She was simply there and responsive in various ways. Their sex was a ritual seldom discussed and always performed in darkness or in the faint natural light coming through curtains. On her part, there had been no sense of abandon, of opening herself up to him on every level. Instead, conscious or not, a holding back that had made him hold back, too—not only sexually but in other ways just as profound. A withholding of self.

With Leslie, sex was a celebration, an act of utter commitment. He didn't have to hold back in any way, and, because he didn't, it was like being freed of the other things locked inside him: so much feeling, the failure of his marriage, the specter of his dead love for Evelyn. Love. For the first time since the divorce, he understood that that was what he had always wanted and needed, that it was the motivating force in his life—the one thing that meant everything if it wasn't cheapened. Not a new job or a new direction; at bottom, he was content enough in the new Bureau despite its history and the taint of Hoover throughout. Just love, to help him accept who and what he was so he could reclaim his life.

Saxon was, all at once, ravenously hungry. Another phenomenon: Making love made him hungry. Just as tension did the same thing to Walker, he supposed. Walker. He reached out to the nightstand, picked up his wristwatch. Almost 11:00. Past time to check in at the inn. He slipped the watch on, shifted around, and leaned up on one elbow to look at Leslie.

In the lampglow, her face appeared calm and flushed, almost radiant. But the strain was still there and her eyes had hints of anguish.

"You okay?" he said. "Psychically, I mean."

"Yes. I'm okay."

"More relaxed now?"

"Yes. How about you?"

"Me too. Okay. I'm also hungry—starved."

"I'll make you something—"

"I can do it. I've got to call Walker anyway."

"All right. There's plenty in the icebox."

"Sandwiches sound good?"

"Not for me. I'm not hungry."

"You've got to eat, baby."

"I suppose so. Maybe a piece of toast."

He kissed her again and swung out of bed. The covers fell away from her, too, and she didn't touch them. He stood looking down at her. "You're beautiful," he said.

A faint smile. "So are you."

"Hah. I won't be long. Late supper in bed."

"Or in the kitchen. I may get up, too, after a bit. We're not going to sleep for a while anyway."

"No, probably not."

He got dressed and clipped his service revolver and holster to his belt; they had been within easy reach on the nightstand. At the doorway, he paused to look back at her.

"Beautiful," he said again, and waited for her smile, and then went out and into the kitchen to the telephone.

11:05 P.M.

After Brad was gone, Leslie got slowly out of bed and padded naked into the bathroom. When she came out again, she pulled a sweater over her head and stepped into a pair of Levi's, not bothering with undergarments, and slid her feet into slippers. Then she stood hugging herself, listening to the nervous stutter of her heart.

The black pulses beat, beat, beat.

Ripples, spots of color, subliminal images. Menace, suffering. Evil. Death.

She had lied to Brad, hidden the truth from him. Again. Because he wasn't supposed to know about the controlling forces, about the inevitability of all this. Or about—

The painting.

Her eyes lifted ceilingward, and for a moment it was as if she could see through the wood and lathe and plaster, into the studio, to where the winterscape sat covered on the floor. In her mind, it seemed to glow, to give off a shimmering bluish light like something charged with radiation. The light had a magnetic attraction; she felt it begin to tug at her, draw her toward it.

No, I don't want to go up there.

Waves of energy beating, beckoning.

Her legs carried her from the bedroom, without will, just as they had carried her out of the house to the covered bridge earlier. Down the hallway. Up the stairs to the studio. One of her hands went out to the light switch and she saw the broken shrouded furniture and the hideous streaks and stains of paint leap out of the darkness. Saw the painting leap out of the darkness. No shimmering bluish light, just a covered canvas on the floor. And yet it seemed enormous, omnipresent, a conductor for the black pulses she was receiving.

It pulled her forward again. Step. Pause. Step. Pause. She stood in front of it, then knelt as if it were a shrine. Her hand extended to the cloth that concealed it. And jerked the cloth away.

The figure on the snow stared up at her.

It had no face, it had no eyes, but it was staring up at her.

Her hand moved toward the surface of the painting, toward the figure, her fingers spreading out, flattening into a vertical plane. Touched the smooth canvas and the rough raised brushstrokes of dried paint. Touched the figure, covered it, covered the staring faceless oval—

Blue black red white screaming terror smell of feces choking pressure Sandra's face screaming Gloria's face Jo's face jelly eyes mouths screaming velvet cord choking terror smell of feces hanging bodies tongues crawling out of bowls of black white red blue

colors congealing

painting coming alive alive not a painting anymore alive the dark figure standing in the snow outside obscured by flurries blackish man-shape in a long coat concealing blackish man-shape staring up at the house winter hat with earflaps hiding the upper half of his face no face no face jelly eyes screaming terror screaming death

Her fingers felt hot, burning, as if the painting were generating palpable heat. A cry came out of her and she wrenched her hand away so violently that she toppled over backward.

Her consciousness reeled away, stuttered toward a confused awareness of where she was. The studio wavered out of focus. Only the painting was clear to her—the painting and the vision of it, come to life.

Not a scene that had happened in the past. A scene from now, from tonight.

Not a symbol, not the dark figure of someone innocent. The murderer.

She struggled upward to her feet and half-ran to the north windows. Her breath fogged the glass when she tried to peer through the nearest one; she tugged at the sash, flung it upward. Thrust her head out into the stinging bite of the wind.

And the dark figure was there in the snow below.

Painting, vision, reality: standing motionless between one of the elms and the woodshed, looking up at the house; a blackish man-shape in a long coat and a winter hat with ear-flaps hiding the upper half of his face.

Already here, already coming for her.

The murderer.

Coming for her.

She recoiled, and her head cracked sharply against the sash; the sudden jolt of pain broke the psychic hold on her, cleared away some of the debris. She backed away from the open window, shivering in the icy drafts of wind that came through it. Telling herself: Don't panic, for God's sake, tell Brad. You can tell him about this, the forces won't stop you from telling him about this.

She ran to the stairs and down them, clutching at the handrail. Ran into the kitchen calling his name.

He wasn't there.

A loaf of bread and sandwich fixings on the table. The telephone receiver off the hook, hanging from its cord against the wall like a dead black body.

She wheeled and raced into the bedroom. "Brad, Brad!" And ran from there into the living room.

His coat and hat and gloves no longer beside hers on the couch.

He was *gone*.

11:05 P.M.

No one had answered the phone at the inn.

Saxon let it ring twenty times before he hooked the receiver.

Scowling, he moved over to the icebox and took out butter and lettuce and the remains of the roast Leslie had cooked last night. Put them on the table, found a loaf of bread and put that on the table. But then he just stood there, slapping the flat of his left hand against the closed fingers of his right.

Damn it, somebody should have answered; Walker should have answered. It just didn't make sense that the Colebrooks would let the switchboard be shut down for the night. Procedure was for Walker to have instructed Colebrook to plug the outside line into Koskovich's room, where he and Iverson were supposed to be sleeping, and Walker would never make a procedural mistake. So why the hell hadn't he answered?

Something's happened, he thought.

The phone drew his eyes again. He could feel tension beginning to seep back into him, to chase his hunger pangs and the last of the placid warmth of their lovemaking.

He went back to the wall extension, lifted the receiver, and dialed the number of the inn again. Five rings. Ten. Goddamn it, pick up the phone! He turned aside in agitation, with the handset pressed to his ear, and leaned forward against the drainboard to stare out the kitchen window. Fifteen rings. Sixteen. Darkness outside. Snow still falling but without the blizzard turbulence of before. Eighteen rings. Movement here and there, barren tree branches swaying in the wind, movement—

Somebody out there.

The realization slapped at his mind, made his nerve endings jangle. He leaned closer to the glass, still holding the receiver. Somebody immobile in the snow fifty yards downrange, near one of the elms: indistinct shape cloaked in the wavering shadows cast by the tree branches; making no effort to hide himself, just standing there and staring toward the house.

It's him, he's after Leslie! Nobody else would be crazy enough to come here and watch the house like that.

Saxon's lips peeled away from his teeth. He let go of the receiver, heard without hearing its clattering dance against the wall. On one side of the drainboard was a flashlight that he'd noticed before; he caught it up in his left hand. And swept his service revolver into his right hand.

All right, you son of a bitch, now it's *my* turn.

He ran into the living room, caught up his coat and hat and gloves, struggled into them on his way to the front door. And ran out into the night.

The wind billowed and swirled the open tails of the coat. He managed to get three of the buttons fastened as he shoved through drifts to the north corner of the house. When he reached it, he eased his head out to scan the area across the yard, near the elm.

The man was still there, still motionless in the snow.

Why was he standing out in the open that way? Why hadn't he taken a position where he couldn't be seen from the house? Too crazy now to think rationally, maybe. Either that, or it was an act of cunning: He *wanted* to be seen. Wanted to draw Saxon out after him just this way, so he could try to elude him and get into the house after Leslie. Or else draw Saxon into a stalking game he was crazy-bold enough to think he could win.

No matter what the reason, it meant going after him with extreme caution.

Saxon squinted through the snowfall, looking for some sort of clue to the man's identity. Too dark to make out anything except lumpish human outlines; he couldn't even guess at height and weight. Had he come here from the inn? Was that why nobody had answered the phone?

The hell with speculation, he told himself grimly. Getting him is all that matters. Not even finding out who he is; that's secondary. Getting him. *Get* him.

Another elm grew thirty feet away, at an angle to the corner of the house. Saxon backed up until it was between him and the man and then went in a slogging, humped-over run to the tree bole. Forty yards separating them now. He looked out around the tree. Couldn't see him from this position; the second elm was in the way. There wasn't any cover between the two trees, nothing but wind-smoothed drifts. With the snowfall slacked down the way it was, he'd be visible crossing that distance in a straight line. But the garage sat off to his right, less than fifteen yards away, and there was heavy shadow along its near wall, beneath the overhang of the roof.

He stepped out from behind the elm, leaning forward so that he formed a low silhouette against the snow. The wind-chill factor had already begun to suck body heat from him; his cheeks burned, his nose and ears burned, his feet felt numb inside his shoes. The icy air stabbed at his lungs with each inhalation and forced him to breathe in shallow pants.

When he got to the garage wall, he had a clear sightline to the place alongside the elm where the man had been standing. Only he wasn't standing anymore, he was just starting to move: not toward the house but laterally, in the direction of the woodshed. Saxon drew back against the wall, but he hadn't been seen. The man's movements were slow, plodding, and he didn't turn his head as he went.

Still forty yards between them. Risking a shot at that distance, on a night like this, was out of the question; and there wasn't enough time to get to him before he reached the shed. Saxon stayed where he was, tense and unmoving, and watched the man approach the line of cordwood stacked along the shed's south wall. Watched him pause there, arched against the wind.

Stay right where you are, you bastard—

The man started forward again, into the shadows beyond the woodpile, and was gone.

Inside his glove, Saxon's right hand, locked tight around the revolver butt, was slick with cold sweat. Along the wall and across to the rear corner? Or away from the wall and a diagonal run in the open to the front corner? Had to be the long way; there was an evergreen tree halfway between the garage and the back of the shed that he could use for cover. Too much risk of being seen if he came out into the open.

Wind-slanted icicles had formed under the garage roof; they nipped like teeth at the top of his hat as he hurried forward beneath them. He stopped again at the back corner and brushed ice crystals off his eyelids and squinted at the shed. No movement anywhere around it; no movement behind it to the north either. A fading line of tracks led from the fence in that direction to the shed, but it seemed certain they had been made coming, not going. He could see the rear porch of the house, part of the field of snow that lay between the porch and the shed. A smooth-rippled plane void of tracks.

All right. The man was still somewhere on the south or east side of the shed. Either that, or he'd kept on going away from it to the east.

Saxon eased out of the roof shadows and burrowed his way to the bole of the evergreen tree. Ice-weighted branches swayed in random gusts. Except for the keening of the storm and the irregular thrumming of his pulse, unbroken stillness surrounded him.

He made his run to the shed, pivoted, and braced his body against the wall, scanning left to right. Made his way along the wall, then, in a sliding sideways walk. The lighted windows in the house glowed a misty yellow, and for the first time he realized that the lights in the studio were on. Had Leslie gone up there to look for him? If she had, she'd seen the man, too, by now. But there was no sign of her at those windows or at any of the others. Each of the lighted rectangles was empty.

His stomach muscles clenched as he neared the white-coated cordwood stack. Three paces from it, he backed out from the wall at an angle. Held a breath and extended the revolver at arm's length in a two-handed shooter's grip. Then shuffled out in quick movements made awkward by the deep snow, to where he could look along the length of the woodpile.

Empty.

The breath came out of him. He took his left hand off the gun, wiped again at his numbed eyelids. The man's tracks led straight to the end of the cordwood, then made a right-angle turn back to the north. The snowfield beyond to the east was unmarred.

Saxon followed in the wake of the tracks, out away from the woodpile by three feet. The cold had begun to send tremors through him; he locked his teeth together to keep them from chattering, took another two-handed grip on the .38 to hold it steady. All of his senses seemed to have grown acute: The sound of the wind was louder in his ears, the smell of winter flared his nostrils, the feel of the gun butt made his fingers tingle with cold-hot sensations.

When he neared the end of the cordwood, he set himself and repeated his actions of before: backed and shuffled out until the length of the shed's east wall became visible.

Empty.

The tracks here led in a straight line, in close to the wall, and at the north corner they made another right-angle turn to the west. Saxon hesitated. What the hell kind of game was this? If the man had seen his spoor, or seen *him*, why hadn't he run? Or made a stand? Unless he was trying to set some kind of trap—but what kind of trap could you set circling a goddamn woodshed?

Cautiously Saxon started forward again, following the tracks. There was a door on this side of the shed, narrow and made of the same weathered gray planking as the rest of the structure. He drew abreast of it, went past by a step before it registered fully on his mind.

Door. Door!

There was a flicker of warning and the half-formed thought *He could have doubled back*, and he was just starting to turn when the door flew inward and the dark body and the long length of cordwood came sweeping out at him.

His head erupted in blinding yellow light. He felt himself spin and start to fall, and then he stopped feeling anything and just kept on falling and falling into yellow, into white, into gray—

Leslie!

Into black.

11:30 P.M.

I'm not going to panic, she thought.

She stood in the living room, the empty living room, and forced herself to take a series of deep breaths to calm herself. If she was supposed to panic, then she would—but she wasn't going to panic, so that meant she wasn't supposed to. Logic in that somewhere. Whatever was destined to happen would happen. Face up to it. Leslie Abbott is a strong woman, remember? She's been through a lot in her life, little girl and woman alone in so many rooms, and she's been through hell the past few days; she's faced all of that and she can face this.

Face it and get through it. Believe that. No fatalism now; none of that. Face it and get *through* it.

It was obvious where Brad had gone. He must have seen the dark figure, just as she had, and gone out after him; he was outside after the murderer. All right. Look out there, look for him. Rear porch, the back door. Walk, don't run. Walk.

She went through the kitchen and onto the porch. Unlocked the main door but left the screen door hooked. Through the thin mesh, she could see the woodshed and the elm, but the dark figure wasn't there anymore. Brad wasn't there either. Tracks in the snow, a lot of tracks, crisscrossing and meandering in a crazy-quilt pattern. Nothing else to see. Brad must have chased him away from the house, out of the yard.

Now—get help. The forces won't stop you from doing that. Call Walker at the inn, tell Walker what's happening here.

Her footsteps echoed hollowly in the stillness of the house. Unnatural stillness, like a mausoleum. Dead house. Raped and violated house. No, don't think about that. Love in this house, too, last night and tonight. Love with Brad. Love *for* Brad? Yes, admit it: You love him. And he loves you, too, you know he does. Endings and beginnings. The end of emptiness, the beginning of love. The end of one life, the beginning of another.

Face it. And get through it.

She caught up the dangling telephone receiver. Why was it off the hook like that? Brad must have been talking to Walker or trying to reach Walker when he saw the man outside, and he'd charged out so quickly that he hadn't taken the time to hang up. Yes, that was logical. Maybe Walker was already on the way. Maybe it would all be over in another few minutes. The ending so that there could be the beginning.

She depressed the cradle, held it down for a second. Dial tone. She dialed the number of the inn and listened to the circuit make clicking and chattering sounds, then ringing sounds in her ear.

Ring-ring. Ring-ring. Ring-ring.

Come on, she thought.

Ring-ring. Ring-ring.

Come on, somebody answer.

Ring-ring. Ring-ring. Ring—

Snicking sound.

And the phone went dead.

Evil in her mind, beating, beating. Screams in her mind; black ripples and black symbols; jelly eyes and black-bowl mouths; faces, and figures without faces. Dead psychics, dead line. Dead line.

He's cut the telephone wires, he's right outside.

Her control began to slip. Outside, outside. Got away from Brad—did something to Brad? Outside, but not for long. Coming for me. *Did* something to Brad? Velvet cord, choking pressure, terror, black tongue, dead and hanging at the end of a rope—

Stop it, stop that!

Believe. You're going to get through it. Believe. Brad hasn't been hurt, he's not hurt. Believe. Believe.

She took a half-dozen more deep breaths. Her control stabilized again; she could feel a kind of calm infiltrate her, swaddling the panic, smothering it. It wouldn't come again. She wouldn't let it come again no matter what happened to her.

But nothing was going to happen to her.

Believe.

What now? What did the forces want her to do next? Leave the house, try to get away in the darkness? No. The murderer was out there, watching, waiting; he would see her if she tried to leave, and she couldn't outrun a man through the snow. Hide? No. There wasn't anywhere to hide that she wouldn't be found.

Fight, she thought.

Yes. Get some kind of weapon, get the biggest, sharpest knife in the house and stab him when he comes in here.

She threw the dead phone away from her and jerked open the utensil drawer under the drainboard. Paring knives, bread knives, steak knives. Butcher knife with an eight-inch curving blade. She caught it up. Reflections of light glinted off the honed steel edge—and she imagined something else gleaming there: bloodstains, intimations of blood. She squeezed her eyes shut, blinked them open again. The ghost stains were gone.

I can do it, she thought. If the forces let me do it, I can stab him, murder him. Kill him so he can't kill me.

Sounds. The house seemed alive with sounds now: creakings, groanings, rattlings. He might already be coming inside. She couldn't just stand here in the light and wait for him. Light. Lights on all over the house. But light wasn't her ally, it was his; darkness was what she had to have. Darkness would give her the advantage in her own house; she could surprise him in the dark.

Holding the knife, she went back onto the rear porch and over to where the fuse box was fastened to the wall behind the washing machine. She'd had to deal with fuse boxes before, living alone; she found the master switch immediately and threw it shut. Cold darkness enfolded her. She reached out, groped for the lid on the washing machine, and opened it. Then she began unscrewing fuses, one after the other, and dropping them inside the washer.

The screen door rattled.

She wheeled around, raising the knife. But beyond the glass panel and the screen, the night was empty black, empty white. Just the wind—a gust of wind.

Where was he? Out back here? Along one of the side walls? In front? On his way *in?*

She couldn't stay on the porch either. Or anywhere else downstairs. Doors, windows—there were a dozen ways for him to enter, a dozen directions he could come at her.

The studio.

The only way up there was the stairs, she'd only have one direction to guard. There was no lock on the studio door, but maybe she could drag what was left of the furniture over in front of it and barricade herself inside.

No, the painting—

Damn the painting!

The black pulses beating, beating. Screams, symbols, colors. She made a fist of her free hand and hammered it against the top of her head. Image of the winterscape radiating bluish light, giving off waves of energy. She wasn't through with it yet; it wasn't through with her. More to come. But what? Another vision? His death? Her death?

Get through it. Believe.

He's out there, or already coming inside.

Studio. Like a voice whispering now. The no-mouth on the figure with no face, whispering from the heart of the painting: *Studio, studio.*

She groped her way through the darkness with the knife held out in front of her like a crucifix. And started up the stairs to the painting.

11:45 P.M.

He was waiting in the snow alongside the bedroom window when the lights in the house went out. Yes: the vision. He put his gloved hand inside his pocket to touch the blue velvet cord. Now she would go upstairs into her studio, close the door, and move furniture over in front of it. And then he would enter the house and climb up after her.

But what then?

He didn't know. The vision had been clear at first, like all the others. Even more urgent and demanding, but still clear. He had seen himself here in the snow by the elm; he had seen Saxon come out and stalk him, himself go around the wood-shed and hide inside and then beat the man down with the piece of cordwood; he had seen himself cut the telephone wires with his pocketknife. But after that, the images had begun to waver, to flicker in and out of focus, to curl up at the edges like pieces of burning film. Waiting here in the snow, Leslie Abbott putting the house lights out and going to her studio with a knife in her hand, himself going inside and starting up the stairs: all just burning, fading flickers. Then nothing. Ashes.

What would happen up there?

He heard screams echoing faintly in his mind, just as he had heard them in the vision, but he didn't know if they were Leslie Abbott's or someone else's. If they were his own. He smelled death, but he didn't know whose death it was. Would he strangle her like all the rest and hang her body from a rafter? Or was it he and the host who were going to die this time?

Obey or die.

Protect the secret or die again.

But even if it was her death, it all seemed so hopeless. Coming apart—the secret and himself and the host. Unraveling. Two visions already today. Out of control, trapped by the visions and hurled by them toward—what? Discovery and death instead of salvation? The one true death from which there would be no return?

He was terrified.

The wind gusted, blew flakes of snow against his numb cheeks. But he no longer felt the cold; his terror and the velvet cord insulated him with bright shimmers of heat. Cold-hot sweat under his arms and between his legs, burning. A taste in his mouth like burnt wool. Fever-jumble of screams and smells and afterimages searing the walls of his mind. Heat. Fire. Fire of purpose, fire of salvation. Fire and ice and death.

Time to go: the vision.

He made his way through the snow to the front of the house. The door was unlocked because that was the way Saxon had come out. Yes. He opened it and stepped into darkness.

When he had shut the door behind him, he took the flashlight from his coat pocket, clicked it on. Long yellow slice through the dark, shadows crouching at its edges. He moved deeper into the house, cutting away more of the gloom, until he came to a center hall. The stairs were there, leading up to the closed studio door.

He crossed to the foot of the stairs and shut off the flash.

End of vision.

The last of the charred images, the last of the screams and the smells, faded and were gone. There was nothing inside his head now except purpose and terror and hot glowing ashes.

His eyes were wet; he wanted to weep. Instead he took out the velvet cord, held it clenched tightly in his left hand. And started up the stairs to the unknown.

11:50 P.M.

Crouched against the studio wall near the door, Leslie waited and listened. Wind. Ice crystals ticking at the windowpanes. Old boards creaking and chattering. Her breath making little rasping sounds in her throat. The skip-thump, skip-thump of her heart. But nothing else yet. He didn't seem to be in the house yet.

It was cold in there. Cold, thick darkness, unbroken except for the black-gray outlines of the windows; the slashed couch and the remains of the catchall table were a formless mass in front of her, where she had dragged them over to block the door. She couldn't see the painting at all from where she stood, but she could feel it: the black pulses from it bombarding her in a relentless stream. She wanted to destroy it, cut it to ribbons with the knife, but the forces wouldn't let her do it. Not done with her yet. More to come.

Get through it.

She wasn't going to die tonight. Brad wasn't dead and he wasn't going to die tonight either.

Believe.

Seconds dragged away. Minutes. And every minute that the murderer failed to come for her was one more minute of life, one more minute of hope that Brad, Walker—someone—was destined to help her.

Her hand, wrapped around the handle of the butcher knife, was slippery with sweat. She transferred the weapon to her other hand and rubbed the palm dry on her Levi's. The wind gusted again and made one of the window frames rattle. Inside the house, silence. A wall board popped. Silence. Skip-thump, skip-thump. Silence.

Banging sound downstairs.

She went rigid, straining to hear in the darkness. Door shutting? Dryness caked her mouth; she swallowed painfully. There was a hollow, wobbly feeling in her legs and she leaned back against the wall to steady herself.

Silence.

More seconds passed.

Thump.

The noise seemed to come from directly below, at the foot of the stairs—as if the toe of a boot had bumped against one of the risers.

Creak.

He's here now, he's coming.

Creak. Creak.

Not minutes. Seconds.

Thump.

Who? Whose face?

Creak.

Sweat stung her eyes; she pawed at them with the flat of her free hand.

The door latch clicked. Wood thudded softly against wood as the door opened a crack and banged against the frame of the couch.

In her mind, the painting glowed and glowed.

Another bumping sound: heavy shoulder thrust against the door panel. A faint grunt. Breathing. Legs on the couch and on the table beginning to ratchet backward across the floor.

In her mind the black pulses beat and beat.

The crack between the door and jamb widened. Something came through it, barely visible . . . an arm with a hand holding a short cylindrical object. The couch and table legs kept on ratcheting backward, yielding to the man's shoving weight. The door opened wider, wider, wide enough for him to get through.

She raised the knife.

Stab him! Do it now!

The object in his hand burst into a cone of glaring light. It was angled away from her, toward the center of the studio, as he swung inside; but the suddenness of it froze her against the wall, blinking. And in the next instant she saw him in dark profile behind the flash beam, saw the color and design of his coat.

A name rose like a scream inside her.

Harmon Colebrook—

11:50 P.M.

Walker found Ephraim Buell hiding in his cellar workshop.

Buell's sudden panicked escape from the inn had caught him off-guard, like a damned rookie. He'd been so intent on Iverson's dramatic revelations that he'd momentarily lost his handle on the suspect. When he had finally recovered and gotten outside, Buell was clear over by Quint's Country Store, running in a wild, awkward gait through the snow. Colebrook had tried to take up the chase with him, but the innkeeper had already gotten in the way and Walker didn't want any more civilians screwing things up. He'd ordered Colebrook to get the hell back to the inn and then gone on alone.

He had lost sight of Buell behind the store, but the man's tracks were easy enough to follow. They led straight to the garage next to his cottage, where an old Dodge pickup was parked. Buell had only gotten one of the doors open against the high drifts before giving up on that idea, and the tracks had led from there around the cottage. Walker had caught sight of him again on the opposite side, running toward the antique shop. Half a minute later, he'd disappeared inside. The only question then was whether he was planning to hide or make a fight of it—whether or not he had a weapon of some kind stashed in there.

By that time Walker was half-frozen and filled with rage. If he didn't come up with a case of pneumonia from all this running around in subzero temperature, it would be a miracle. He kicked in the back door of the shop and spent a lot of long minutes searching the place because he didn't want to walk into a trap. Only there wasn't any trap. There was just Buell hiding down here in the workshop. Huddled inside an old claw-foot bathtub, under a piece of canvas.

Walker pointed his service revolver at Buell's right eye and said, "All right. It's over now, Buell. Come on out of there."

All the aggression had gone out of the man. He looked beaten and sick and trapped. A frozen smear of something that was probably vomit stained his mouth and chin; his eyes were jaundiced. When he crawled out of the bathtub, he was shaking so badly that his legs wouldn't support him. He thumped down on the edge of it and made whimpering sounds.

"I never killed nobody," he said. "You got to believe me. Jesus, you got to."

"Then why did you run?"

"I was scared, I lost my head. Because I done them other things, I admit it. I been selling fake antiques for years. And I made the calls to Leslie Abbott and tore up that painting studio of hers last night. I was drunk; it was a crazy thing to do, but I was drunk and scared. I been afraid ever since she come here and I found out what she was that she'd have one of her visions and know I was phonying up antiques. That's why I been deviling her, just like Iverson said. But I never killed any of those other psychics. I ain't a murderer. I never hurt nobody in my life."

Walker studied him. And an uneasy feeling began to replace the anger in him. After thirty years in the Bureau, you got so you could judge whether or not somebody was telling the truth. It was part of your survival equipment: You learned to read their eyes and their expressions and the inflections in their voices. There was plenty of guilt in Buell; he was a liar, a swindler, a vandal, and any number of other things. But a psychopathic murderer? Iverson had been right about everything else, but that didn't necessarily make him right about Buell being the killer.

"I swear to God," Buell said, "I ain't a murderer!"

Damn it to hell, Walker thought.

If it isn't Buell, then who is it?

11:55 P.M.

It *wasn't* Harmon Colebrook.

It wasn't him at all.

The dark figure raised the flashlight, started to swing it around toward Leslie, and in the backspill of its glare she realized the mistake she had made.

And recognized who it really was—

11:55 P.M.

The Prince stood in the snow near Leslie's house, looking up at it and knowing she was about to die inside.

Just the way I saw it in the vision, he thought. He stomped

his legs up and down, shivering inside his coat; it had been a long trek here and he was numb with cold. Besides which, he *really* had to urinate now. But he just wasn't going to expose his pecker on a night like this. It was liable to freeze solid if he did and maybe break off like an icicle. How could the Prince of Psychics go through life without his pecker?

There wasn't time to urinate anyway. Leslie was about to die inside the house; she could already be in Buell's clutches in there. He had to go in and save her. He wasn't armed and he didn't know anything about stalking psychotic murderers, but he had to go in and save Leslie.

Didn't he?

He wasn't sure. That was certainly what he ought to do—the final heroic act—and the Prince wanted to do what was right. But those psychic birds were pecking away at his consciousness again, fluttering their wings and battering their beaks inside his third eye. One of the birds seemed to peck out *Saxon,* like a message. Saxon. Where was Saxon, anyway? He'd taken Leslie home from the inn, the Prince was sure of that. Maybe he was inside, saving her at this very minute. But then again, maybe he wasn't. Maybe he was somewhere else around here.

Saxon. Saxon. Now all the birds were pecking out the name. Saxon. Saxon. Saxon.

The Prince pushed forward through the drifts. But he wasn't going toward the house; the birds were taking him parallel to it. Past the garage, past a couple of bobbing elms, on a line to where the woodshed loomed at the rear of the yard. The snow here had a pocked look, as if somebody had been slogging around in it a while ago. The wind and the new snow had covered up part of the tracks, but he could see that there had been a lot of activity around the shed.

I really ought to go save Leslie myself, he thought. At least I should *try* to save her. If I don't, it might make the Prince look like a coward, being near the scene of a murder he knew was about to happen and not even making a serious attempt to stop it. It could screw up my whole career.

The psychic birds kept pecking and fluttering, leading him to the woodshed.

He went past rows of stacked firewood along the near shed wall. There weren't any tracks in the snowfield beyond; he could see that as he neared the east corner. Where they went was around on the shed's far side.

The birds were frantic now.

He started around the corner.

A dark, curled-up shape lay in the snow fifteen feet away, in front of the open shed door. Lay there like a black rock draped in a thin layer of white.

Saxon! Saxon! Saxon!

The Prince ran to the shape, lost his balance on the slick crust, and sprawled down on top of it. "Uff," he said. The shape didn't say anything. He pulled back on his knees, turned the shape over; his bladder felt as though it were inflated to the size of a cantaloupe.

Saxon's face stared up at him: a frozen white-caked grimace.

MIDNIGHT

The dark figure behind the flashlight was wearing a man's coat, a man's clothing that Leslie had seen before. *But it wasn't a man.* They had thought all along that it had to be a man, but they had been wrong. It was a woman.

It was Myrna Colebrook.

Leslie stared in amazement and confusion, and for another second she was locked in position against the wall. Then the light swept around toward her, the rim of its glare reached her. Her breath spilled out in an anguished hiss and she made a convulsive lunge forward, the knife held high over her head.

The light jerked and struck her full in the face, blinding her, then flew up in a slashing diagonal across the front of her body just as she brought the knife blade hacking downward. The flashlight's metal lip slammed against the bone in her wrist, sent an explosion of pain through her; the knife flew from her hand and went skittering and clattering into darkness.

For an instant, the cone of light danced away from her. Then it danced back and a muscled forearm struck her just above the left breast, drove her into the wall with jarring force. She dropped down it in a boneless slide to one knee.

Waves of pain and dizziness. Tears squeezed out of her eyes. She clutched at her wrist, blinking against the glare of the flash beam—a hot white circle with blurred aureoles around the center, the fuzzy shape of Myrna Colebrook's stocky body behind it in the darkness.

"Stay away from me," Leslie said. "Stay away from me."

No answer. Just heavy panting breaths. The light held steady, pinning her against the wall.

Black pulses beating. Screams.

Painting glowing like fox fire.

Face it, get through it, believe!

Pain ebbing. Fear and confusion ebbing.

Deep breaths. Now stand up, get off the floor. Slow. No sudden movements. Slow.

Myrna Colebrook didn't move. But the light lifted to follow Leslie as she balanced shakily, leaned her shoulders tight to the wall.

The knife. Where was the knife?

"I'm sorry, Leslie Abbott."

The voice, thick and whispery, seemed to come out of the light. Desolate. Desolate voice, as if the woman were as confused and frightened as Leslie herself.

Find the knife. But how?

"It's all over now," the voice said. "For you, not for me. For you."

Talking. Not attacking, just talking.

"It has to be that way, there's nothing I can do."

Keep her talking. Back up a step at a time, follow the pace of her voice. Slow, no sudden movements. Let the light find the knife, watch the floor for it. Light, knife; knife, light.

"Why?" she made herself say. "Why do you want to kill me?"

"I have to. To protect the secret."

Small sliding step. Stop. The light moved with her, hot and bright in her eyes.

"What secret, Mrs. Colebrook?"

"Mrs. Colebrook? Oh, no. No. That's the secret."

Step. Another patch of floor became visible as the light shifted. No sign of the knife.

"Tell me what the secret is."

"No. I can't."

Step. "You can tell me. It won't matter now."

Silence. Then weeping sounds. Madwoman crying in the dark? "You know already, don't you? Don't you?"

Step. Light moving. No knife.

"Tell me, Mrs. Colebrook."

"I'm *not* Mrs. Colebrook." Hoarse blurted words, like a confession. "I'm her brother, Jason. I'm Jason Haggers and I live here inside Myrna's body. Myrna's the host and I live inside her."

Chills on Leslie's neck. Step. Light moving.

No knife.

"Myrna killed me in nineteen forty-six," the woman said, "but I've been back for a long time. I came back from the dead in nineteen fifty-one to live with Myrna."

Black pulses. Screams.

"How?" Step. "How did Myrna kill you?"

Light moving. No knife.

"We were playing cowboy and Indian." The voice still had tears in it, but it was stronger now. And madder—thick with madness. "Up in the attic of our house one Sunday while Mother and Dad were away. I was the Indian. I wanted to be the Indian, and Myrna let me, and then she tied me up with a blue velvet cord from some old drapes we found. But she tied me too tight, too tight around my throat, and I started to thrash around and turn purple. Myrna was frightened. She tried to untie me, but her hands shook and she couldn't do it fast enough, and by the time she finally got the velvet cord loose, I was dead. I was all purple and black and dead."

Oh, God. Step. Light. Knife? No knife.

"Myrna cried. She cried and cried. She was so scared. She was thirteen and I was eight; she was my big sister, she was supposed to watch over me. And I was Mother's favorite. Myrna and I both knew that. Myrna loves Mother very much, but Mother never loved Myrna, she thinks Myrna is a witch. Myrna couldn't tell her she'd strangled me with the velvet cord, she was afraid Mother would do something terrible to her. So she went out to the barn and found some rope and came back and hung me up from a rafter. Then she went away and pretended she'd been doing chores. She pretended that I did it all to myself and she'd never even been playing with me."

Step. And Leslie felt her right shoulder butt up against another wall, south wall: She had reached the corner. She eased her body around, took another sliding step along—

Myrna Colebrook moved; the flash beam came closer.

Leslie stopped and stood rigidly, scanning the floor in desperate sweeps. Where was the knife? Where *was* it?

The woman and the light were still again.

There was a sick, brassy taste in Leslie's mouth. She blinked away trickles of sweat, took another deep breath. Don't move now, don't move. Wait until she starts talking again.

"Mother was the one who found me hanging in the attic. She screamed and cried, and Dad had to come and cut me down and call the doctor and the police. Mother was never the same afterward, it teched her to find her son hanging like that. Everybody thought I was playing up in the attic alone and hanged myself by accident, but Mother blamed Myrna anyway. She said it was all Myrna's fault and beat Myrna and told her she was a witch and she'd go to hell someday."

Step. Light following her. *Where was the knife?*

"Myrna doesn't want to go to hell. She knew it was all her fault, but she couldn't help it, she didn't want to kill me.

It was an accident. She's not a witch either. She can't help it if she has visions. They just come to her. The visions just come to her."

Visions. Dear God, Leslie thought, she's psychic, she's a clairvoyant. That's why the vibrations have been so strong. Mad, sick, evil. *Psychic.*

Step.

"That's part of the secret, too. That Myrna sees things. It doesn't happen very often, not very often, but she sees things. Mother is the only one who knows. Myrna never told anybody else, she never told Harmon. Especially Harmon. She kept the secret all these years."

Step. Light. Empty floor.

"One day she had a vision where she saw me come back from the dead and live inside her, and it came true. I came back and she was my host. I don't hate Myrna, you see. She didn't want to kill me, she was just playing, and she tried so hard to save me. I love Myrna, I want to help her, I want to keep on living inside her so I won't have to die again."

Step.

"When the death visions started, she was afraid to make them come true. She didn't think she could kill anyone else. But I could. I said I would do it for her. It wasn't so bad at first; I didn't have to kill very many people. Just once in a while, that was all. But then you moved in here and you brought the others and we were afraid for the secret. I was afraid. And the death visions came and came, faster and faster, and everything started to go out of control. I could feel that everything was going out of control. But what could I do? I had to keep making Myrna's visions come true. I still have to. If I don't, I'll die again and Myrna will die and I won't be able to come back anymore."

Step. Light moving—

The painting.

The light touched it and made it spring out of the darkness two paces away against the wall; it seemed to glow the way it had in her mind, reflecting glints of light and color. And the dark figure seemed to have a face now, it had Myrna Colebrook's face—

"That's why I have to kill you," the woman said.

And came forward in a sudden rush.

Leslie tried to run, but Myrna Colebrook was in on her before she had taken two strides. The light was dazzling, blinding. Something brushed her ankle, touched her thigh—the painting—and then the light was gone, it fell away in a wavering arc, clattered on the floor, and hands grabbed her, arms went around her and twisted her body and pulled her backward, hands and arms that were as strong and insistent as a man's. They slithered upward over her breasts, bent her back like a bow against an upthrust knee. An object slender and soft touched her throat, caressed it. Velvet cord!

A thin cry tore from inside her; she flailed wildly with her heels, felt one of them strike flesh, heard a grunt and felt breath sear her neck. Kicked again as the cord tightened, missed, kicked again and hit something that wasn't a leg, heard it make a ripping sound—the painting—and one of Myrna Colebrook's feet scrabbled backward, the knee dropped away from Leslie's buttocks, there was a banging noise and a bleat of pain.

The velvet cord slid away from her throat; the encircling hands and arms were suddenly loose on her body. She lunged forward—and she was free.

She stumbled away, gagging on her own breath. More sounds behind her: clattering and ripping, thud of a body hitting the floor, a shriek that was more animal than human. The dropped flashlight was somewhere behind her, too, laying a long yellow strip across the floor, letting her see emptiness, no sign of the knife, no time to look for the knife. Letting her see the vague black outlines of the door that led up into the belfry.

Belfry.

Stored things up there—weapon, weapon!

She fell against the door and fumbled for the knob. Found it, turned it, flung the door open. Flung herself inside.

A shout behind her.

She threw the door shut. Lockless, like the studio door; it was no barrier. She pivoted, almost tripped over the first of the risers, got a grip on the handrail, and ran up the stairs.

Terror flooded her, but the black pulses were muted now and the image of the painting was gone. Gone. Myrna Colebrook had fallen over it; it had saved her life. Deviled her all this time as if it were an instrument of her destruction, and then saved her life.

But for how long?

Get through it, believe, get through it.

She came up off the last step, onto the attic floor. Masses and lumps of shadow loomed around her; the blackness was absolute except for the gray-black contours of the belfry windows. What was stored where? She couldn't seem to remember. She veered over to her right, and her knee struck something and threw her off-balance against a stack of boxes. One of her grasping hands dislodged the top box and sent it toppling over. Glassware shattered as she caught herself against another of the boxes and regained her balance. Echoes rang and faded in the darkness. She pulled back and felt frantically with her hands among the litter on the floor.

Below, the belfry door rattled and was hurled open.

Boxes, unused canvases, boxes, suitcases—nothing, nothing.

A finger of light jabbed upward along the stairwell.

She whirled into a crouch, panting, trembling.

Heavy thudding footfalls on the stairs.

The finger of light brightened, cutting away some of the blackness inside the belfry, giving substance to the shapes around her. Boxes, boxes, broken stool, broken easel, broken spider web dangling from one of the rafters—

Broken easel.

The light and the footfalls neared the top.

She threw herself across to where the broken easel sat propped against an empty crate, folded into a slender four-foot length. Caught it up and whirled with it drawn back over her shoulder like a baseball bat.

Myrna Colebrook's dark form appeared at the head of the stairs, making sobbing, wheezing noises. The flash beam in her hand swept around, guttering through the belfry, bringing shapes into odd, poised clarity.

Leslie took two running steps and lashed out with the broken easel. The upper half of it sailed past the light, struck the woman a glancing blow across the arm and chest; knocked her backward into the boxes of old glassware. The flashlight spun out of her hand and hit something and went out, plunging the belfry into darkness again. More glass shattered. Boxes clattered against each other as Myrna Colebrook struggled frenziedly to untangle herself.

Leslie dropped the broken easel and went in a blind run toward the stairs. Plowed into the wall on the near side of the stairwell, caromed off, and groped around the corner and touched the railing, got her fingers over it. Her right foot came down on the first of the risers.

The woman lunged at her out of the dark.

A hand caught her ankle and spun her, throwing her legs up from under her.

She would have plunged headlong down the stairs except for her grip on the handrail. Instead she hit the edge of a riser on her left hip, slid, and bumped downward a half-dozen steps before she could break the momentum. Dizzying pain flared along her spine, in her hips and left elbow, and wiped her mind clear of everything but terror.

Scrabbling sounds above her. Footfalls on the stairs, running.

She got her feet anchored on another of the steps and heaved herself upright, clinging to the rail. Lurched downward on wobbling legs, gasping, making involuntary mewling noises deep in her throat. Staggered off the last of the steps and through the open door into the studio.

Hands caught her from behind.

No! Oh, my God, no!

Arms wrapped around her, hot pulses of breath burned her

neck again. She felt herself being yanked backward, tried to struggle, tried to kick at the braced legs as she had before. But her strength was gone, she had no more strength.

"Now," Myrna Colebrook's winded voice said in her ear. "Now."

Leslie screamed.

And screamed again.

The arms moved upward over her breasts. The velvet cord bit into her throat.

No!

She tried to scream a third time, but the pressure at her throat increased and she had no voice, she couldn't breathe. Odors in her mind, colors swirling, blue black red white, choking pressure, jelly eyes black-bowl mouths screaming screaming screaming—

NO!

"I'm sorry, Leslie Abbott," Myrna Colebrook whispered.

The velvet cord tightened.

MIDNIGHT

Saxon clawed his way up out of darkness. Somebody was holding him propped against a curved arm and slapping his face with a gloved hand, saying over and over, "Wake up, Mr. Saxon, wake up. Wake up."

He couldn't open his eyes; the lids seemed frozen shut. Tremors racked him. Cold. Agony in his head. Cold.

Leslie!

He struck out at the hand slapping his face, heard a voice say "Hey!" and felt the supporting arm slide away from beneath his shoulders. He fell back, rolled over immediately, and came up onto his knees. Pawed at his eyelids and got them unstuck. His vision was blurred; he saw two Neal Proof Ivers-sons kneeling in the snow and staring at him through ice-streaked glasses. Two woodsheds, two houses in the distance.

The pain in his head was savage. Nausea overtook him; he gagged, turned to one side, and vomited up a thin stream of bile and saliva.

Leslie!

He got one leg planted and levered himself up. Stood swaying and trembling, still half-retching, still pawing at his eyes. His gun—where was his gun? His eyes began to focus; he saw the .38 lying half-buried in the snow, leaned over painfully to pick it up, and rubbed it between his gloved palms to clear the ice from it.

"You'd better hurry, Mr. Saxon," Iverson said eagerly. "Buell's in the house with her, he's going to kill her like he killed all the other PSYCHICs. I was ready to go in there myself and save her, but I found you instead because you're a trained agent. . . ."

Buell. In the house with her.

Jesus God, if anything happens to her, it's my fault—

He staggered past Iverson. His legs didn't want to work right; the joints felt stiff, atrophied. Each step sent more agony through his head.

The house was dark. All the lights had been on before, but now it was dark. What had happened to the lights? Buell in there, it was Buell. Or was it? What was Iverson doing here?

Leslie, Leslie.

He veered toward the rear porch. By the time he got to it, urgency and desperation had cleared some of the pain-fog from his mind. He mounted the ice-slick steps, caught hold of the screen-door handle, kicked away enough of the frozen snow to brace his feet, and yanked the door toward him viciously. The screw eye ripped loose from the wood inside, squealing, and the door wobbled open in his hand. He held on to the handle to give himself leverage and drove his foot against the frame of the inner door, just above the latch. Had to do it twice before the lock snapped and the door flew inward. He stumbled through into darkness.

Sounds above him. Thumping, banging.

Studio, she was in the studio.

He started forward through the heavy black. Remembered the flashlight he had taken with him from the kitchen, slapped at his coat pocket: it was still there. He dragged it out, turned it on, and ran through the kitchen and into the center hall.

Somebody screamed upstairs—a sound full of terror.

Leslie!

A kind of wildness came into him, a frenzy of love and hate. He heard himself make a bellowing cry as he raced to the stairs and charged upward.

She screamed again.

The door at the top of the stairs was ajar; he hit it with full force, was thrown off-stride when it slammed against something inside and failed to yield. He recovered, fought his way through, and swept the room with the light.

Over by the belfry stairs—Leslie struggling in the grip of someone that wasn't Buell, that was Myrna Colebrook, it was Myrna Colebrook, goddamn crazy cunt was sobbing and garroting Leslie with a cord—

He flung himself across the room. He was almost on top of them before the woman saw him, and when she did she grunted in surprise and tried to use Leslie as a wedge between them. But he got there first and hit her with his shoulder, knocked her aside, and she let go of Leslie. Leslie dropped, gagging, to her knees, and he went after the woman and hit her with the gun, threw her against the wall, and moved in on her to hit her again, but she was crying, moaning, her arms up to protect her face, and he drew back and pointed the gun at her head and wanted to pull the trigger, but she was *crying*. . . .

The tension drained out of him; sanity came flooding in. He thought: My God—and backed away from her. Held the light on her, but backed away to where Leslie was kneeling on the floor, holding her throat, retching dryly. He knelt beside her, put his arm around her, and said her name. Said it again.

"Brad." Choked whisper. "Thank God."

Thank God.

Clumping on the stairs. He swung the light over there as the footsteps reached the top—Iverson, the kid had followed him at a distance—and then put it back on the Colebrook woman.

"Mrs. Colebrook?" Iverson said incredulously. "*Mrs. Colebrook*'s the psychotic murderer?"

The woman straightened against the wall. Her face was grotesque in the flash beam, twisted into a rictus of madness and fear, glistening with tears. "The secret," she said, and the madness was in her voice, too. "You all know the secret!"

"What secret?" Iverson said.

"They know, Myrna, they know! Protect the secret or die! Oh, Myrna, Myrna!"

She spun away and ran wildly toward the windows in the north wall.

Saxon came up onto his feet, shouting "Stop!" and started after her.

But she didn't stop; she kept on running with arms flung up over her head. The light was full on her back, reflecting off the glass ahead of her, reflecting the madness in her face, when she hit the center window head-on.

Winking shards of glass exploded outward. The sound of it breaking was thunderous, overridden in the next instant by the woman's scream as she went through. Then she was gone. But she screamed all the way down; it seemed to Saxon he could still hear it seconds after it stopped, echoing in the night and the dark studio.

"Son of a bitch," Iverson said in awe.

Chills worked up and down Saxon's back as he ran to the shattered window. He shoved his head out into the wind and snow, looked down.

Myrna Colebrook lay in a broken sprawl below, unmoving, like a black stain on the surface of the snow.

Iverson came up beside him and peered out, his head against Saxon's in what was almost a posture of intimacy. "I just can't believe it," he said. He sounded disappointed. "I just can't believe it wasn't Ephraim Buell."

Saxon shoved him aside, holstered his revolver, and went back to Leslie. He felt empty, nauseated, weak with pain; but he also felt a relief and a tenderness that went beyond his suffering. He helped her to her feet, turned her against him. Held her.

And heard her say something against his chest that he didn't understand.

"I believed," she said. "I believed."

PART THREE

After the End

CHAPTER 6

Monday, January 29

ARLINGTON, VIRGINIA—11:25 P.M.

In Brad's apartment—her apartment, too, now—Leslie sat close to him on the couch and watched Neal Iverson on television.

The program was a live, non-network talk show out of New York City called "American Revelations," hosted by Marvin Martin. Neal had been on for ten minutes, discussing what he called "the Whitehall clairvoyant murders" and explaining how the Prince had helped solve them with his psychic gift. The Prince. That was how he kept referring to himself, in the third person. He was wearing his vision hat and he had his usual excited look, but otherwise he seemed to be fairly poised and not bothered at all by the cameras. Marvin Martin and the guest who had preceded Neal, an aging blond sex-symbol actress, listened attentively, but it was obvious that they were both skeptical of and amused by Neal's account.

Five people were dead, including Myrna Colebrook, and the Prince was on television and Marvin Martin and a stupid roundheels actress were amused. God.

". . . and yesterday I went to see Oscar Koskovich in the

hospital here in New York," Neal was saying. "What happened to him was that the visions he had were so powerful, he got all confused inside and went into what the doctors call a state of catalepsy. But it's in remission now. That means he's getting better. He knew who I was when I went to see him. I told him I was going to be on your show, Marvin, and he said he was going to watch if they let him have a television set in his room." Neal paused. "Well, I guess that's about it. That's the whole story of the Whitehall clairvoyant murders and how the Prince helped solve them."

"Fascinating, Prince," Marvin Martin said. He looked out at the studio audience. "Don't you agree, ladies and gentlemen?"

Applause. Neal beamed.

Marvin Martin said, "One of the most interesting things to me, Prince, was your description of the visions you had in Whitehall. The psychic birds fluttering in your third eye and the dazzling light and the falling birds of knowledge. Could you tell us if any of those birds are in your consciousness right now?"

"Right now?" Neal said. "Well, no, my psychic eye is closed. But it could open at any time. The birds could come in at any second."

"Really? Do you suppose you could *will* them to come in, Prince?" Marvin Martin winked at the studio audience. "We've had a number of unusual things on 'American Revelations' over the years, but I can truthfully say that we've never had any psychic birds."

Laughter.

Neal didn't seem to notice. "Actually," he said, "you can't will a psychic experience to happen. But sometimes, when I'm wearing my vision hat, I can touch things or people and it will trigger my gift. That's what's known as psychometrics. I think I told you about psychometrics, didn't I?"

"Yes, indeed," Marvin Martin said. He looked at the blond actress. "Rose Ann, would you mind helping the Prince try to summon his psychic birds?"

She tittered. "Oh, not at all, Marvin."

"Prince, suppose you take Rose Ann's hand." He winked at the audience again. "Maybe that will trigger your gift. Or *something*, anyway."

Laughter. Applause.

Neal seemed to blush slightly. "Sure," he said, "maybe it will at that." He took the actress's hand and then closed his eyes, touched his cap with his free hand, and began to frown in concentration.

Marvin Martin and the actress grinned at each other.

The camera moved in for a close-up of Neal's face. Little beads of sweat broke out on his forehead. Then, abruptly, he said, "Something's happening. Yes, my psychic eye is starting to open. The birds are trying to form an image. Wow! I'm having an experience, Marvin, I really *am*."

"Wonderful," Marvin Martin said. "What do you see?"

"I see . . . Rose Ann," Neal said. "And you. You and Rose Ann doing something in a room."

The actress's smile began to fade. So did Marvin Martin's.

"I think it's your dressing room backstage," Neal said. "The image isn't too clear, but you're standing in front of the mirror—"

Marvin Martin looked startled, frightened, and angry at the same time. The actress looked horrified.

"—and Rose Ann is kneeling on the floor. You're saying something to her—"

Marvin Martin made a frantic slicing gesture at the camera.

"—I think you're saying 'Hurry up, we haven't got much time'—"

The screen went blank for an instant; then a commercial for Shower Massage came on.

Leslie shook her head. "Turn it off, Brad."

"So much for the Prince and his show-business career," he said as he leaned forward to darken the set.

"I never want to see him again, anywhere," she said. "I never want to see another clairvoyant."

"You don't have to, baby."

I never want to have another vision, either, she thought, but didn't put it into words. There would be other visions—the curse was hers for all her life—and some of them would be painful and ugly. There might even be another situation, good or bad, which was predestined by whatever those forces were that controlled the universe. But she had gotten through the ultimate test in Whitehall; she could get through anything from now on.

At this moment, she had essential control of her life again. And she had Brad. That was what mattered. That was *all* that mattered.

He put his arm around her, and they sat in good, warm silence.

Endings and beginnings, she thought again. The ending of one life, the beginning of another. The ending of emptiness, the beginning of love.

Here, together, the two of them.

Beginning.